WAYNE of GOTHAM

Batman created by Bob Kane

WAYNE OF GOTHAM

™

TRACY HICKMAN

!t
itbooks
AN IMPRINT OF HARPERCOLLINS PUBLISHERS

*it***books**

A hardcover edition of this book was published in 2012 by It Books, an imprint of HarperCollins Publishers.

WAYNE OF GOTHAM © 2012 by DC Comics.

HarperCollins books may be purchased for educational, business, or sales promotional use. For information please write: Special Markets Department, Harper-Collins Publishers, 10 East 53rd Street, New York, NY 10022.

First It Books paperback published 2012.

Designed by Paula Russell Szafranski

Library of Congress Cataloging-in-Publication Data is available upon request.

ISBN 978-0-06-221986-2

12 13 14 15 16 OV/RRD 10 9 8 7 6 5 4 3 2 1

This book is dedicated to Ryan Hickman.

Because he asked.

CONTENTS

MAKING A MAN

Wayne Manor / Bristol / 4:24 p.m. / September 21, 1953

"Damn it, boy! Stand up!"

Thomas Wayne shrank once more from the voice. It was a reflex ingrained in him. In all his fifteen years of life, that flinch had been as natural as breath, as unthinking as a blink.

"That's no way to hold a gun!" Patrick Wayne was a big man in a big town, with strong, wide hands that had, Thomas had no doubt, bent and shaped the very steel that formed the foundations of Gotham City. His voice outdid his size, roaring into the darkness, bounding off the unseen walls in a cascade of echoes that reached into the bowels of the earth. The column of yellow light from the old man's handheld flashlight hurt the boy's eyes. "Grip the stock by the trigger with your right hand so you can lift the barrel up by the forestock! And for hell's sake, hold it across your body with the barrel down."

Thomas dutifully repositioned his hold on the shotgun. His hands were shaking so violently he was afraid he would drop it. Sweat was pooling between his shoulder blades beneath his collared shirt and sweater vest despite the damp chill of the cave. Some part of his mind registered the fact that his new jeans would be ruined. It was a diversion of his mind. He sensed what was coming next.

The big hand slammed into Thomas's back, propelling him forward into the cavern. The young man hated the dark. The unseen cavern walls and roof pressed down on him. He hunched up his shoulders, drawing tighter within himself as he stumbled over the loose shale crumbling beneath his feet.

"Hell or high water, boy, I'm going to make a man out of you," Patrick roared behind him. Thomas knew the mix better than the cocktails his mother had him make for her every evening— and, of late, in the afternoons as well. His father had achieved balanced parts of rage and liquor soured with a twist of disap- pointment. It never mattered where it came from—who or what had set the old man off was irrelevant, Thomas knew. All that mattered now was that Thomas had become the focus of his father's displeasure . . . again. His own manhood had been somehow threatened and now manhood would be impressed on his son at any cost. "Do you think those comic books are going to keep you alive in Gotham? It's kill or be killed out there—not like that comic book world you live in! And you're gonna learn how to kill today, son. You're gonna kill *something!*"

He could hear them.

Even over his father's thunderous voice, he could hear the waking bats.

It was afternoon, and he had disturbed their rest. The dim light from the failing Evereadys in his father's flashlight reflected in a thousand pairs of eyes blanketing the ceiling above them.

The bats were at home beneath Wayne Manor, and in their coming Patrick and his son had upset the quiet balance in the cavern between the world above and the world below.

"Get on with it, boy!"

The cringe was deepening. He couldn't stop his hands from

shaking. He tried to raise the barrel of the shotgun but the foreign thing felt impossibly heavy, and he could not will his arms to move. Tears stung his eyes, welling out and spilling down his cheeks in the darkness.

Thomas tried to speak through shivering lips.

"What did you say, boy?"

Thomas could feel the massive presence of his father looming up behind him as the dimming flashlight shifted in his hands.

"Speak up, boy!" Patrick's voice shook the cavern.

He froze, but Thomas knew disobedience would only make it worse. He blurted his response loud enough to clear his clenched teeth.

"I—I *can't!*"

"You CAN'T?" Patrick raged. "You're the descendant of knights who fought in the crusades! Waynes have participated in every battle fought in or about America—given their blood for this country. We build the weapons that make this country strong and great . . . and you tell me you *CAN'T!*"

The big hand. The strong hand. The hand that had bent the steel of Gotham smashed down across the boy's face, driving him to the ground.

Thomas lay on his back sobbing. He could taste his own blood from the corner of his mouth where Patrick's ring had dragged as it drove him to the ground. The side of his face would sting for a while but the pain in his soul would never diminish, only be compounded.

The shotgun lay across his body as he wept; his eyes closed against the darkness of the cavern around him . . . the deeper darkness of his father standing over him. The watchful darkness of the keening bats beyond.

The big hand. The strong hand.

Thomas felt the gathering of his collar at the back of his neck.

It stretched the sweater, dragging him to his feet as the gun clattered on the shale ground.

The hand of Patrick Wayne held his son in an iron grip, dragging their faces within inches of each other. The flashlight flickered as it shone upward, casting both their faces in heavy contrasting shadows. Thomas stared into the eyes of his father.

"You're a *Wayne*, boy!" Patrick growled into the face of his son. The words smelled like rotted fruit falling from his father's scotch-soaked tongue. "There are only two types of people in this world: the hunters and the hunted—and you had better make up your mind right now that you're going to hunt! I won't allow the empire I've built to be taken apart by the government, and I sure as hell won't turn it over to a bookworm son with a head full of comic books and no stomach for survival."

Patrick swept up the shotgun. The polished barrel reflected the dimming light as the man pushed the weapon into young Thomas's hands.

"Be a man! *Show me* you're a man!" Patrick growled into the face of his boy. "Use this! Kill something!"

Thomas stopped shaking, his eyes suddenly focused and unblinking. His lips split apart revealing clenched teeth. His hands gripped the stock without thinking.

"*Show me!*" Patrick screamed.

Thomas turned, raising the shotgun up in a quick motion as he had seen his father do a dozen times on the skeet range behind the Manor.

The barrel crossed Patrick's face in its arc.

Thomas froze—the barrel wavering on his father's face.

I could make it stop. I could pull this trigger and make him stop. He would go away and stop hurting me . . . hurting Mother . . . hurting anyone. Everything would be better if I could make him stop . . . make him stop . . .

But the boy's finger did not move.

Patrick stepped around his son, standing behind the youth as the barrel shifted uncertainly in the air. Thomas could almost feel the hairs of his father's mustache on his neck, smell the sour breath.

"What are you waiting for?" Patrick urged, his voice rumbling in his son's ears. "Do you think they'll wait for you? Do you think they would hesitate a moment if they were after you? Go on, son. Kill them . . . kill them before they kill you."

Thomas's hands began to shake once more.

"KILL THEM!" Patrick screamed.

The shotgun roared. The recoil from the shotgun blast slammed the butt of the gun into the boy's shoulder, pushing him back as he stumbled awkwardly against the mass of his father behind him. The ceiling exploded in noise and motion, the bats filling the air with their own sound and confusion. The walls of the cavern vanished in the flow of leather wings and the outraged cries of the bats.

"Again, boy!" Patrick yelled. "Do it again!"

Thomas felt the hand on his shoulder. The steel-bending hand . . .

He had no choice.

Tears streaming down his face, he fired again . . .

And again . . .

And again . . .

CHAPTER ONE

SPELLBOUND

You can't run . . . you can't hide . . .

Batman dropped down onto the square of cement, landing in a strong crouch, his cape settling around him. It softened his silhouette in the darkness. His right fist pressed against the ground, and he raised his head.

Come out, come out, wherever you are . . .

It was a nightmare landscape dragged from an M. C. Escher drawing. Iron stairs leading away from the small cement balcony connected in impossible ways with still other stairs. The mind-tortured stairs led to more landings and more impossible stairs, a cascade of metal works extending into infinite space. Hooded work lights hung at cross angles from one another. Their feeble rays barely illuminated the shadowed figures that stood beneath them. Some were on opposite sides of the same stairs as though gravity were a matter of personal perspective. Their shadowy outlines twisted nervously in the dark. Revolver, automatic, shotgun, rifle—a variety of weapons pointed at bizarre angles into the space. Each was different and each was alike in important aspects.

Nervous hands held them.

Nervous fingers twitched on the triggers.

An image flashed through his mind of another time and place far away yet never far from him. *Joe Chill's hands did not shake. They were steady as granite. His eyes as relentless as a glacier* . . .

Batman settled lower into his crouch. The Batsuit was new, and he was pleased at the response. It was essentially a form of power armor, although its ability to deflect damage had yet to be field tested. The exterior of the Batsuit still used a light variation of the Nomex/Kevlar weave, but gratefully much of the weight had been shed by dropping the armor plating. In its place now was a complex set of exomusculature beneath the exterior weave. It was his "muscle" Batsuit, one that could artificially enhance his natural movements and strength. The bidirectional neurofeedback loop maintained a dynamic stability that was tied at once into both the voluntary and involuntary neural responses from his body. That he could use the *arrectores pilorum* on his body hair as a neural source for control was all the more convenient. The electroactive polymers were liquid bound ionic EAPs, which kept the voltage low throughout the Batsuit and the heat generation at a minimum. Kevlar was always passive; this Batsuit had an active defense, a blast-ion charge reacting to force trauma. The downside was that the Batsuit could bleed if it did not react quickly enough.

The Batsuit could die on me.

I could die in the Batsuit.

A smile played on his lips at the thought.

What a wonderful symmetry.

The cape shifted around him. Its fabric was of the same reactive polymer material and moved as though it, too, had a will of its own. It shifted around him as a living thing. Its original purpose had been as a heat-sink for the exomusculature, but the ever-inventive and adaptive mind of Bruce Wayne had found other creative uses for the cape.

It's the hunt. Stalk the stalker. Prey on the predator.

Batman raised his head, searching the mad maze stretching to infinity in all directions. His mind raced. Time slowed. He was setting up the game in his mind.

The pieces were clearer to him now. He set each of them up in his mind. Evaluate. Strategize.

Jillian Masters. Anchorwoman for the WGXX news at eleven. She robbed four banks in three days. Walked out each time. Everyone thought she was covering the stories. Turned out she was the story. She holds the automatic sideways and steady. When she moves the muzzle, it stops rock solid. The 9 mm cannon in her arms appears to be an old friend to her.

Aaron Petrov. Head of the diamond exchange. Led the investigation into the thefts throughout the Diamond District. Nobody thought to look in his bags. Assault rifle with cover and good firing position. Clear field covering all the platforms between regardless of their orientation. Hand unsteady. No marksman and unfamiliar with the weapon. Three or four shots before he finds his mark on a stationary target.

Batman continued to catalogue the obstacles between him and his opponent on the other side of the twisted board. Whom he sought was obvious to him. Spellbinder—the former Fay Moffit—had somehow managed to get a release from Arkham Asylum six weeks before and promptly vanished. Fay wasn't the first to take on the Spellbinder racket. She had learned the hypnotism powers from her lover and the previous Spellbinder—a third-rate criminal by the name of Delbert Billings. She won the title after retiring Delbert with a shot through the head. Now she had used her talents to convince a number of the upstanding citizens of Gotham to do her robbery for her . . . again.

Old story . . . not even an interesting one. Just a test of the new Batsuit . . . with a walk in the park.

He continued listing off the opponents, in his mind.

Angel Jane-Montgomery, socialite with a shotgun . . . William Raymond, fireman with a full-automatic . . . Diana Alexandria, pop-music celebrity with a grenade launcher . . . James Gordon . . .

Batman frowned beneath his cowl.

Gordon would require some finesse.

Batman closed his eyes.

The cowling over his head was also new. Using it had required considerable training, but it had been worth the trouble. The sensors at the edge of the cowl eye openings read his eye closure, activating a subsonic imaging system—like the sonar of a bat—that communicated directly to an implant connected to his optic nerve. The image was still unclear in its details, but he had adapted to it, and it gave him a field of vision that he could interpret three-dimensionally in all directions around him. It was like having eyes in the back, side, and front of the head, a tactical awareness that extended in all directions.

Justice is blind. Batman's lips parted over his set teeth.

The sonar imager had one additional advantage. It was based on sound, and the light-bending illusions of Spellbinder's Fun House would vanish.

Too easy . . .

Batman sprang, the synthetic muscles of the Batsuit enhancing his powerful legs. He shot across the open space, spinning through the warped light of the mirrors fixed throughout the hall.

Gunfire erupted from every direction. The assault rifle spat slugs from its muzzle, issuing deep, loud "chuff" sounds with every burst. Several cries of rage and fear pierced the cascade of gunfire—for Batman suddenly looked to be everywhere at once, his dark form flying through the mirrored space of the illusions and suddenly multiplied a thousandfold.

Mirrors of safety glass were holed by the rain of lead. Several shattered loudly, the round glass of their pebbled remains falling like glittering snow among the now-swinging worklights.

It's a place to start.

Jillian Masters swung her 9 mm automatic around just as Batman dropped his shoulder toward the cement platform. His tensed shoulder muscle translated into the exosuit, which tensed as well, buffering the impact as he rolled. The 9 mm barked only once before Batman's momentum carried him to his feet, striking her gun hand with the back of his forearm. The enhanced musculature of the exosuit struck the handgun with such force that the weapon tore a long gash down the newswoman's hand.

Chuff . . . ping! The slug from the assault rifle kicked off one of the metal stairs.

That's one, Aaron.

The other enthralled citizens continued to fire, but the maze was still in their way, throwing off their aim. The mirrors continued to suffer the worst for random carnage. More shattered with each passing moment.

No more time.

Batman grabbed the wrist of the enraged newswoman, rotated his body around and then threw her to the ground next to one of the metal stairs. She rolled quickly face down, pushing herself up with her hands. Batman quickly dropped his knee down on her back as he reached for his Utility Belt.

Chuff . . . clang! The strike was on the stairs only a few feet away.

That's two, Aaron . . . you may be better than I thought.

The Dark Knight pulled a long, black strip of plastic from his belt. Grabbing Jillian's hands, he wrapped the plastic strip around both her wrists and the metal riser for the stairs. With a quick pull and a ripping sound, Jillian was secured to the riser.

Zip ties. Sometimes simple is best.

Chuff . . . crack!

But Batman no longer knelt where the cement was chipped by Aaron's third round.

His black shape rushed again, bounding from platform to platform . . . Montgomery, Raymond, Alexandria . . .

Gordon. Where's Gordon?

Aaron Petrov stood sweating on the platform. A single work light remained, shining down on his glistening hairless head. He shouted into the darkness.

"You can't have them! They are mine, and you can't take them from me! You can't . . . You—you can't."

Aaron looked up.

The light vanished as darkness enfolded him.

Batman stood up. Aaron Petrov was bound hand and feet beneath him, whimpering and sobbing like a child.

"FREEZE!"

He was waiting for me. He's behind me. Service automatic. Gordon was always a great shot. Somehow I've always known in my soul that he will be there when I die. But not today . . .

Batman began to turn slowly.

"I said FREEZE!"

Batman stopped. "Calm down, Gordon. You're being played by Spellbinder."

"Like hell!" Gordon answered. There was a quiver in his voice. "Spellbinder's tucked away in Arkham . . . I saw her there myself yesterday before . . . before you . . ."

He's angry. He's in pain. What's he seeing? What's Moffit convinced him to see?

Gordon's words cut like the shattered glass that lay around them. "How could you? You bastard, you killed her!"

"Who? Who did I kill, Gordon?"

"You can't even remember her name?" Gordon's voice went cold. "Barbara. My little Barbara . . . You put her in that wheelchair, and now you've finished the job!"

"Gordon, think! Joker put her there . . . remember? She's still alive, Jim."

"I ought to just put you down right now!" Gordon screamed.

"But you won't. You'll take me in."

"No! I'm gonna save this city a lot of trouble and expense . . . I'm gonna . . ."

"You're a good cop, Gordon." Batman moved ever so slowly, raising both hands. "You're going to take me in. You're going to see that justice is done."

Batman placed both hands behind his head. He closed his eyes.

Justice is blind.

Gordon raised his weapon, stepping forward. The muzzle of the service revolver jabbed against the base of Batman's neck below his fingers.

At the base of his skull.

No amount of armor—active or otherwise—would protect him at this range.

"That's right, Batman!" Gordon seethed. "I *am* going to see that justice is done! I *am* justice, you son of a—"

The cape reached up, suddenly flying in Gordon's face.

Not just for show anymore.

Gordon fired just as Batman's head shifted aside.

The muzzle blast exploded in Batman's ear as he spun around on Gordon. The neurobionic interface was disrupted, and for a moment Batman was truly blind as he opened his eyes. The cape was still affixed around the police commissioner's wrist, pulling him forward and into Batman's reach.

The spin kick cost Gordon his glasses, but the commissioner was fueled by rage, revenge, and despair. He managed to fire his weapon twice more in wild rage before Batman could force it from his hands. It tumbled into the void around them as they locked in combat. Gordon had nothing to lose in the death of his opponent. Batman had everything to lose.

At last, Gordon fell quivering beneath the careful blows of his old friend. Batman secured him as he had the others, although perhaps not so tightly.

He stood up and closed his eyes.

The cowl was responding once more.

The game was over.

It was time to claim his prize.

"I've done your bidding, master," she mumbled. "Everything exactly as you asked. Did it please you, master? Did I please you?"

Batman found her in a small room with a single, high-back winged chair. She was seated before a shrine.

On the shrine, a ventriloquist dummy stared at the intruder with dead, glass eyes as he approached.

Batman set his jaw. He knew the wooden doll too well to turn his back on him.

He had been called Woody when he was first carved in Blackgate Penitentiary. The gallows had been dismantled after a botched execution in 1962, and a "lifer" by the name of Donnegan had salvaged some of the wood to keep his hands busy. Donnegan was a big fan of noir and gangster films, and managed to dress his puppet creation in a miniature gangster suit with wide pinstripes and lapels to match. As Blackgate became more crowded, Donnegan and Woody were joined in his cell by a rather unlikely murderer, a usually timid man by the name of Arnold Wesker. Wesker tried to hang himself but, according to the prison psychiatrist reports at the time, was "talked out of it" by the dummy, who Wesker claimed had started speaking to him. Woody convinced Wesker to attempt an escape with him using a tunnel that Donnegan had abandoned digging the year before. Donnegan agreed to help finish the tunnel for Wesker to use. However, when Donnegan discovered that Wesker was planning to take Woody with him, Donnegan became upset. He was happy and safe in his cell with Woody and would not let him go. Wesker, under delusions that the mute dummy was actually goading him on, attacked Donnegan in their cell with a corkscrew. His initial lunge missed Donnegan but slashed Woody's face, leaving a long, ugly scar. Wesker killed Donnegan and escaped with the dummy. The escaped lunatic and his puppet both took on new personas: Wesker became the Ventriloquist, while Woody was billed as "Scarface" because of the irrepairable gash left by the corkscrew. The Ventriloquist turned out to be a terrible performer—mispronouncing all his Bs and Gs—but he always claimed that the advice of Scarface made him a criminal mastermind. Both eventually vanished into the dark underside of Gotham. Wesker eventually was killed by his own gang, but Scarface continued on as a strange icon among Gotham shadow society. The dummy was said to have been cursed or possessed, and there were those in the criminal underworld who swore that it spoke to them, too.

The dummy's eyes seemed to follow Batman as he walked around the chair.

Fay Moffit sat staring blankly at the dummy as she mumbled a one-sided conversation. "You really are too kind, Scar-boy! Thank you. Thank you . . ."

She lapsed into silence, her eyes unfocused and her breath shallow. Her head lolled to one side in the chair.

Spellbinder . . . is spellbound? Who hypnotizes a hypnotist?

Batman bound her wrists. She barely moved, let alone resisted. He slung her limp body over his shoulder and turned to leave.

"Solved another one, eh, copper?"

Batman turned at once.

Scarface was talking to him.

"You missed the mark, flatfoot." The dummy's mouth moved as it spoke, the dead eyes fixed on Batman. "Lettin' the big fish get away. I'm the brains of this operation, and you're just pickin' up the crumbs. But then, you never did see straight."

It's a device. Audio player coupled to actuators. But it's aimed at me. This whole thing was to deliver a message . . . but what's the message and who's it from?

"Take your folks, fer instance! Salt of the earth! Saints of Gotham! So sad that some crazed hood gunned 'em down in Crime Alley." The dummy's head shifted back and forth. "That's the way they told it to you—a nice bedtime story so you could sleep at night in your nice warm bed in Bristol."

Batman froze.

Whoever is behind this knows who I am.

Scarface shook his wooden head violently from side to side. "But you're a big boy now, aren't you? You have new toys to play with, so maybe you don't need fairy tales anymore. Maybe you can wake up and know that all saints pay a price and that their souls ain't always clean. I'm gonna throw a party, just for you. Do you think you're old enough to come?"

The dummy suddenly stopped moving.

It was only then that Batman noticed the card held in the dummy's hand. He would take the dummy with him along with any of the audio equipment. It would not do to have those words replayed during any subsequent police investigation.

But first he reached down with his gloved hand and picked up the offered card. To his eye it was a standard size, blank on the back with a single line of text on the front.

"You are invited."

CHAPTER TWO

COLD CASE

Batcave / Wayne Manor / Bristol / 5:51 a.m. / Present Day

Batman opened the gull-wing door of the Batmobile, gripped the titanium frame, and tried to stand up. His legs shook under him but held as he painfully rose out of the low-slung seat. He had exhausted the capacitors for the Batsuit's power in Spellbinder's Fun House, which was on Amusement Mile, on the north shore of the Newtown District. Normally he would have recharged the Batsuit during his return using the vehicle's onboard power, but it had been too short a trip from Newtown under the Kane Memorial Bridge and into Bristol. So now the Batsuit hung on him as extra weight that his aching body was struggling to support.

He slowly rose to his feet next to the car, tapping the release points at the base of his cowl in sequence. The smooth collar fitted to his neck loosened and he pulled the cowl off with urgent vehemence. His dark hair exploded outward at odd angles, sweat dripping down off his brow. The mask was off, and he was Bruce again, breathing a little harder than he would like and staring down at the cowl in his hand as though it were a part of him removed. He reached up, rubbing the back of his gloved hand across the prominent stubble on his face. The new Batsuit worked well, but it could be improved.

Everything needs to be improved. It's not right. Not yet.

Bruce looked back at the Batmobile.

Batmobile . . . what a joke. It was a name that the Gotham press had given his specialized vehicle when he had first appeared in one. It defied their classifications of standard transportation systems, and so they slapped a name on it that they could handle: the Batmobile. In truth, there had been many different Batmobiles at his disposal down through the years, some specialized and some made obsolete by the passage of time and technology. One of his favorites was a heavily converted 1955 Lincoln Futura. It had been his father's car originally, and Bruce had managed to salvage it from the junkyard just in time. He had spent years working on the car. He never used it, but he liked the look. Most of the vehicles were more practical, designed for the specific requirements of the time, and nearly all were in a constant state of rebuild and upgrade. Many were easily recognizable as a Batmobile—their bodies sweeping into the ubiquitous sculpted and scalloped fins that somehow always made it into his designs. The models from the 1980s were muscular, built around jet engines or enormous power plants that screamed in the night. He had been younger then and relished the power under his hands. As the Batmobiles evolved, they were becoming subtler if not less muscular, with stealth technologies incorporated into their brute strength.

The current version was, as always, an improvement over the last. Gotham was largely an island severed from the continent by the Gotham River. That meant there were only a handful of bridges connecting the boroughs of the city proper to the outside world, many of them a commuter's nightmare during drive time.

Bruce flashed a rueful smile. The image of a Batmobile—black fins, menacing angles, and screaming engine—crawling along across the Trigate Bridge while stuck in traffic was laughable.

Justice must be swift . . . and sure . . . and final.

So this particular incarnation of the Batmobile was a modification he knew as TS8c. It had started from a military scout vehicle frame. He had married it to a modified aircraft power plant and a custom-engineered combined gearbox and differential. It normally ran on RP-1 kerosene rocket fuel—relatively common and easy to obtain. Keeping the sound dampened from the screaming, high-torque engine had been a major problem that was solved, in part, with a secondary electric drive system when distances away from the power conduits were short and stealth was required. There were also four sets of modified RCS rocket motors mounted on gimbals—each shrouded by the vehicle's shell and drawing on the same RP-1 rocket fuel used for the drive engine—that could give him some control over the vehicle's attitude should it become airborne. There were also four downsized PAM-D solid-rocket boosters fixed to the back of the frame in a cluster. He could use those one at a time in case he needed a significant push. The deployable weapons hard-points were specifically designed to allow for different load-outs depending on what Batman considered to be required for the mission at the time. The cockpit had its own layer of passive armor, while the shell of the car used an active armor similar to his own Batsuit—not only protecting the control, weapons, drive, and sensor systems, as well as the Caped Crusader himself, but also allowing the exterior shape of the vehicle to shift. It could find its own aerodynamically optimized shape at high speeds or could modify its look at lower speeds simply to confuse his prey in the middle of pursuit. There were no windows in the vehicle at all, and no lights—the driver depended entirely on an array of cameras, radar, and sonar sensors to give him a picture of his surroundings. However, as the exterior surface could become alternately polished or dull from one plane to the next, it could impersonate the look of smoked glass found in more common vehicles—temporarily blending in with traffic when necessary.

It did nominally look like a "mobile," Bruce admitted but, that, too, was something of an illusion, because the wheels on the vehicle were not solely designed to operate on streets. Bridges were choke points too easily cut off by civilian traffic or the misguided vigilance of the Gotham City Police Department. So for the last year, Gotham Power and Light had been upgrading—thanks to the influence of a number of Wayne Industries subcontractors— power, water, and sewer systems throughout the Gotham network. The real purpose had been to install rapid access points at key locations throughout the city where the TS8c could turn a corner and vanish from the street, the suspension shifting the wheel positions as the vehicle plunged down abandoned subway tunnels, utilities-access conduits, or even main subway lines, if traffic permitted. His favorite system involved a pair of rail clamps that could extend upward out of the front and rear of the vehicle and attach themselves around the specially designed power conduits that ran the length of each of the Gotham bridges. The variable suspension could then rise upward against the bottom of the bridge structure as though it were an upside-down road, allowing him to cross the river beneath the bridges unimpeded, while above him the snarled traffic contended with the occasional roadblocks set to catch him.

Bruce walked slowly to the test bench. It was set on the walkway that partially surrounded the turntable on which the car now rested. He set down his cowl, leaned against the bench, and took in several deep, painful breaths. He looked down into the glossy surface, his reflection staring back at him.

I was young once . . . or was I? I don't remember being young. The face is still strong but there are more lines in it than I remember. Dusk to dawn, fall to spring . . . Did the wheel of the years turn and I never noticed? There are no seasons in this cavern tomb where my soul resides. Does Gotham exist in an eternal rain-soaked night, or do I only see it that way?

Bruce turned around, leaning back against the bench. The Batmobile was resting in the center of the turntable. The original entrance to the cavern was flanked now by six dark tunnels— four black maws on the left and two more on the right—that led away down into the forgotten veins beneath Gotham. Older models of his vehicles had once exited through the waterfall beyond the natural access, careening through the night-shrouded woods and onto the back roads of Bristol Township, with the forbidding silhouette of the city just beyond the riverbanks, calling him back toward Crime Alley. Calling him on to the chase once more. He used to relish driving through the cleansing water of the falls—a ritual baptism that sanctified his quest.

Time changes everything. Time changes nothing.

Bruce listened to the falling of the water echoing toward him down the cavern's natural exit. The gentle green of the surrounding forest on his estate lay beyond. It was a different world.

The tunnels are better than the water. Not perfect . . . but better.

"Master Bruce!"

The irritatingly familiar voice echoed down through the industrial platforms, suspension rods, and turnbuckles throughout the cave. Bruce closed his eyes, considering for a moment whether he would simply not answer, but thought better of it.

"On the vehicle platform, Alfred," he called back. The noise of his former butler's clattering hard-soled shoes on the metal platform grating sounded like the jabbing of an ice pick. "This version of the TS8 performed well tonight."

"It should, considering what the components cost," came the echoing reply. "Mr. Fox wanted me to mention that there may have been some cost overruns—"

"Don't sweat the ledger, Alfred," Bruce chuckled. "It's not in your job description."

"My job description, as you put it, has always been a bit nebulous," Alfred responded, stepping lightly from the metal staircase on the far side of the vehicle turntable. He was a tall, slender man with an anachronistic thin mustache and a mane of white hair combed straight back. Alfred Pennyworth moved in his exquisitely tailored Collezioni charcoal pinstripe suit with an agile confidence that belied his years. He spoke with an upper-crust British accent that had a hint of London about it despite the fact he had been largely raised on the Wayne Estate and only visited London occasionally. His father, Jarvis Pennyworth, had been the family retainer, as such men were so quaintly called during the time of Bruce's grandfather. The accent, it seemed, came with the family business. To Bruce, the Pennyworths had simply come with the house, like the grounds or the furniture. They had always been there, although to Bruce, Alfred had become the only breathing link to his own past . . . the only family that he knew.

Family relationships can be complicated.

"What is it, Alfred?" Bruce sighed. "Why are you bothering me?"

"There are matters that require your attention, Master Bruce, and I had hoped . . ."

"Don't call me that," Bruce snapped.

"But, sir, I've always . . ."

"Just how the hell old do I look to you?" Bruce raged.

"We both know your age well enough, sir, and you will be yet another year older this coming February 19," Alfred said with his nerves suddenly placed on ice.

How long have I been running this mad race? Has it really been that long?

Bruce raised his head, the vertebrae in his neck cracking as he did. "I'm the president of the largest multinational corporation based in the United States, and you still talk to me like I'm wearing short pants. You would never have talked to my father this way."

The words fell between them.

"You are not your father, Master Bruce," Alfred said.

"So you never fail to remind me," Bruce replied, shaking his head as he stood upright and stretched. "I don't suppose you have come this far below your station just to polish the brass?"

"No, sir," Alfred responded in his best businessman tones. "As you so eloquently put it yourself, you *are* the head of the largest multinational corporation in the United States . . . although perhaps not for long."

Bruce stepped around the platform, drawing the fuel nozzle out of its cradle, the hose slinking along behind it toward the vehicle. Bruce touched the pattern on the surface of the car and the fuel cap enclosure opened where the surface had previously appeared seamless. "Is it the board of directors again? Are they singing that old song about ousting me?"

"No, sir . . . well, yes, sir, but this time the pressure is coming from the Securities and Exchange Commission," Alfred pressed on. "You remember the scandal involving Tri-State Home and Hearth?"

Bruce pushed the fuel nozzle into the opening and activated the pump. He leaned back against the side of the vehicle, feeling its malleable surface give slightly under his weight as he crossed his arms. "You would think that with all this power *and* a butler standing at hand, I wouldn't have to pump my own gas, would you?"

"Sir, if you would please just concentrate for a few—"

Bruce released the seals on his gloves and began pulling them off. "Yes, I remember Tri-State . . . it was the mortgage-holding division of our finance side. They were the ones who issued all those subprime loans. Carl Rising was the CEO, and together with his CFO, Ward Olivier, they approved that policy against our corporate directives."

Alfred raised an eyebrow.

"I *don't* just wear this cape, Alfred," Bruce said, rubbing his eyes. The nozzle clicked and he pulled it from the car, sealing the opening again. He continued talking as he placed the fuel line back in place. "We cleaned up Tri-State and kept their doors open. I fired both Rising and Olivier and, as I recall, both of them are under federal indictment."

"Yes, but the SEC isn't satisfied with them," Alfred said, nervously adjusting the cuffs of his tailored shirt, the onyx cuff links flashing even in the spare lights of the cave. "They've approached both Federal Trade and the Department of Justice to come after Wayne Enterprises under the Sherman Act."

"Antitrust?" Bruce chuckled. "Really?"

"They're also talking about RICO, sir," Alfred swallowed hard after pushing out the words.

"Racketeering?" Bruce shook his head. "They can't be serious."

"Sir, they are looking for an excuse . . . ANY excuse . . . to take apart Wayne Enterprises." Alfred reached up and tugged at his collar. "And with public sentiment running against big business and all the negative publicity that we've had about Tri-State—"

"Alfred, that *is* your job," Bruce said, reaching back into the vehicle. He pulled out the Scarface dummy, which still held the invitation card. "We all have a job to do. Yours is to be my public relations director and personal assistant. Those were the titles that I gave you with the raise. You seemed pleased enough at the time, remember?"

"Yes, sir, I remember it well," Alfred replied with a sniff. "Although I do still seem to be making your meals and dusting the banister."

"Exactly." Bruce held up the horrific gangster dummy with the card attached to its hand as he walked quickly past Alfred up toward the main investigation platform. "I, on the other hand, have got to do *my* job and fathom why the Spellbinder was herself spellbound by the Ventriloquist's Scarface dummy and the meaning of this strange invitation."

"But I already have one, sir." Alfred shrugged.

"What are you talking about?" Bruce said, setting the dummy down on the testing bench.

"This invitation," Alfred replied, pulling an identical card out of the breast pocket of his jacket.

Bruce frowned. "Where did you get that?"

"Where did *anyone* get them?" Alfred shrugged, turning the card over in his hand. "Everyone in Gotham and the surrounding municipalities received one today. It's taken over the news reports."

"Everyone?" Bruce asked. He moved to the Batsuit locker as Alfred spoke, pressing the release points on the new Batsuit as he moved. The arms' exomusculature released from the attachment points at the shoulders, unsealed, and pulled free down both arms. The shoulder segment released next from the torso manifold, taking the cape with it over his head. He quickly placed each in its supporting rack position.

"They say there was a computer error at the Gotham Powerball Lottery offices that generated the mailing of these defective cards to everyone in the city. There is one on the foyer mail table addressed to you as well."

"That's no computer error," Bruce said, sitting down on the bench next to the locker, releasing his boots, and then pulling them free. The Utility Belt—a power supply for the Batsuit—he set into the charging station built into the locker. "It's a cover story and a rather hastily baked one at that."

Bruce stood up. Still wearing the long microtube garment that kept him cool beneath the powered armor, he stepped back to consider his latest incarnation of the Batsuit.

It's a good design. Not perfect. It will be better next time.

"Master Bruce?"

Bruce reached over and snatched the invitation out of Alfred's hand. "I've got work to do, Alfred. That will be all."

Alfred's eyebrow seemed to pull his nose into the air as he started climbing the stairs. There was a secured elevator that would take him up to the Manor but not until after another two-story climb up into the darkness of the cavern. "Of course, sir. Will you be expecting breakfast?"

Bruce sat down on a stool at the lab bench and switched on the light of his large magnifying glass. He turned the card over and over beneath it. The card appeared to be common except for the printing. There was something strange about the ink . . .

Bruce looked up.

"Alfred, did you say something?"

"Just asking if you wanted your breakfast, sir."

There was a plaintive quality in Alfred's voice that Bruce could not remember having heard before. "Yes, I would. Thank you, Alfred."

Alfred nodded and began again to climb the stairs.

Bruce tried to look closer at the card but was suddenly distracted by a smell that connected in his memory. It was a warm, musty smell of autumn leaves and green grass. It reminded him of laughter.

"Alfred?"

The old man stopped on the stairs. "Yes, sir?"

"What is it like outside?"

A second silence stretched between them filled with thought.

"It is the promise of a beautiful day, Master Br— It is a beautiful day, sir," Alfred responded as he looked down on the circle of dim light illuminating Bruce alone in the midst of the cavern. "Indian Summer today, I believe they call it. The storm has cleared off to the east and we're expecting slightly warmer temperatures under clearing skies. Breezy, cool, but pleasant."

"Pleasant." The word rolled off of his tongue like a foreign, unknown thing. A sunny day in Gotham. No, he thought, there was no such thing. Gotham was a never ending night. Gotham was a rain that never healed, never cleaned. Gotham was dirt and decay and rot that festered, a disease for which he alone was the cure; he alone stood between the great abyss and justice for those who called the darkness home.

The darkness is Gotham. The darkness is my world.

"Will there be anything else, sir?"

Bruce looked up.

The smell of leaves.

The sound of laughter.

"You can call me Master Bruce, Alfred," he said quietly. "It's all right, if you like."

"Thank you, Master Bruce." Alfred smiled as he turned and continued up the stairs.

Bruce Wayne continued to hold the card in his hand, but his eyes were fixed on the exit from the cave, the rushing sound of the falling waters . . . and the smell of a bright autumn day.

CHAPTER THREE

AMANDA

Bruce Wayne, playboy of Gotham, with inexhaustible wealth, had become the Howard Hughes of the new century.

For more than a decade, he had disappeared from public life. National news commentators collected their appearance fees by filling in the gaping blanks in the meaning of his absence by tracing his disappearance to September 11, 2001. Local newscasters, on the other hand, would annually and at regular intervals fill a little more airtime by pulling out the file footage on his parents' violent deaths—lately with computer-generated reenactments of the murders—and trace the reclusive peculiarities to these understandable roots. Articles in the financial section of the *Gotham Globe* sold their papers with the claim that the Wayne heir's mental aberrations were rooted in the mid-1990s and the rise of neoliberalism. Their competition, the *Gotham Gazette*, took a completely different point of view, insisting the underlying causes that had unhinged him were to be found in the economic explosiveness of a 1980s marketplace released from the restraints of ethics or social conscience. Several biographies— each unauthorized and always the subject of a perfunctory lawsuit—insisted it was a former lover, either female or male, who had jilted the unbalanced Wayne. Two of these had hit a little too close to the mark. *Tarnished Princess: How Julie Madison Became Portia Storme Without Really Trying* had been a bestseller exposé that centered as much on Bruce as it had on his former college girlfriend's strange and meteoric life. The other one, the far more lurid *Slain Manor: The Strange Case of Vesper Fairchild*, had revived interest in the sensational murder of the popular television reporter and personality whom Bruce had dated briefly before trying to cool things off . . . only to be arrested when her body was discovered in his home. Those books were the exception; for the most part the players in these fantasies were shadows. The public, it seemed, was ravenous for any lurid ink regarding the Prince of Gotham and was willing to pay tabloid and paperback prices to read it. Each one promised to spotlight a new damsel in distress or hooker with a heart of gold. Their identities were always known only to the author, who was only willing to divulge the secret to anyone willing to purchase his book, pad his royalties, and wade through the shocking, fictional details.

They knew absolutely nothing about Bruce, but that was not permissible for the media maw that had to be fed, and so they filled the silence with their own wild imaginings and sold all the more airtime, newspapers, books, and blogs in the process.

They would have all been outraged, however, to know the truth: that Bruce reveled in it.

It all added to the mystery and never approached the truth—an even better cover than before. The connection to Hughes was an obvious one and only needed a little push. Alfred was promoted from "gentleman's gentleman" to press agent and public relations manager at about that same time. Alfred Pennyworth became the face the media associated with Bruce Wayne whenever anyone came calling or needed a statement. Bruce even reveled in the game, appearing from time to time in a latex mask he had fashioned for himself, hunching over in a wheelchair and wearing large dark glasses, a wide-brimmed panama hat, and an afghan draped around his shoulders. He had forced Alfred to push him around the east gardens in the costume at random intervals until one of the paparazzi showed up on the grounds and managed to snap a slightly out-of-focus image of the two of them going for a stroll. The security sensors placed throughout the grounds of Wayne Manor had alerted Bruce to the intruder's presence long before the paparazzo saw them. Still, the picture had become the iconic image of Bruce Wayne, the recluse: an incredibly wealthy but broken man. Bruce and Alfred were occasionally forced to repeat versions of this charade whenever other photographers took a chance on the grounds, but that first photograph had become iconic.

Now maybe they'll leave me to my work.

It had been a wonderful dream, but Bruce discovered there is nothing so public as being too private. In time, however, Bruce Wayne faded from interest, only to become a mythic figure whose image had been so reshaped that no one knew any longer what the real Bruce Wayne even looked like.

Wayne Estate Grounds / Bristol / 6:32 a.m. / Present Day

Multibillionaire Bruce Wayne climbed out of the ravine in the cloth canvas jacket, a flat cap on his head. His face was covered in rough stubble. The eyes squinted in the bright, clear morning as he moved from shade to dappled shade beneath the forest of trees. He allowed the footfalls of his hunting boots to smash down through the undergrowth . . . an unaccustomed luxury.

The great lawn is across the slope. Father used to host enormous gatherings on that lawn behind the manor.

The lawns were always impeccably manicured, but now their silence was broken only by the occasional trill of a meadowlark. The magnificent view down toward the north branch of the Gotham River and across the waters to the unique skyline of Gotham itself remained unappreciated. There would be no music. No laughter would disturb a single blade of grass.

It would make a fine cemetery.

He needed to think. He had been scanning the invitation card when suddenly, in the darkness of the caverns, his memory had taken him back to a different time.

Mother enjoyed planning the lawn parties more than all other events; she said the desired result was inevitable if the event was properly arranged. She never could think in the house . . . she always had to go somewhere she could clear her mind . . . clear her soul . . .

Bruce turned down the slope, away from the lawn just visible through the trees. He had not thought of his mother's garden in more than a decade. Dead and rotting leaves from unnumbered seasons obscured the old path.

Bruce stopped, cocking his head to one side.

The wall was almost completely obscured by tall brush and vines, still full of foliage despite the lateness of the year. He might have missed it altogether except for the fact that the doorway had been completely cleared of brush. The door was weathered and showed only the slightest vestiges of the emerald paint his mother had chosen for it so long ago, but it was free of any debris.

He had half wondered if the succession of gardeners down the long years had forgotten its existence, as he had. It would seem the garden had been tended after all.

"If you need to think something through, Bruce," Martha Wayne said, *"you had best find someplace pleasant."*

Bruce reached for the keys in his jacket, pulling out a large, tarnished padlock key and stepping to the door.

The lock was open . . . the door slightly ajar.

Bruce froze, his senses heightened.

"Ting-a-ling-a-ling-tum, ting-tum, ting-tum . . ."

Singing. Someone is singing in my mother's garden.

"Ting-a-ling-tum, ting-tum-tae . . ."

I know that song . . . I remember that song.

Bruce put the key slowly back in his jacket pocket. He reached forward with his left hand, pressing it against the door gently and testing its resistance. It moved with surprising ease, the hinges only popping twice as the door swung open before him.

The garden was dead. The roses had gone wild and died during the succession of winters without care. Their gnarled limbs reached up like claws from the edges of the footpaths, which were covered in dead leaves decomposing into dirt. The prize lilacs his mother had been so proud of now reached up menacingly over the walls. The garden had gone native, weeds choking and obscuring the careful planning that now lay buried and barely recognizable.

The gazebo was still there. Its wood was rotting and one side of the roof had collapsed, charred, it seemed, from either a lightning strike or a flaming branch falling from one of the surrounding trees, which may have been struck during a storm. The stone benches around the gazebo's inner perimeter were still standing.

A woman sat with her back toward the door.

Bruce set his teeth.

The woman's hair was a platinum blond.

Her hair was a platinum blonde. She had always adored Kim Novak, changing her own dark hair to imitate Novak's look. She wore a camel-hair coat with a high collar turned up at the back.

He could still hear his voice when he said it. "Martha, that coat looks stunning on you!" She never wore another coat after that . . .

"Ting-a-ling-a-ling-tum, ting-tum, ting-tum . . ."

Hand mother a baby and she would break into that song. She sang that to me as early as I can . . .

The woman swayed back and forth on the bench, her voice listlessly murmuring the lyrics. "Ting-a-ling-tum, ting-tum-tae . . ."

Mother in the garden . . . Mother in the garden to think . . .

Bruce lunged forward. He crossed the dead garden in five quick strides, reaching for the woman even as he passed between the cracking posts of the gazebo. He grabbed the woman by her coat, hauling her to her feet in front of him.

"Who are you?" he shouted into her face. "What the hell are you doing here?"

Her skin startled Bruce at first. Her face was a creamy alabaster that registered in his mind as being almost ghostlike in its pale complexion. She may have been in her mid-thirties, yet her face had a quality of timeless beauty that made placing her age difficult. Her eyes were large and gray, but as he looked into them they were unfocused and slightly dilated. Her nose had a slight upturn with an almost imperceptible dimple at the end, and her eyebrows had been carefully plucked. Her hair was long but pulled back into a tight bun. She was beautiful and elegant, but in a way that was completely out of fashion with the times.

"Please," she said. "Help me. Help me find Bruce."

"What?"

"You're hurting me—"

"Yes, I am. Who are you?"

"I don't—please, help me find him."

"Help you find who?"

Her eyes suddenly focused on him with a bright intensity. "Bruce!"

She knows me? I've never met this woman before.

"I told you, I have to find Bruce," she continued glancing around her. "Please, he's lost . . . he's lost and he's frightened and I have to bring him home. Whoever you are, can you help me?"

More than you know . . . I hope. Bruce relaxed his grip on her shoulders slightly. "You don't know who I am?"

"Well, how could I?" she said indignantly. "We just met!"

An identity . . . an alias . . . who shall I be today?

"I'm Gerald Grayson . . . I'm the gamekeeper here."

She looked around as if for the first time. "Here . . . Where am I?"

"You don't know?"

She flushed slightly. "No, I . . . I really don't know how I got here."

"Well, here is somewhere you're not supposed to be—you're trespassing," Bruce said, letting go of her shoulders and hooking his thumbs through the loops of his jeans. "Old 'Hermit Wayne' wouldn't appreciate you coming in unannounced."

"Bruce, you mean," she said, as though the word tasted odd on her tongue. "I . . . I need to find him. Warn him."

"I see him now and then," Bruce said with a shrug. "I could get your message to him."

Her smile was slightly wry. "Thank you, but . . . could you just show me the way out?"

Bruce considered for a moment how she possibly could have gotten in. The number of alarm and surveillance systems in place, not just on the perimeter but within the grounds, including seismic sensors, should have made it impossible for anyone to pass around the estate unnoticed. Indeed, while Bruce had engineered the system himself, he had more recently come to feel he was a prisoner in a cage of his own design. The once comforting thought of being able to track anyone on the grounds had eroded over time, until Bruce felt he was constantly being watched by Alfred.

Things had been slowly changing between them in recent years. Alfred's elevation in title and position within the company had been necessary but strained the tightrope balance of their relationship. Bruce had begun to feel vaguely unsettled in Alfred's presence, like the hair standing up at the nape of one's neck for no discernable reason. Alfred was deferential and efficient as always, but now there was something irritating about the uncanny perfection of his former butler's service to him that made Bruce want some space in his life where Alfred could not reach—something the security of the Manor, the grounds, and even the caverns under it could not afford him.

But Bruce's jacket had something in its lining that would facilitate the solution: a low-yield bypass transmitter sewn in just for such occasions. If he wanted to wander the grounds without Alfred knowing where he was, he had to be a ghost to his own surveillance systems. As long as this woman stayed within five feet of him, he should be able to get her off the grounds without tripping any of the multiple alarms.

And maybe then he could discover how she managed to get *into* here in the first place.

"If I may escort you," Bruce said, extending his crooked arm.

She smiled as she slipped her elegant, long hand through his arm. "My knight in shining armor."

Hardly shining, lady.

"So you're a gamekeeper?" she said as they strolled out of the walled garden and further down the slope. She arched her right eyebrow even further. "Do they still have those, Mr. Grayson?"

With his left hand in his pocket, he fingered the invitation card.

The card mystery . . . now the woman mystery. I wanted to come to the garden to . . . why did I come to the garden? Why didn't I stay in the cave where it was safe and dark? Why did I have to come into the light?

"*They* do," he replied. "Here they do. And you still haven't told me your name."

"Richter," she said turning her head away slightly as she spoke. "Amanda Richter."

Means nothing. New to me. File it for reference later.

"Well, Ms. Richter, I'll see you to the servants' gatehouse," Bruce said. "It's at the bottom of the hill, and we can call for a cab from the guard's room there."

"Won't the guard mind us intruding on him there?" she asked.

"No guard," Bruce smiled. They had already passed over more than a hundred different automated alarm and intruder-response systems. "Still, I wouldn't advise you coming back for another try over the fence."

"Is *that* how I got in?" Amanda asked. "Climbed over the fence in my designer jacket and tailored suit?"

"Well, if you did," Bruce nodded, "I'm sorry I wasn't there to see it. Here is the gatehouse."

They were at the base of the enormous slope of the back lawn. The twelve-foot-tall stone fence emerged from the woods to their left and extended across the back of the property and into the woods on the far side of the lawn. The line was broken only by the gatehouse and the wide iron gate next to it, thwarting the road that wound up the edge of the woods toward the manor, which was nearly two miles distant at the top of the rise to the north.

If Amanda heard the door unlock at their approach, she didn't show it.

Bruce showed her through the gatehouse and out the other side. He placed the call for the cab and then stepped out to where she was standing next to the road.

"They say they'll be here in about ten minutes," Bruce said. "Must be a gathering of the upper-crust somewhere in Bristol tonight if the cabs are that close."

Amanda nodded, then turned her gray eyes on him. "I really must see Bruce, Mr. Grayson."

"Call me Gerry," Bruce corrected.

"Gerry, then. Isn't there any way that I—"

"Well, you can ask," Bruce said.

Remember to flash your charming smile. It's been such a long time.

Bruce leaned against the gatehouse, folded his arms, and nodded toward the intercom mounted next to the gate.

Amanda gave him a "thanks for nothing" smile and stepped up to the intercom. She jabbed the button with a long, elegant finger. "Yes?"

Alfred sounds upset. He's probably wondering why he didn't get any proximity alarms at her approach.

"I am here to see Bruce Wayne," Amanda said.

Bruce raised his eyebrows and nodded approvingly.

"Mr. Wayne is not taking callers," Alfred's tinlike voice replied from the box.

"I have a message for him—a very important message," Amanda said.

"I shall be delighted to take the message, madam," Alfred responded. "Whom may I say the message is from?"

"It is from me. Amanda Richter."

The metal box went silent for a moment.

That's not like Alfred. Reporters and writers trying to make their mark approach him every day, and usually a lot more creatively than this.

"Could you give that name again?" Alfred said at last.

"Yes. I'm Amanda Richter."

Silence again? Did I hear stress in Alfred's voice?

"Miss Richter, please stay where you are," Alfred said. "I'll be down directly."

Bruce continued to smile, but there was definitely something wrong. Alfred had strict orders never to greet anyone on the property nor allow them in unless they had been cleared by him personally. There were no exceptions.

"It looks like you won't be needing that cab after all," Bruce said.

"I suppose not, Mr. Grayson," Amanda said.

"Oh, and I shouldn't have let you out through the gatehouse,"

Bruce added. "If that butler catches me here, there'll be hell to pay. I could lose my job."

"I promise not to say a thing," Amanda nodded.

"Thanks," Bruce replied. "It's been a pleasure, Amanda."

"Thank you, Gerry."

Bruce turned and stepped back through the gatehouse with studied casualness. He stepped back on to the grounds out the other side, registering the sound of the locks on the doors snapping closed automatically behind him. Amanda was now properly locked outside his domain, though he still did not know how she had managed to get *into* the grounds in the first place.

Moreover, there was the question of Alfred.

Alfred had been with him from the beginning. Every relationship has its strains. He and Alfred had been through it all together for as long as Bruce could remember. Sometimes it was easy and sometimes it was hard. Of late, the warm relationship between the retainer and his master had cooled somewhat and the silences between them had lengthened. Even so, Bruce believed Alfred Pennyworth had been steadfastly honest in his service.

But now Alfred was reacting contrary to Bruce's direct orders because of a woman he obviously knew—one who somehow had managed to slip undetected onto the grounds.

"They are all just pieces to the puzzle, Bruce," Mother said so often. "Just put together the ones that make sense and the rest will follow in time . . ."

Bruce moved quickly back toward the ravine. He could hear the motor of the Bentley approaching from the Manor, no doubt with Alfred behind the wheel, and wanted to be out of sight before it arrived.

Bruce settled down into the massive chair in front of his research console. The air in the Batcave felt oppressive now compared with the morning outside, but it was also familiar and somehow comforting after the strange encounter he had on the grounds.

Don't let yourself get distracted. Hold onto the greater picture and let the pieces fall into place when you see where they fit.

He pulled the card out from the pocket of his jacket and set it down in front of him. Then he pulled on the gloves of the virtual interface. The array of screens awoke in front of him and he started pulling data out of the air with his hands. It shifted in the space in front of him as he examined it. The first was the card itself. He pulled the chemical analysis of the card and the printing which displayed in a cascade to his left.

The laminate coat over the cards was actually a bonded protein complex, permeable and releasing its bond under heat. It was an unusual substance for a card laminate, and understanding its properties would take some additional consideration. He let the sequencer continue chewing on that one while he moved on.

The paper itself was a plastic derivative rather than actual paper. The grain was a fine embossed simulation of the feel of paper down to a very fine surface level, and a comparison of the card he had pulled from the Scarface dummy with the one he took from Alfred showed their texture patterns were identical down to microscopic levels.

That's an unusual amount of effort for an invitation. Fine detail . . .

He pulled the high-resolution optical scans of the cards to examine the printing side by side, looking for variations in the ink.

There were none. No bleeding, print smudges, or blur variations one might expect in a mass-production press run. The printing was identical right down to the highest magnification of the—

The highest magnification . . .

He pushed the scan in as far as the magnification would go.

The ink was not contiguous. It was a half-tone imaging at the most miniscule microprinting scale he had ever encountered. Each of the letters was made up of a series of spaced dots. Not only were there distinct dots, but the dots appeared to be the same size in each case, although their positions and the spaces between the dots varied.

No . . . they don't vary at all. They are an entirely uniform spacing of black dots and white spaces. It's a digital stream. It's data!

He pushed the chemical analysis aside and pulled down a graphic parser module, coupling it to the cryptography node. The parser would scan the micro image into a data stream, and then the cryptographic software would process it searching for recognizable patterns. The graphic parsing would be almost instantaneous, but the cryptographic node could take days to chew through the data before coming up with possible recognizable patterns. Bruce set up the parameters, started the program run, stripped off the gloves, and spun around in his chair.

He had barely started to stand when the consol began chiming.

I must have made a mistake in the comparison loop sequence.

He sat back down and turned to the consol, pulling the gloves back on in annoyance. The display was flashing "Run complete." He reached for the image, tapped it, and waited for the garbage data to display so he could push it into the trash.

"What the hell?" Bruce muttered, staring at the display.

It was a congruous PDF file.

"It can't be that simple." His eyes narrowing, Bruce reached forward and tapped on the file to open it.

It sprang open.

Gotham City Police Department
Case Number: VR/01/04/05/1689
Investigating Officer: Detective J. Gordon
Vice & Racketeering Division
June 28, 1974

Two days after my parents died. Two days after I died with them.

Bruce leaned forward, reading the fuzzy type on the digital page floating in front of him.

> Telephone tip received from one Marion Richter / 1429 Pearl Street / Upper West Side re: Wayne killing. Partner Detective T. Holloway and I conducted the interview in Richter's apartment at 10:36 a.m. Richter asserted the death of Thomas and Martha Wayne had been contract killing motivated by Thomas Wayne's alleged business with her father, Dr. Ernst Richter (deceased). She further claimed Thomas Wayne had ties to the Moxon mob and had been conspiring with them over several decades. She presented six of her father's bound journals in evidence, as well as a number of contracts and papers that appear to have been signed by both Wayne and her father. She also included a number of bank deposits and account statements indicating when payments to her father and, after his death, to her and her young sister, Amanda, had been made by Thomas Wayne through the intermediary of the Wayne House managers, Jarvis Pennyworth and subsequently his son, Alfred Pennyworth. These items were catalogued by Holloway and accepted.

Bruce sat back in his chair, his frown deepening.

No wonder, then, that Alfred came down to the gatehouse to see to Amanda Richter personally. But I've never heard of these Richters before, and certainly not in conjunction with my parents' deaths. Why didn't Alfred tell me about this?

He read on.

> Miss Richter further stated that, according to her father's journals, Thomas Wayne also kept extensive journals of his own that could corroborate her testimony. We concluded the interview with Marion Richter at 11:46 a.m.

We then proceeded to Wayne Manor in Bristol with the intention of interviewing Alfred Pennyworth regarding the payments made to the Richters and the alleged journals. Mr. Pennyworth consented to the interview, which we conducted in the library at Wayne Manor. Alfred acknowledges knowing the Richters and conveying financial assistance to the Richters at the behest of his employer, Thomas Wayne. He denied the existence of journals by Thomas Wayne in any form, electronic or otherwise. (Search warrant filed / pending.) He further denies any association between the Moxon mob and the . . .

The typewriter text ended at the bottom of the page.

Bruce stretched his hand out, tapping the document to flip to the next page.

Nothing happened.

He looked at the lower right corner of the displayed page. It read "1 / 14," meaning that he had read page one of fourteen pages. He quickly checked the file size. The single page was all the data that existed in the microprint on the card.

Bruce cross-referenced the case file number against the Police Evidence Archives database.

The file referred to in the document was missing from the archives.

Bruce pressed his hands together, his forefingers tented in front of his pursed lips. He reached forward, stabbing at the intercom switch on the console.

"Alfred."

"Yes, Master Wayne."

"You mentioned something about breakfast earlier . . . and I feel like we should talk."

"Of course, sir," Alfred's voice was smooth as cream.

"I'll be right up then."

"Oh, I beg your pardon," Alfred responded at once. "I apologize that your meal will be ready a few minutes later than I had anticipated. I fear I am required to run to the market for some fresh cilantro. It shall be another hour, sir."

Cilantro? In an hour?

"Oh, that's quite all right, Alfred," Bruce said in practiced, even tones. "I'm more of a brunch man myself. By the way, was there someone at the back gate just now?"

There's a pause in his response. He never pauses . . . never hesitates.

"No, sir," Alfred replied brightly. "Not that I am aware of."

"I just thought I heard the proximity alarm is all."

"No, sir," Alfred replied. "Perhaps a malfunction. I shall look into it at once."

"Of course," Bruce replied. "Let me know when breakfast is served."

Bruce released the intercom button, a dark shadow covering his face as he again sat back in his chair to consider.

The evidence file is missing. Thirteen pages of Gordon's report are missing. Alfred is lying to me about Amanda Richter. My parents' lives are missing and now the why behind their deaths is missing, too.

Reluctantly, Bruce reached forward, spun the display down to a file he had long ago closed.

BC001–0001
Wayne, Thomas & Martha

CHAPTER FOUR

GOOD-LOOKING CORPSE

James Gordon stood on the roof of police headquarters facing the high-load circuit breaker box. The lock was dangling from the open panel door. It had long since stopped swinging. The night was chilly, his breath forming clouds in front of him as he stood in the clear autumn night.

How the hell did it come to this?

Gotham City police commissioner James Gordon knew the answer better than anyone else. He had grown up with his brother Roger in Chicago, the two of them playing "cops and robbers" up and down the block of their brownstone-lined Lincoln Park neighborhood. It had not mattered much to the boys then who played the "cop" and who played the "robber," and they often tossed a coin to see which one would be which.

It was not until much later in his life that Gordon—a newly minted police lieutenant moving his wife and son to a new job in Gotham—discovered just how arbitrary that coin toss was in the G.C.P.D. His first partner on the job was Arthur Flass—a cop as

dirty as they came. Gordon dutifully reported his partner's extortion racket to then-commissioner Gillian Loeb. He soon had
his naïveté beaten out of him by a number of his brother officers
wielding baseball bats; it seemed that Loeb was skimming a cut
of his own off the top of every corrupt cop in town. The beating
only managed to forge the young lieutenant into tougher steel.
Gordon became known as an "untouchable" cop, but with Loeb
running the police and his hand firmly in control of the Internal
Affairs Division, it was obvious that the career of James Gordon
had died in the baseball bat beating even if his body had not.

Then Gordon's fortunes all changed at the hands of a different kind of bat.

Batman had been hailed as a valiant citizen by Commissioner
Loeb when he first arrived. Loeb believed this Batman could
be bought and controlled just like nearly everyone else, and
his antics were a nice distraction from the commissioner's more
shadow-prone deals. Loeb had not counted on this "nut-job in
a cape" actually prying into his own racket. So when "the Bat"
opened up the commissioner's can of worms, Loeb responded
by branding him a criminal, vigilante, anarchist, and terrorist.
Batman became Gotham's most-wanted criminal.

And who better to bring down such a menace to law and
order than the squeaky-clean, untouchable Detective Lieutenant
James Gordon?

It had been like trying to hose down a fire with gasoline.

It was the beginning of a volatile friendship.

They were different men with different approaches to the
problem, but they both agreed on what the problem was.
Gordon could never condone Batman acting outside the process of law. Batman was often frustrated by Gordon's insistence
on a process that so often thwarted justice. But together they
managed to turn the tables on both Flass and, eventually, Loeb,
bringing both of them down.

Batman, it seemed, was the salvation of Gordon's career, so long as Gordon could justify to himself allowing the Batman to exist. It required him to compromise his principles in order to achieve them, a dichotomy that made him question and sometimes hate himself every day. He had come to view the Batman as his friend and yet he hated him—hated him for the compromise he represented in his life and for the things Gordon was forced to ask this outlaw to do when justice could not be served by the very institutions he had vowed to honor and protect.

The Batman had made him a success at the cost of a piece of his soul.

Gordon's fortunes rose in the police department, though at a high personal cost. The beating he had taken had also been the beginning of the end for his relationship with his wife, the strain of being a principled police detective eventually showing as cracks in his marriage. His brother Roger and his wife Thelma both died in a horrific automobile accident, leaving their daughter Barbara without a home. The Gordons adopted the thirteen-year-old girl partly out of duty and partly out of a hope that it might help them save their marriage. When Gordon's wife finally left him, Gordon had doted on the girl, raising her into a fine young woman with a bright future.

Then the Batman swept onto the porch of her apartment and shot her in cold blood . . . she died alone, bleeding out in that hallway . . .

Gordon stared at the breaker arm that would power up the Bat-Signal on the roof of police headquarters.

"It's been fifteen minutes, Gordon," came the raspy voice from above him. "Can't you decide?"

The police commissioner jumped at the sound, his hand instinctively going for his service weapon. Some delicate inhibition in the back of his mind snapped. He knew he should stop, but he was already past that, the weapon drawn from its holster, rising up toward the silhouette that blocked out the stars with its hated, too-familiar shape.

I'm going to do it this time, Gordon thought with detachment. *I'm really going to do it . . .*

Cold gel shot out from the shadow, encasing the gun and Gordon's hand in a terrible mass. Gordon's finger pulled against the trigger but the gel was hardening too quickly. The commissioner pulled back the gun, staring down through his glasses at the barrel, now plugged and encased in the hard, rubbery glob.

Gordon cried out in rage, trying to get the gun free of the thick mess encasing both it and his right hand. "Damn you! You son of a bitch!"

"You need to calm down, Gordon," the Dark Knight said roughly, his cape shifting slightly behind him. Batman was perched atop the stairwell casing looking down on the commissioner. The wide lens of the Bat-Signal—the name another press affectation—stood dark at the edge of the roof, its beckoning eye shuttered. "If you manage to pull the trigger, the bullet has nowhere to go. The gun will explode and you could lose that hand . . . and it's probably best not to bring my mother into this."

Emotionally exhausted, James Gordon fell to his knees. "What are you doing here?"

"I came because you need me," the Bat whispered. "Because the chase isn't over . . . The monsters are still out there."

"The monster's right here," Gordon responded. He hated the Batman more than anything he had ever hated in his life. He needed him just as badly. "I should have killed you when I had the chance."

"Hold out your gun hand," Batman said, slipping down quietly from his perch to stand on the roof in front of Gordon.

The commissioner raised his arm. Batman took Gordon's wrist in an iron-vice grip with his right hand, pulling a small aerosol canister from his Utility Belt with his left. He sprayed the solvent on the commissioner's encased hand. The gel crystallized and then crumbled away in a heartbeat. Batman was ready for it, snatching the gun out of Gordon's grip before he had time to react. The Caped Crusader took a step back into the shadows of the rooftop, his eyes fixed warily on his old friend.

"Barbara is still alive, Gordon," Batman urged. "She's upstate at school. She was put in a wheelchair, but she *is* still alive—and I didn't do that. Joker did."

"Don't lie to me," Gordon seethed.

"I've never lied to you," Batman replied in a voice like gravel. "It's a false memory, Gordon. A phantom conjured by the Spellbinder to make you and the others commit crimes all across the city."

"No, you're wrong—it wasn't the Spellbinder," Gordon smiled with smug satisfaction. "That maniac uses hypnosis to control her victims, and we both know that hypnosis wears off if it isn't reinforced. Besides, we've got Spellbinder, I mean, Fay Moffit, back in Arkham, and she's suffering from her own set of delusions."

"She's a psychotic sociopath," Batman grunted. "Delusions would be a step up for her."

"She says you seduced her into stealing the Scarface dummy," Gordon replied. "She believes it, too."

"Then it isn't hypnosis," Batman replied. "Psychotropic drugs, perhaps with a memory or behavioral modification component. Someone cast a spell on the Spellbinder, eh? So now you have a mess, and you want me to clean it up. Is that why you wanted me?"

"I don't *want* you at all," Gordon seethed.

"Then let's just say that's why you're standing on the roof," Batman replied, *"not* using the Bat-Signal to summon me."

Gordon blinked, trying to see past his rage. "About three months ago, everyone who was committing these crimes got a card in the mail. It read, 'This card will bring you luck.' Nothing else, and each with a Gotham Central postmark."

"Let me see it," Batman demanded.

"I don't have it," the commissioner replied. "Threw it away months ago."

"Show me your wallet," Batman demanded.

The Commissioner reached back and pulled the wallet out, spreading the folds with his fingers.

Batman reached forward, swiftly pulling out the card.

"Hey," Gordon said. "I would have sworn that wasn't there."

"But that's not why you came to the roof *not* to use the Bat-Signal," Batman said, examining the card carefully. "These are the same type of cards that are now all over the city."

"That's right," Gordon responded. "We were able to trace their manufacture to Lunar Products in their plant down by Dixon Docks off Englehart Boulevard. It's a property registered to a Dr. Chandra Bulan. Both words are aliases for . . ."

"Moon," Batman spat the word. "Both are Southeast Asian words for moon."

"Dr. Moon," Gordon agreed. "He was an expert in memory tampering, and this looks like his M.O."

"*Was* an expert is the point," Batman agreed. "Moon is dead and has been for years."

"He's been pretty active for a corpse, then," Gordon responded. "We have been getting reports there's an Eastern cult growing in Chinatown with Dr. Moon at its head."

"I don't suppose you mean Sun Myung Moon and the Unification Church." Batman smiled beneath his cowl.

"Would I be asking *you* if I did?" Gordon grumbled.

"You think Dr. Moon's come back from the grave and is

spreading these cards all over the city," Batman stated, slipping the card into an evidence pouch on his Utility Belt.

"*Someone* is spreading these all over the city," Gordon stated, "and if that's true, then this last little crime spree will have been a tame preview to the storm that's coming."

Batman nodded, then held the gun out to Gordon, grip first.

Gordon stared at the gun for a few moments, then shook his head. "You had better take it with you."

"It never happened, Gordon," Batman insisted. "It's a memory that is only a dream."

Gordon drew in a deep breath. "Not for me. I remember every detail . . . seeing her fall in the entry to her apartment . . . the blood spreading out beneath her on the tile . . . you standing in the doorway. My rational mind knows it's all a fake . . . but if I take that gun, I also know I'll use it on you. It hurts too much and it seems too right."

Batman nodded. He released the clip and tossed it across the roof, then released the slide, pulling the recoil rod and spring from the pistol frame. He scattered the components around him in an arc. "I'll let you know when it's done."

"What are you going to do?" Gordon asked.

"Pay a visit to a dead man," Batman said.

Gordon was going to ask how . . . but Batman was gone.

Dixon Foundation College / Gotham / 9:42 p.m. / Present Day

Batman sweated. The Batsuit was overheating badly, the charge levels of the Utility Belt drawing dangerously low despite the additional capacitors he had mounted. The Batsuit's cooling system was taxed to the limit, but beneath it all, Bruce Wayne reveled in the challenge and gloried in the exertion.

Eight young cultists had managed to converge on him at once in the sound booth of the crumbling auditorium. Their blows were starting to penetrate the weakening active armor of the Batsuit, reaching his ribs.

Batman smiled.

This was his kind of fight.

The Lunar Cultists were drawn largely from the gangs of nearby Chinatown, and Moon's guard had been well trained in martial arts. Their enthusiasm for their leader was fanatical and absolute, driving them with the same kind of zeal that fueled Batman. He had the advantage of experience, but his body was aging. They had the advantage of numbers, but were not trained in group combat. Neither side would relinquish the field.

It was the balance that made it interesting for him.

With a cry, Batman pushed outward with all his strength. The Batsuit responded, drawing more power from the fading capacitors. The cultists exploded away from him, two of them crashing through the glass of the booth and falling limp among the broken seats below.

Batman was at once on his feet. Two of the remaining cult guards regained their stance, their shaved heads glistening with blood, nunchucks appearing in their hands in a sudden blur.

Too many movies. Maybe not their first mistake . . . certainly their last.

Batman stepped into the first, the hard end of the chain-bound weapon whistling toward his head. He shifted, twisting, and then blocked the nunchuck with his forearm at just the right moment, causing it to rebound into the face of his assailant, whose nose broke with a satisfying crunch. Batman spun, adding injury to injury, as his elbow rose up under the broken nose and drove the bones upward into the face.

The turn left him facing the second remaining opponent, whose own nunchucks were wheeling in a blur toward the panting Dark Knight. Batman crossed his forearms in front of him, arresting the sweeping nunchucks between the gauntlets of his gloves. His arms slid down the polished wood, wresting the weapon from the hands of the young, surprised cultist.

"Never spin the weapon," Batman instructed, wheeling the sticks around their metallic link until both came together side by side in his hand. "It's better to hold it firmly."

Batman smashed his fist, still gripping both sticks, across the youth's face, driving him to his knees. His smile grew on his face as he drove the fist clenched around the nunchucks again and again, hammering down on the cultist.

When the boy quit moving, the fist stopped.

Batman jumped through the shattered window, the cape dutifully billowing to slow his descent as he landed ten feet below on the bodies that had preceded him.

Dixon Foundation College had once been a private institution, but when the funding left, so did the students. The teaching auditorium was crumbling, but bright red cloth had been draped in bunting along the crumbling Sheetrock of the walls. There was a podium, the focal point of the empty auditorium.

Dr. Moon stood at the podium.

I have to admit he looks pretty good . . . considering he's been dead for ten years.

His facial skin was drawn back into a leathery mask, the lips pulled into a hideous grin. Moon stared back at the approaching Batman from empty eye sockets. He wore a jester's hat, colorful with bells at the ends of five different points. The hair sticking out beneath it was unkempt and his fingernails long, but that was understandable for someone dragged from the grave. He wore resplendent red silk robes. He did not appear to mind at all that he and his robes were supported by means of an iron pipe affixed vertically to the floor, thrusting into his lower back and up into his chest cavity. Moon's hands rested on the podium, his bony fingers wrapped around a stack of papers.

Batman's face fell into a scowl.

The papers on the podium were yellowed with age, dry, and fragile, but the old-fashioned letterhead was easily recognizable.

WAYNE ENTERPRISES

FROM THE DESK OF DR. THOMAS WAYNE

Batman felt the sweat pooling at the base of his spine, a chill coursing through him despite the residual heat of the Batsuit. He gave the corpse of Moon a shove, dislodging the clavicle bone from its perch and causing the cadaver to slide down the pipe into a heap at his feet.

Batman and all the layers of his Batsuit could not shield Bruce Wayne from the words on the pages he took up in his hands.

To: Dr. Ernst Richter

Dear Ernst,

I can understand your reticence to proceed with this project and write to you today in the hopes of shedding some light for you on my apparent obsession with your work. I am having this letter delivered to you personally by my servant, in whom I have complete trust, so I may be assured it come into your possession only.

Perhaps for you to fully understand, I have to explain about how Martha introduced me to Denholm Sinclair in the first place and how that led to my friendship with Lewis Moxon . . .

CHAPTER FIVE

BLIND DATE

"Welcome to the Koffee Klatch, Mr. Wayne."

He almost turned around and walked out.

Thomas Wayne was impeccably dressed for anywhere but here. His trim frame supported the white dinner jacket and the black tie perfectly, and he had taken extra care with the Brylcreem to make sure his dark hair swept back from his brow and stayed in a flattop. His dress slacks were elegantly tapered, tailored down to break perfectly atop the shine of his patent-leather dress shoes. A red carnation in his lapel gave color to his otherwise monotone ensemble, and his face was rapidly approaching the same hue.

He would have fit in at any of the finest clubs and restaurants in town—only he wasn't in any of those places.

He was standing on the brink of anarchy.

At least he was if anarchy was defined as the upper level of this basement coffee house in the Bowery. The Koffee Klatch was in a run-down section of Uptown south of the Park Row theater district but not quite south enough to be fashionably adjacent to Riverfront Park. The theater district was booming with bright lights, heralding first-run productions of *My Fair Lady*, *Auntie Mame*, and *Bells Are Ringing*—stagings that reflected the veneer of optimism that glossed over the nation as a whole. But feeding those nightly dreams were an army of actors, musicians, choreographers, and playwrights who preferred Jack Kerouac's *On the Road* and Allen Ginsberg's "Howl" to Rodgers and Hammerstein. The Bowery had become the center of the counterculture Beat Generation in Gotham: a nexus of intellectuals, artists, and freethinkers who celebrated nonconformity and spontaneous creativity. These lofty words were themselves a thin coating over hedonistic excess, bohemian lifestyles, and dabbling in recreational drug use. The Beat Generation was not so much *for* anything in particular as they were *against* everything that remotely could be defined as a boundary. They saw the ordered concrete and steel of postwar United States showing stress fractures and were determined to bring it down and break free.

So from the basement balcony that looked down into the large rectangle of the sub-basement below, it looked a lot like anarchy to the Harvard Medical graduate in his formal evening clothes. The place was packed, and the ventilation nonexistent. The smell of the unwashed in the room was overwhelming. The July evening had been a cool one outside, but now, in the confines of the Klatch, the heat was oppressive and the smell of booze and cheap perfume cloying.

"Tommy!"

Wayne cocked his head, his eyes narrowing. He had heard his name from somewhere, but it was nearly drowned out in a sea of voices and bongo drums.

"Tommy! Down here!"

Thomas looked down over the railing into a seething pool of dark knit T-shirts, jeans, and hair. It took a few moments before he saw her, looking up at him with a beaming smile as she waved for his attention.

Martha Kane had literally been the girl next door for as long as he could remember, although in his case next door was about a quarter of a mile through a woodland preserve. Her father was Roderick "Roddy" Kane, who had built his business, Kane Chemical, on two world wars, boundless ambition, and an uncanny talent for knowing just how far to bend to make the deal. It was said of him that he did have a personality but that only his wife, the former Maureen Vandergrift of the Pennsylvania steel Vandergrifts, and his daughter knew where to find the switch to turn it on. The Kane holdings, according to the jokes bandied about at all the best cocktail parties, consisted of "that half of Gotham not already owned by the Waynes." It was a gross exaggeration in truth, but reality seemed to have gone out of fashion at the moment. What was true was that Martha was the heiress to both old and new money from both sides of her bloodline. It was, as her parents so often put before her, an enormous responsibility for which Martha, typically, cared not a whit. Her dark hair and liquid brown eyes were ubiquitous in the Gotham press, although just as likely at times to be appearing in the *Daily Inquirer* tabloid as on the society pages of the *Gotham Globe* or the *Gazette*. But to Thomas she was simply Martha, the strong-spirited neighbor girl who could and had talked him into just about any mad scheme she could concoct from the time he was eight.

Thomas wound his way carefully down the metal stairs. The cast-iron railing seemed to be coated in something unpleasantly sticky, which, he reflected, was not unlike the crowd itself. He waded into the shifting bodies on the floor of the club, a white speck adrift on dark waves. He maneuvered with only moderate success around the small tables grouped too closely together and managed at last to reach the corner that Martha had established as her realm in which to hold court.

"You're such a fashion plate!" Martha chimed. She looked him over with one carefully plucked eyebrow arched. She was wearing a dark cardigan sweater and tight denim jeans that displayed her body to her considerable advantage.

"You said we were going on the town." Thomas tried to temper his shrug with an embarrassed smile.

"And we *are*, ducky!" Martha beamed, flipping her hair back out of her face as she twined her arm around his. "Just not the town that you're used to—and it's about time you made it. Here, I have some friends you just *have* to meet!"

Thomas leaned closer to Martha's ear. "I thought it was going to just be us tonight."

"Oh, nonsense, Tommy," Martha laughed, slapping his arm with her right hand. "Two people alone are entirely too serious. We're here to celebrate. Here, may I introduce Denholm Sinclair?"

The man stood in the corner on the opposite side of the small café table. He was approximately the same height as Thomas but with slightly broader shoulders and a more muscular build. He had wavy black hair that was carefully coifed and an artist's goatee that was expertly trimmed. He wore a sports jacket over an open-collar shirt and pleated gray slacks with loafers. He held his hand out toward Thomas, his face breaking into a bright smile. "Nice to meet you, sport . . . call me Denny."

Thomas took the offered hand and regretted it. Denholm had the grip of a gorilla. Before he could say anything, Martha answered for him. "And you can call him Tommy—I always have. And this is Celia, my very best friend!"

Thomas managed to extract his hand and turned to follow Martha's gesture.

"How do you do, Mr. Wayne?" Celia said from her chair, offering her hand with her pale, lithe arm. She wore a sad and distant expression, her large brown eyes not quite looking at Thomas as he took her hand. Her hair was cut short, the curls lying tight against her head. She had full, pouting lips under a prominent nose, and while the eyelashes were obvious fakes, they looked good on her."

"Fine, thank you, Miss . . . ?" Thomas's voice trailed off into the question.

"Kazantzakis," Martha interjected. "Celia Kazantzakis."

"Ah." Thomas floundered for a moment.

"Please, Celia will do just fine," Kazantzakis said with a slight nod.

"And please call me Thomas," Wayne said. Denholm had already pulled the chair out for Martha, into which she quickly sat, sliding closer to Sinclair. Her arms snaked around the sleeve of Denholm's sports jacket, leaning into him. "Now isn't this just about perfect? I just knew the two of you needed to get together the moment I met Celi."

Thomas nodded with as gracious a smile as he could manage. Martha had done it again, and now he found himself as the blind date for another of Martha's projects. To Martha, Gotham was her playground; everything in it either belonged to her or would if she bothered enough to buy it. There were marvelous places in her playground that irritated her parents, in whose discomfort she took private delight because it meant they were at least paying attention to her.

"So," Thomas said turning to the young woman next to him. "How is it that you know Martha?"

"The orphanage. Copper Street Orphanage. Have you heard of it?"

"Sure, I think it's one of our endowments," Thomas nodded,

his eyes stinging from the smoke. "Over in Burnley near the botanical gardens, isn't it?"

"That's right," Celia nodded, reaching for her cocktail and taking a halfhearted sip. "I was raised there."

"Oh," Thomas said, "I'm sorry."

"Don't be," Celia shrugged. "I didn't really know any different. Anyway, I'm a secretary over there now trying to keep the place on its feet. Martha breezed in one day with a check that set us up rather well and the promise of more when we needed it. One thing led to another, I guess, and we just started ending up in the same places accidentally on purpose."

Thomas glanced back over at Martha, who was curling up closer to Sinclair and whispering something into his shoulder. Celia stopped speaking, letting the conversation stagnate on the table between them and die.

Thomas tried to revive it. "So do you like your work?"

"Huh?"

"Nothing, really . . . I just asked—"

"Listen, I'm sorry—"

"Thomas," he prompted.

"I'm sorry, Thomas. I'm a little distracted tonight," Celia replied waving her hand slightly in the thick air. The smoke in the room was settling thicker than a London fog. "A friend of mine's gone missing, and I just don't know what to do about it."

"Missing?" Thomas said, raising his eyebrows. "Who's missing?"

"Lorenzo," Celia said, biting her lower lip. "He's just a guy I know named Lorenzo Rossetti. He vanished about ten days ago. No call. No postcard . . . nothing."

"That sounds serious. Have you notified the authorities?"

"Actually, it's probably better if we left the authorities out of this one," Denholm said from across the table.

"Why?" Thomas asked. He had not been aware that Sinclair was listening to their conversation.

"Well, because in his line of work it probably wouldn't be very profitable in the long run," Denholm said with a slight arch to his eyebrows. "I think he's just away on business and he'll be back when he's finished is all."

"You mean . . . you mean he may be involved in some nefarious activities?" Thomas said with incredulity.

"Oh, honestly, Thomas! You are such a *square!*" Martha laughed, her own martini sloshing slightly in her hand as she waved it. "Loosen up a little, will ya? We're celebrating!"

"And thanks for coming to my place to celebrate," chimed the nasal voice. Thomas caught the flash of disdain on Sinclair's face before he turned around.

He was a shade under five foot six, barrel-chested, with large, strong hands. His head was shaped like a block, and he appeared to have no neck. He wore a black formal jacket, but the collar of his shirt was open and the bow tie hung completely undone round his neck. His dark hair in a crew cut of bristles from which his ears stuck out slightly. He looked like a fullback slightly scaled down, and he was young; Thomas guessed he must have been in his late twenties at the oldest.

"Hiya, Lew!" Martha beamed, raising her glass.

"Miss Kane, it's nice to see you again."

"You know my friend Tommy?"

The crew cut gestured for Thomas to stay seated. "It's all right, Mr. Wayne. Don't trouble on my account. Just happy to have you here. Moxon's the name, Lew Moxon."

"Thank you, uh, Lew," Thomas said as Moxon pumped his arm. "Have we met?"

"Nah, but a guy would have to be blind not to recognize a Wayne in this town," the man said. "I appreciate you coming and classing up the joint. You need anything at all, just call for Lew."

"Generous of you, Moxon," Sinclair said through a tight smile. "I didn't know you kept up with the social set."

Lew's smile chilled slightly. "Oh, I didn't see you there, Sinclair . . . but then Miss Kane has a habit of taking care of the needy."

"We all have friends," Sinclair answered. "Some are bigger friends than others, and we all need a little help now and then. How about you, Moxon? You buy this place all by yourself or did your friends help you?"

"You're barking up the wrong tree, friend," Lew replied, a chill in the air despite the heat in the room. "I been working nights since I was twelve. This place is a hundred percent mine."

"And just how much *did* your old man pay you for those jobs when you were twelve?" Sinclair sniffed. "I mean, surely the big Julius Moxon with all that money trickling up to him from so many low places has enough to finance a swank place like this for his baby boy."

"Not cool, cat," Moxon replied, his fists clenching and unclenching at his side. "My hands are clean, and my joint's on the up and up. By the way, how are things working out with you and old man Rossetti? I haven't seen Cesare's boy around here for a while. Did you send him on a vacation?"

Celia caught her breath, her lower lip trembling.

Sinclair slowly started to stand, pushing Martha away from him.

"My house," Moxon said through a smile. "You really wanna do this here?"

"Excuse me," Thomas said standing up suddenly, the metal legs of his chair squealing over the sound of the bongo drums.

Both Sinclair's and Lew's heads snapped in his direction.

Thomas held up both hands as he spoke. "I'd just like to interject something here, if I may."

Sinclair froze with one hand in his coat pocket. Moxon's right hand hovered just inside the lapel of his jacket.

"I'd just like to point out that we're celebrating my graduation from Harvard Medical School which, as you probably know, is a really big deal for me . . . and thank you for your congratulations, but the thing is, I don't start my internship until tomorrow morning, so I'm technically not supposed to actually *use* any of that medical stuff they've been pouring into my head for the last, oh, eight years or so. I mean, you would think it counted for something, but apparently I need some additional on the job training."

Moxon gave Thomas a look of bewilderment. Sinclair blinked.

"So it all comes down to this: I've got this really swell white dinner jacket on and, yes, I know I probably should have worn something leather or torn, but it's what I'm stuck with for the evening. And it would be really hard to get bloodstains out of this, and I'm not supposed to save anyone's life for a few more weeks at least. So, Lew . . . how about getting me a drink so we can toast my future instead of making my coat all messy?"

Lew stared at Thomas for a moment.

"Please?" Thomas urged. "Coffee would do. I can toast myself with coffee . . . Do you serve coffee here?"

A wide grin grew on Lew Moxon's face. "Sure, Mr. Wayne, whatever you say. You're all right in my book. If you ever need a favor, I'm your guy."

Sinclair sat back down, chuckling as he did. "Nice moves, Tommy!"

"Call me Thomas," he said as he fell into his own chair. Wayne reached across the table, snatching Martha's partial martini from the table and downing it in a single gulp.

Denholm nodded. "I think I'm beginning to like you, Thomas. What say I show you a few places I know about?"

"Great," Thomas answered, setting down Martha's martini glass. His hand was shaking slightly. "But first, let's order Martha another drink."

Martha looked into her empty glass and started to laugh.

CHAPTER SIX

UNTOUCHED

Kane Estate / Bristol / 6:22 a.m. / October 5, 1957

Dawn was breaking as Thomas drove the Lincoln Futura across the Kane Memorial Bridge. The theater district of Gotham proper and Sheldon Point receded behind him quickly in the light traffic. The Futura was a concept car—the car of the future—and his father had financed a second version of it from the Ghia plant in Turin, Italy, when it was being built two years before. It had the opalescent pearl-white finish that could only really be appreciated in person; the long, flat back deck and the forward and rear fins were dramatic, but it was the clear Plexiglas double-teardrop top that always turned heads whenever he drove it. It was both an icon of the age and of its problems: the Plexiglas roof acted like a greenhouse under the sun. Worse, it was designed to seal the passenger compartment so tightly that a microphone actually had to be mounted in the center of its "futuristic" circular radio antenna on the back deck so the driver could hear sounds coming from outside the car through a speaker placed behind and between the bucket seats. A safety feature made it so the bubble top could not be opened unless the automatic transmission was in park, which meant there was practically no ventilation inside the car. The air conditioner was always faulty and never quite kept up with the ant-under-a-magnifying-glass interior. Worse, the stylish exterior restricted airflow around the engine, constantly causing it to overheat. Still, such practical matters hardly impacted the thinking of Patrick Wayne; anyone could purchase a production Lincoln, but to spend a quarter of a million dollars on one of only two hand-built cars of the future? It was not simply transportation to the senior Wayne; it was a demonstration of power and wealth that could not be ignored. Giving it to his son provided more than a photo opportunity for the press; it was Patrick's way of saddling his son with the responsibilities of being a Wayne and pushing his boy to acknowledge the superior and unquestioned authority of his father.

Thomas had responded to his father's most impractical gift by taking a screwdriver and a wrench to the unique concept car and removing the automated section of the roof. It improved the airflow considerably, he liked the convertible aspect it gave to the otherwise enormous car, and it simultaneously demonstrated, in Thomas's small way, an act of defiance.

This early morning, however, with the dawn just breaking over the ocean to the east, the long vehicle was a bit chill even for Thomas. He reached over to the left of the steering column—with its unique speedometer sitting inside the hub of the wheel—and pushed back the cover on the heat controls. They slid back into the console like a jet-aged rolltop desk. He adjusted the knobs to pour heat over the floorboard and glanced across the center console between the bucket seats to the form snoring softly on his right.

Thomas reached forward, turning up the volume on the radio dial. The close-harmony male duet sang louder about the troubled reputation of two teenagers falling asleep at a drive-in movie.

Thomas glanced once more at the voluptuous, makeup-smeared mess sprawled next to him that was Martha Kane.

Her dark hair was piled over her face. Her lipstick was smeared, and her mascara had made her eyes reminiscent of a raccoon. She lay as she had been put into the car, Thomas doing his best to put her form into some semblance of a passenger and failing utterly. She was a restless sleeper, and it had been all he could manage to keep her arm inside the car while he closed the door.

Thomas reached over casually, trying to push the hair out of her face as he drove. The wind whipping through the open top of the car, however, prevented any success in that either, and so he gave up. Martha would have to remain wild . . . as he had always known her.

From the bridge, he turned right at the northern exit and followed the coast highway a short distance around Breaker's Point before turning between the brick pillars that supported the gold-painted iron arch fixed with a single *K* in the center. He sped up the private road, a few rebellious leaves defiant of the wishes of the groundskeeper having fallen to the ground only to be spun into life as the car sped past. The canopy of trees would provide shade later in the day, but for now the low angle of the rising sun cast intermittent patches of light and dark across the car as it sped past the trunks and the orange hue of the morning.

He knew the house itself was nearly a mile further on. Thomas reached forward and switched off the radio, letting the engine fill the silence in the morning.

He had driven down this road many times before, and truth be told, he had brought Martha back down it in similar states before. They were so very different and yet bound together in strange ways. Both of them were wealthy and both of them carried that wealth on their backs like modern versions of Heracles, bound by fate. They both reacted to this burden with their own ways of rebellion: Thomas by turning his back on the business world of his father to become a doctor and Martha by spending as much of her parents' money as possible, either by burying herself in her charitable causes or by finding the bottom of a bottle with friends as willing to spend her money as she. She was notorious for being as likely to appear on the morning police report as she was on the social pages at some gala. She tended to be a loud drunk and had an uncanny knack for attracting trouble. He had always thought her beautiful, although not nearly so after a long drunk, and Thomas had found his mind wandering to what might be discovered beneath the suggestive lines of her cardigan sweater and tight blue jeans.

Thomas's attention jerked back to the road. The car had drifted off to the right, and one set of tires was thumping in the grass off the gravel drive. He gripped the wheel and with a firm hand eased the car back onto the road.

Martha might give him the time of day, Thomas thought, but she would never see him as anything but that gawking boy next door who was a good friend to have around when everyone else had deserted her like vampires with the rising of the sun, when she had thrown up the expensive dinner hitting both the alley wall as well as her shoes and she needed someone to drive her home. He was Tommy, the boy who would always be a chum and nothing more.

Thomas frowned, wondering why the hell that should bother him.

The tree tunnel ended at the edge of the manor's lawn. Kane House stood as a monument to excessive Georgian architecture, so opulent it might have made Carnegie blush. It had two enormous wings extending from the main house, reaching forward like an American Versailles. He followed the curve of the road toward the courtyard for a while, but turned off short of the house, following instead the service road that went around the back. He parked short of the grand ballroom, which jutted out from the house like a cathedral, its tall, dark windows reflecting the rising sun. The enormous lawn at the back was shrouded in a thin layer of fog.

Thomas switched off the car, hopped up to stand on the seat and, with both hands on the rims of the Plexiglas windows, front and back, swung his feet over the side and dropped to the ground. The gravel made a slight hissing sound as he landed his dismount.

"And a four from the Russian judge," he muttered to himself as he straightened up, checked his bow tie, and quickly stepped down the servants' stairs to the door entering the basement. Thomas knocked emphatically with five quick taps and then waited. The distant sound of a meadowlark answered. A few quick additional knocks were answered by a shuffling sound beyond the door, the bang and squeal of a table followed by a muttered swearing. Thomas waited. The door opened slightly, stopping at the end of its lock chain.

"Yes?"

"Bertie, it's me . . . Thomas." His voice sounded loud in the stillness of the morning.

"Master Wayne?" the voice seemed puzzled for a moment. "Again?"

"I'm afraid so, Bertie," Thomas confessed. "Shall I bring her in?"

"Don't you always?" Bertie replied. The door closed quickly and Thomas heard the lock slide free of its plate. The door opened wide to reveal the gaunt face and disheveled white hair of the aging retainer standing in his bathrobe, striped pajamas, and slippers, which he had put on the wrong feet in his haste.

"Take her up to Mary's room. She's off taking care of her mother and no one will bother her there."

"Or see me," Thomas added.

The old butler chuckled. "The staff knows to keep their silence, but if Mr. Kane sees you coming out of Miss Martha's bedroom, there's not so much as that we can do for you. I suspect there are grounds enough about the house to hide a dead Wayne just as easily as a dead pauper."

"Cheerful as always," Thomas said, shaking his head. He turned and dashed up the cement steps back to the car.

Thomas opened the passenger door and half expected Martha to pour out of it, but she obligingly remained in the seat. He straightened her upright as best he could and then, bending over, set his shoulder against her stomach and shifted her arms and head down his back. He carefully leaned back, gaining his balance and was at last, with some struggle and the help of the car's body for leverage, able to stand up with Martha draped in a fireman's carry over his shoulder.

He was keenly aware of her body touching his, the faint smell of perfume mixed with vomit coming from her sweater, and the placement of his arms across her thighs.

Thomas drew in a deep breath and moved quickly around the car. He knew the way well enough. Down the servants' entrance stairs, through the kitchen and servants' rooms to the back, and then up the servants' stairs to the fourth floor and the servants' bedrooms. It was an arduous climb up a narrow winding staircase, and twice he had to stop to catch his breath before reaching the upper hall. The servants had not yet arisen for the day, although Thomas suspected the cook would arrive shortly. Fortunately, Mary's room was nearest the staircase, and he quickly opened the door and, shifting Martha on his shoulder once more, entered the room.

The bed was simple in the sparsely furnished room. Thomas crouched at the bedside and carefully rolled Martha off his shoulder and onto the bed, which squeaked slightly under her. He arranged her legs and arms more comfortably as she groaned slightly. He knelt next to the bed frame and brushed her hair away from her face.

He considered undressing her.

He stood up in a rush.

"You're a doctor, damn it," he muttered to himself. He had seen naked bodies before, alive or otherwise. Male or female they all tended to look remarkably the same when they were lying on a table in the laboratory. Her clothing reeked, and it would have been a kindness for him to take them down to Bertie and have them washed before she came around and had to face both the hangover and her own stench. All these good rationalizations were firing in his mind but he could not move to touch her.

He could not because he wanted so desperately to touch her, to experience the texture of her neck, the round firmness of her breast, the curve of her back, and the contour of her legs. He ached to gather her in his arms, clothed or otherwise, to feel her heart beating against his chest and know that neither of them rattling about in their enormous, empty lives was alone. He wanted her eyes to open—really open—and see him as though for the first time not as the awkward boy who fell silent and withdrawn before the senseless battering of an obsessed father but as a man who longed for an intimacy that had been denied him his entire life.

Thomas gazed down on Martha as she stretched out before him on the bed, oblivious to him as a man, as she had been all along. How could she know that more than anything he wanted to be seen, to have his existence recognized—to *matter*—and to be the focus of a pair of languid, large brown eyes.

He realized that here, in the silence of the morning, with the house asleep, he could touch her. She was barely an arm's length from where he stood. He could reach down with both his hands, slip them beneath the cardigan, and find the warmth of her skin. He had been a pal to her, the boy next door whom you might let look, but never, ever touch you *that* way. No one would ever know . . . Not even Martha would remember, given how passed out she was from the drunken binge of the night before.

A chill ran through Thomas.

Martha would not know . . . She would not even see him.

Thomas bolted from the room and down the stairs. He rushed past Bertie, who said something to him, but he could not hear the words for the ringing in his ears. He pushed out through the servants' entrance door and bound up the steps two at a time. The door was stubborn to open and he managed with some frustration to get into the driver's seat. He turned the car engine over with the ignition.

It churned twice and then died.

Thomas banged the wheel in a fury, pumped the accelerator twice to reset the choke and tried again.

The engine groaned once . . . and then caught, roaring to life. The tires kicked up gravel as he wheeled the car around, roaring back around the house and down the tree-lined road back toward Breaker's Point.

By the time he reached the front of Wayne Manor, the tears were gone but his face was still flush. He got out, slamming the car door as Jarvis Pennyworth came out the front door.

"Master Tom," Jarvis said in a British accent that managed to convey both serenity and alarm at the same time. "We were concerned for you. I trust your evening went well, sir."

"I had a fine evening, Jarvis," Thomas lied. "It is always a

delight to be out in the company of Miss Martha Kane. Is my father home?"

"No, sir, he left about an hour ago. Some pressing business downtown."

"Good," Thomas rejoined, tugging his bow tie loose from its knot. "You know how he loves pressing business. This may be a record for him—I haven't even been home a day and he's uncovered some pressing business to keep him away."

"Yes, Master Tom," Jarvis bowed slightly as Thomas passed toward the main doors of the mansion. "But he left instructions that you were to come to his office at eleven thirty, following your meeting with Dr. Horowitz at Gotham University Hospital."

"Horowitz?" Thomas stopped. "He's the chief of staff. What does he want with an intern?"

"I wouldn't know, sir," Jarvis answered with diffidence.

Thomas drew in a long, tired breath. "Okay, Jarvis. I'm going upstairs to try to excavate a clean, doctor-to-be from this wreck of a night on the town. Would you see that the car is put away? I'll drive the Buick back to Gotham. Did my father say when I was supposed to meet with Dr. Horowitz?"

"He said that he had arranged the appointment for you at ten o'clock this morning with Dr. Horowitz and that you were not to be late."

"Fine," Thomas said, pulling off his tie. "Anything else?"

"Yes, Master Thomas," Jarvis continued. "Dr. Horowitz's office called to confirm your appointment and said they wanted you to keep your afternoon calendar clear. Dr. Horowitz wants you to meet a gentleman by the name of Dr. Richter."

"Ernst Richter?" Thomas frowned in thought.

"Yes, sir; I do believe that was the name the gentleman gave," Jarvis said in his flat, British tones.

Thomas pushed back the tails of his dinner jacket and jammed his hands into his tuxedo pants. "Richter is a research chemist working on special projects. He's got a reputation as a screwball, but his work was being discussed in our graduate year. Something really out of this world about virus mutation, as I recall. I wonder why Horowitz wants me to meet him?"

"Again, sir, I wouldn't know."

Wayne Manor / Bristol / 6:29 a.m. / Present Day

"_. . . was of course the first morning that we met at Gotham University Hospital. I had only met Denholm Sinclair the night before. How could I possibly have known that within three months of our . . ._"

Bruce Wayne sat at the table in the kitchen and turned the page over. He had reached the end of the pages found on the podium. Obviously, more were missing. He waited patiently, shuffling the sheets of paper again and again as the old pendulum clock ticked against the wall. It was nearly four o'clock.

He is a creature of habit. He will be here.

The door to the kitchen opened.

"Alfred?"

The old man was visibly startled, nearly dropping a bag of groceries.

"You always cook on Sundays," Bruce said from where he sat, still gazing at the yellowed papers in his hands without seeing them. "You could have dinner brought in from any restaurant in town and have hired and fired more cooks than I can remember—but you've always, always insisted on cooking my dinner on Sunday at four o'clock. I used to set my watch by it."

"Old habits are the hardest to break, Mr. Wayne." Alfred stood in the doorway, looking at Bruce. "It was always a pleasure to cook for the Waynes."

"The Pennyworths have served in this house a long time," Bruce nodded, still shuffling the dry, yellowed papers. "Haven't they, Alfred?"

"My grandfather was the first to serve this house, yes, sir," Alfred replied, walking over to the counter and setting the bag down carefully.

"But your father served my father, did he not?"

Alfred was pulling fresh vegetables from the paper bag, his back to Bruce. "For a time, sir. He served the family from 1946 until I assumed his stewardship in 1967."

"So you were ten years old in 1957," Bruce continued, shifting the papers front to back continually examining each page in turn. "Do you remember much about that time, Alfred? Do you remember my father?"

Alfred stopped his work, putting both hands on the counter, his back still turned to Bruce. "He was a great man, Master Wayne."

"So now I'm back in short pants again, eh?" Bruce said without a smile. "Well, Alfred, tell me if you know anything about this Dr. Richter."

Bruce watched the elder man with a studied eye. Alfred did not move a muscle for a heartbeat and then spoke.

"I don't recall the name, sir," Alfred said.

"It's right here," Bruce said, his voice flat. "Correspondence between my father and this Dr. Richter. It seems to be about my father's early life. I just thought that if I could find this Richter—"

"He is dead, Master Bruce," Alfred said abruptly. "I recall now that he did some work with your father, but he died when I was young. It was a long time ago, Master Bruce—and if I may suggest, there is nothing to be gained by looking into this."

"You think I should drop it?"

"The past is the past—and we have troubles enough in our own time. Your father was upset at the passing of a friend, if memory serves me, and that was about all there was to it."

"Ah, that explains it," Bruce said, folding up the papers and slipping them into the pocket of his jacket as he got up. "Thanks, Alfred."

"Sorry, but I just don't recall much more than that," Alfred said, turning with a smile.

Bruce nodded and walked away, knowing they had both finished with a lie.

CHAPTER SEVEN

SINS OF THE FATHERS

The shadow near the crest of Wayne Tower stood motionless astride the carved head of an eagle jutting out from the upper bulwarks of the dark structure stabbing into the night sky.

The shadow watched over the city.

The streets were broad threads of light far below, weaving the fabric of Gotham at night. The skyscrapers stood out with their illuminated windows—not nearly so many lit up as there were earlier in the evening, but enough to suggest the outlines of their towering, dark forms. The silhouetted figure had chosen the northern face for his perch, affording him an unobstructed view over the lesser buildings of the Diamond District and Robinson Park beyond. Each of the bridges crossing over the Finger River, linking the downtown districts with Midtown, were jammed with evening traffic. Some were moving north toward the theater and dining district near Burnley in Uptown, while the southbound traffic was most likely headed toward some of the more trendy dining in the renovated areas of the Financial District waterfront or in Chinatown. Many may simply be escaping the downtown environs of Gotham, searching out the different bridges leading out of the city proper. Beyond Robinson Park were the high-rise buildings of Coventry District, hiding from view the dark towers of Arkham Asylum.

The city was filled with life tonight, busy and bustling beneath him, but for the Batman, this was his temple of peace, far more of a sanctuary than the Batcave or his reclusive home. Here, or atop a number of different vantage points he cherished above the city, he could rest his soul, watch over the city he treasured, and, in his vigilance, know that balance had, for the moment, been achieved. In every other place he felt himself in constant motion, anxious and restless. But here, holding perfectly still in the night with the city spread below his watchful gaze, he could stop and allow himself the luxury of contemplation and true rest.

Here, he thought, was balance in watchfulness.

But tonight the balance would not come.

He let his eye wander over the city, and it came to rest for the first time in a long time beyond the shores of Gotham, upon the dark rolling hills of Bristol across the river and the dim glimmer of flickering light, obstructed by haze and distance, of the Wayne Estate.

The papers he had recovered from the corpse of Dr. Moon—his father's papers—and their words took him back more than a half century to the grand paneled office now six stories beneath his perch.

Wayne Tower / Gotham / 11:28 a.m. / October 5, 1957

Thomas stood before the familiar burled wood paneling that decorated the enormous art deco doors. He reached up without thinking to adjust his tie yet again and then, realizing what he was doing, sighed in frustration, clasped his hands together behind his back, and tried consciously to slow down his shallow breaths.

"Mr. Wayne will see you now, Thomas."

"Thank you, Liz," Thomas said to the secretary behind the desk. She had been with his father for as long as he could remember, though he could not recall her last name. She wore her mouse-brown hair pulled back into a tight bun and wore an enormous set of horn-rimmed glasses. She always wore the same gray business suit in the office. Thomas had given up speculating just how many of this same outfit she must have in her closet. She was a virtuoso when it came to the enormous, complex intercom box sitting at the corner of her desk, and both her stenographic and typing skills were legendary. Still, he thought she might appreciate some human interaction. "It's nice to see you again."

"Best not to keep him waiting," she replied evenly.

I guess not. Thomas shrugged, turned toward the twelve-foot-tall double doors and pulled the left one open. He knew his father always kept the right one closed with locking pins at the top and bottom. Visitors always chose the wrong door when entering. It was more than an amusement to his father, of course; it was another way of putting everyone else off balance.

The office extended upward two stories, a vaulting space of art deco extravagance. A large globe sat on the floor in its frame beneath the built-in bookcase lining the right wall of the room; it opened into a bar the elder Wayne found convenient both for clients and for personal use. The books were an elegant selection, although so far as Thomas knew, his father had never once deigned to take one of them down from their perfectly organized shelves. The opposite wall featured a gallery of painting, an eclectic collection of original Matisses, Monets, and Renoirs that had been purchased more as an investment than for any appreciation of the art involved. At the far end, opposite the doors, an enormous cherrywood desk, highly polished, sat before a towering glass window rising up to the full height of the room. Two overstuffed, red-leather chairs sat facing the desk like stooped acolytes in prayer. The high-fidelity stereo system lay dormant. The only sound in the room was a chattering of ticker tape near the desk, behind which sat a swivel chair, its winged back facing Thomas.

It was the cathedral of Patrick Wayne, Thomas thought, and he always felt like an infidel when he entered it.

The chair swiveled around silently, its occupant deigning to acknowledge the young man's presence at last.

"You're late."

Not late enough, Thomas thought. "Dr. Horowitz kept me longer than expected . . . and good afternoon to you, too, Father."

"Good afternoon, then," Patrick answered with a single, humorless chortle. Patrick Wayne's shoulders were still broad but had become somewhat bowed with time and the weight of carrying Wayne Enterprises. His hair had gone white and was thinning perceptibly at the crown. His large hands had grown somewhat gnarled with arthritis, but they still looked strong enough to tear the Gotham phone book in half twice. His tone was casual, even pleasant. "I trust you had a good time last night?"

"Yes, thank you," Thomas crossed the long floor over to stand in front of his father's desk. "It was Martha Kane's party."

"From what I hear, she has a lot of them," Patrick said, and seeing his son's look, he raised a hand. "No, I don't mean anything by it. She's always been a spirited girl, Thomas, you know that. Sit down. I think it's about time we talked, you and I."

Thomas raised his eyebrow and then sat down on the arm of

one of the leather chairs. He had learned long ago that his father had a full inch cut off the bottom of these chairs just to ensure that anyone who sat there would be slightly below his eye level. "What would you like to talk about, sir?"

Patrick reached across the desk, pulling a large folder out of a stack and opening it in front of him. "Well, actually it's about Martha Kane . . . and the company she keeps."

"Sir, you are way out of line."

"Damn it, boy, stop talking and pay attention for once," Patrick barked, picking up the sheaf of papers in front of him. A number of black-and-white photographs spilled out from between the pages. Some of them looked as though they were not quite dry. "The Kane family are our neighbors. Hell, Roddy Kane and I have been trading golf scores for more than a decade now, but that girl just seems to attract trouble. She doesn't take to the right people, boy. She's brushed off every matron of Gotham society, including your mother, yet she has time to go slumming in the Bowery or that little apartment she keeps in Otisburg for who knows what purposes! And now she's started running around with this Sinclair hood—"

"I know all about Denholm Sinclair, sir," Thomas countered, standing up.

"Do you, boy?" Patrick shuffled through the papers, quickly finding the one he wanted. "Then I suppose you know that he's working for the Rossetti mob. He's into them for the kind of money he can't hope to pay off."

"Denny and Martha are both full grown, sir," Thomas countered. "They know what they're doing."

"Oh? And I suppose that means you do, too?" Patrick shot back across the desk. "You haven't been home more than a day, fresh plucked from almighty Harvard Medical School, and I wake up to hear that you've been hanging around Lewis Moxon's

little café. Damn it, boy, the man's Julius Moxon's kid, the big-
gest crime lord this city's ever seen."

"So what?" Thomas shouted. "So they're not your kind of
people? They've got problems, sure, who doesn't? But what's
wrong with them?"

"They're criminals, boy!" Patrick roared, standing up behind
the desk. "What do you think? With all the knowledge they
stuffed into your head up there and all your medical voodoo,
you're gonna just give them a couple of aspirin and make them
all better? You can't cure them like they're some case of the
measles. I've known these kind of people all my life—had to
work with them, watch out for them, protect *you* from them—
and I can tell you, boy, that they do *not* change! They are just
out to take you down, feed on you, suck you dry, and then spit
you out."

Thomas was staring at the photographs spilled onto the desk.
Photographs of him from last night at the Koffee Klatch . . .
of Denholm and Martha . . . of her passed out in the front of
Thomas's car. He reached down and touched the photograph as
he spoke. "Real nice, Dad. You had me followed?"

"Oh, wake up, boy!" Patrick grumbled. "You're a Wayne!
You have a responsibility to the business and to the name . . .
and these people will *never* be worthy of you. Leopards cannot
change their spots, and these parasites can't, either. I supported
you all through this medical school nonsense and you managed
to get through that just fine, but you need to wake up to your
responsibilities. There is an empire here you need to learn how
to run. You had better get your life in order, son, stop the day-
dreaming, and get a vision of your future before these vermin
strip you clean."

"You think I don't know what I want?" Thomas said. "There's
a better way to live than this, sir, and I'm going to find it."

"This *is* life, boy," Patrick said in a tone that defied contradiction. "There are predators and there are prey, and the sooner you learn that, the better."

"Sir, you just don't—"

"Did Dr. Horowitz talk to you about administering that endowment?" Patrick said.

"Yes, sir," Thomas answered, feeling the wall fall again between them.

"Good. Go on and get out," Patrick said, looking away as he sat back down. "I've got work to do. Maybe I'll see you for breakfast."

The audience was over.

"Yes, sir," Thomas said with a sigh. "Maybe."

Thomas stepped out of the doors of Wayne Tower and onto Moench Row. He took in a deep breath, though he still could not quite escape the feeling of claustrophobia that had come over him in the building.

The Buick was parked at the curb with one of the doormen standing next to it. Upon seeing Thomas, the man quickly opened the driver's side door and came to attention. Maybe the man had been a soldier during the Korean War, maybe he was a veteran . . . or perhaps just as likely he had watched a lot of war movies and was pretending to be the hero of the Buick door. Was the young man a thief or a slacker or a con man? Would he pick Thomas's pocket or die defending him? What makes a man who he is? And if there really was something wrong with how he thought, why couldn't he be cured like anything else?

Thomas moved around the Buick and slid into the driver's seat. The doorman already had the motor running for him and closed the door firmly as soon as Thomas was in.

Thomas sat considering things for a moment and then reached inside his coat pocket.

Dr. Richter—Kane Lecture Hall / Monday, 2 p.m.

Thomas slipped the note back into his pocket and shifted the transmission selector into drive.

COINCIDENCE

Curtis Point / Gotham / 10:16 a.m. / Present Day

A laughing couple walked past. Their eyes were bright and fixed on each other as the rhythm of their conversation continued to be their entire world. The skies were clear in their three-foot universe, with no room for the nameless figure with his shoulders hunched slightly into his light jacket and a knit cap on his head despite the unseasonably warm weather.

They might have expanded their universe considerably had they been aware that Bruce Wayne, the most celebrated recluse in all of Gotham, was quietly and determinedly slipping by them. More airtime, bandwidth, Internet posts, chats, forums, and column inches had been written, typed, blogged, podcast, or broadcast about what the world did not know about Bruce Wayne than any other celebrity citizen of Gotham, with the exception of the Batman. The rare paparazzi would win the fame lottery and achieve their cherished goal of taking a fuzzy photograph through an extremely long lens past the barred gates or towering fences of Wayne Manor, their obscure and hastily focused images of an older man, frail with long, ragged hair sticking out from beneath a wide-brimmed hat. Sometimes he would be discovered packed in blankets as he sat in a Nantucket wooden lawn chair or with Alfred pushing the feeble figure about the manor's gardens in a wheelchair. Each of these images could fetch a fine commission from the various media outlets, regardless of its legitimacy, and had spawned something of an industry in false Bruce Wayne images.

Bruce enjoyed these intricately and carefully choreographed "exposures" of his reclusive alter ego. There were considerable challenges to choreographing these paparazzi events so that the photographers set up to take these pictures never suspected they were being used. Now the image the city had of the heir to the Wayne fortune was of something like a cross between Howard Hughes and Charles Foster Kane.

The one thing no one in the city expected was a nondescript, late middle-aged version of Bruce Wayne in a cloth jacket and a knitted cap moving with athletic ease down the cement walkway along the shoreline of Sprang River Park, his shoulders hunched slightly despite the unseasonably warm weather. Alfred had insisted that some contingency planning be in place for Bruce when he decided to go on these walkabouts. Bruce's solution had been a miniature ELT—an emergency locator transmitter similar to those used in aircraft—that Bruce had implanted under the skin of his right ear. Bruce had engineered the device and had the implant done overseas under the guise of a hearing aide. The result was a subcutaneous transceiver that he could trigger simply by tapping the sequence behind his right ear. Always monitoring the specialized frequency whenever Bruce was walking in the city, Alfred was ready to call in the cavalry whenever necessary. He could even speak to Bruce through the device with complete privacy, his voice transmitted through bone conduction directly into the cochlea of Bruce's inner ear and thus heard by him alone. It had never been used, but at least it made Alfred feel he had the option and stopped him from worrying about his charge when he was out.

The Sprang River was on his left, separating the Burnley district of Uptown Gotham from the downtown districts to the south. The apartment towers overlooking the river on the north side lay across Riverside Parkway, the sounds of its afternoon traffic a muffled encroachment on the peace of the park itself. Autumn leaves from the great maple trees lay scattered across the blush of green lawns and the walkway beneath his feet. It might have been pastoral, but that was not within the sphere of Bruce's own world.

He had come with his own purpose, his own vision colored and narrowed by his focus. His intention had been merely to observe the house at the woman's address, but then she had emerged alone, walking down the street of facing brownstones and continuing into the riverside parkland beyond.

He approached Curtis Point, a small section of the park that jutted out beneath the high, double-arched span of the Schwartz Bypass bridge almost directly overhead. Curtis Point was the perfect overlook for downtown Gotham. Most of the benches had been placed facing southward toward the might and majesty of the skyscrapers across the river, and several of the city's tourist brochures featured images of that vista taken from this vantage point.

One bench, however, in deference to the original design of the park, faced to the west and was usually studiously shunned by its patrons from the brownstones across the parkway who brought visitors or tourists to the park for the view. It faced an aspect just beyond the point where the tidal Falstaff Branch of the Gotham River converged with the Sprang River. There, the island known as the Narrows was formed by these two tidal rivers and the greater Gotham River to the west.

There, on the eastern point of the island, rose the dark collection of Georgian and Gothic towers known as Arkham Asylum.

There, on the usually shunned bench, sat the lone figure of the woman.

"We seem to always be meeting in parks," he said to her.

Amanda Richter did not turn to face him, but she did smile as she replied. "Of all the parks in all the towns in all the world . . . you walk into mine. Gerald . . . Grayson, isn't it?"

"Yes," Bruce lied as he sat down on the bench with studied, casual ease. "You remembered."

"Surprised?" Amanda said, still facing the towers of Arkham. "I remember everything . . . too many things. What brings you to me, Gerald Grayson?"

"Just chance, I—"

"Fate," Amanda interjected with conviction, her smile fading. "Fate brought you to me."

"Actually, it was more like Ms. Doppel," Bruce said, turning toward her and lying his arm along the backrest of the metal bench. "I tried to find you at home, but instead encountered Ms. Doppel, herself on her way out to look for you. I told her I'd bring you home."

"Home . . . where is home?" Amanda said. She wore an outdated cardigan sweater, pearls, and a long skirt. Her hair was pulled back and her eyebrows thinned to narrow lines. She looked as though she had stepped out of the past. "Some people call Arkham home. For some, it's the only home they know."

"Is it home for you?" Bruce asked.

"It was home for my father," she answered, her voice wistful and her eyes slowly shifting focus to another time. "His life was there . . . even when he was home. Arkham was where his heart resided, deep and locked away. There he truly lived . . . and there he died so completely that even his memory was buried with him. And my father was where my heart lived, and I died there, too."

"Your father, Ernst Richter?"

Amanda slowly turned toward him. "What do you know of—"

"People like the Waynes are very careful about their visitors, but they don't often keep too close a watch on their gamewarden," Bruce shrugged. "After you visited their grounds the other day, they did a complete dossier on you, the most curious thing about which was how thin it was compared to most."

"You regularly read the Wayne security reports, Mr. Grayson?" Amanda asked with narrowed eyes.

"Only when they interest me personally," Bruce answered. "I know your father was a research doctor at Gotham University Hospital and that he worked with Thomas Wayne—"

"There," Amanda said, looking back across to the Narrows. "They worked there together."

"In Arkham?" Bruce replied, raising an eyebrow. "No, I'm sure that Dr. Wayne never worked at Arkham."

"I used to sit here and watch for them," Amanda said, a deep sadness coloring her voice. "My mother would bring me here because Papa would meet us in the afternoons. He would walk across the Murdock Bridge for lunch and we would meet him here. He would always smile when he saw me, call me Mari."

"Mari?" Bruce looked at her oddly.

"Then he was gone and Mama ended up in Arkham and she died there, though not like he did. Then I followed to Arkham hoping to make it all right . . . and eventually it killed me, too."

Bruce followed her gaze. "Marion Richter died in 1997. She was a behavioral psychiatrist at Arkham at the time, having been the principle caretaker of your mother, Juliet Renoir Richter, who passed away—also in Arkham, in 1983 while suffering from a mental collapse. Amanda Richter was born in 1947 . . . which would make you about sixty-four years old. You seem to carry your age very well."

"I invaded your place and now you've invaded mine, Mr. Grayson," Amanda said, shaking off the dream. "I prefer to wander on my own."

"Perhaps we can wander for a time together," Bruce offered.

"One person wanders, Mr. Grayson," Amanda replied. "Two people are always going somewhere."

"It seems I heard that in an old movie once," Bruce chuckled.

"Really?" Amanda asked. "When did it come out?"

"Oh, I think it was 1958," Bruce replied.

"Ah, that explains it," she said. "I'll see it after it premieres. I suppose Miss Doppel sent you after me."

"Miss Doppel?"

"My nurse. The woman who lives with me," Amanda insisted. "She sent you after me, didn't she?"

"I was looking for you anyway." Bruce shrugged. "So, can I see you home?"

"Yes," Amanda replied with a sigh, standing up. "We may as well go. Papa isn't coming today."

"Maybe I can find him for you," Bruce said as he too stood up. "It is my day off, and I'm pretty good at finding lost people."

"Yes, I believe you are, Mr. Grayson," Amanda replied, her gaze unfocused on the dark towers of Arkham across the river, her voice whispering as though she were murmuring through a dream. "I'm more lost than anyone and you managed to find me. How far did you have to come? Was it miles or years? How far do you think I'll have to go before I can be home, too? Before I can find my way back among the living?"

Bruce stood up, his eyes fixed on her. "Where are you, Amanda?"

She turned suddenly toward him, her eyes bright and pleading. "I don't want to die . . . I want to live! Please, I've got to find a way back. You've got to help me find my way back."

"Back from where?" Bruce demanded.

"Back from this hell," she pleaded. Her voice was frantic and rushed, her eyes darting. "Back from wherever they've put me. Back from the grave and the dark and the cold, Mr. Grayson. I see the shadows as they pass—young and old all at once—and I see you, too, the echo of your father as the echo of mine driving me to do things I do not want to do and say things I do not want to say. We're only echoes, shades, shadows of our fathers, you and I, but their sins still run through our veins and now the blood is calling us back . . . back to a past that is better forgotten. You've got to stop the ghosts. They're coming for us—both of us—in our dreams at night and they will devour everything that we are or ever will be!"

Bruce reached his hands up, grabbing her firmly by the shoulders. "I'll take you home, Amanda. It's just across the parkway and—"

"NO!" Amanda screamed, pushing away from him. A few of the people admiring the view glanced in their direction. "I don't believe you, Thomas! You said you would help! You said you would be there! You said it was our dream, but the nightmare came and it never went away."

Bruce blinked. *Thomas?*

"Amanda," Bruce said in a firm, quiet voice. "I am here to help now. I'll take you home—"

"Stop calling me that!" she yelled. "My name is Marion and you too well know it! *You* did this, Thomas! It's *you* who will pay for it, not me! You . . . you will pay for . . . for . . ."

Suddenly, Amanda threw her head back in a spasm. She shook violently and then collapsed so quickly that Bruce barely managed to catch her before she fell to the ground.

Bruce swept Amanda up into his arms, feeling the muscles in his back protest as he straightened up. The other people in the park had studiously moved away from where he was standing or were pointedly looking in other directions.

Bruce turned with the woman in his arms and started across the parkway toward the rows of brownstone homes on the far side of the Sprang River Drive and Burnley district beyond.

It was, indeed, time to take Amanda home.

CHAPTER NINE

WHAT ARE LITTLE GIRLS MADE OF?

Bruce pressed the doorbell awkwardly with his extended right index finger, the rest of his hand otherwise occupied holding the limp form of Amanda Richter.

The dawn had not yet broken over the Atlantic to the east. All the streets in the early morning light were bathed in a rosy morning glow. A few citizens were stirring and a number of lights shown through the windows up and down the street, but among those early denizens no one took particular notice of the man in the flannel shirt and jeans carrying the woman up the brownstone steps.

He had secured the Batmobile in a side tunnel of the Gotham mass transit system specifically designed to keep the vehicle—and his Batsuit—away from prying eyes or hands. It was as close as he could get to Elm Avenue and Murphy Street and be sure his equipment—especially his Batsuit—would be safe. Walking to the park had been a casual distance. However, the park had been four blocks from Amanda Richter's brownstone steps and

Bruce was feeling the exhaustion from the effort of carrying the woman this far. Now, standing on the stoop with the woman in both arms and struggling to press the doorbell, he wished not for the first time that he were back in the exomuscular Batsuit and letting it take away the years that he was feeling now in his complaining arms and legs.

He managed once more to find the doorbell and leaned against it.

The door opened at last.

"What in the name of . . . !"

"Delivery, Ms. Doppel," he grunted.

"Who are you?" the nurse demanded at once.

"Gerald Grayson," he answered, sweat beading on his forehead. "Do you mind if we come in?"

"What have you done to her?" Ms. Ellen Doppel, RN, was a frumpish middle-aged woman who had the general appearance of having just been shaken in a large paper bag and rolled out of it. Her dark cotton skirt and white blouse were both rumpled, and a bright pink sweater was draped over her shoulders unevenly. Her eyes were also uneven; one appeared slightly lower than the other and drooped perceptibly. Her iron gray hair was sticking out of its loosening bun at odd angles. Despite her worn appearance, Bruce noticed she moved surprisingly well.

"Nothing compared to what's going to happen to her if I drop her on these stone steps," Bruce replied through gritted teeth. "You want to get out of the way?"

Ms. Doppel did not want to get out of the way but did so anyway. She dropped back against the entry wall, clutching her sweater closed as she did. "Straight down the hall and the first door on the left. There's a couch in the study. Put her there."

Bruce obeyed quickly, uncertain as to how long his legs would hold out.

There was a time when I wouldn't have given it a second thought. There was a time long since past . . .

He crabbed sideways down the narrow hall and rotated through the open doorway. The study had stained panels up to a chair rail with a light khaki paint above running to ornate crown molding along the ceiling. A heavy desk stained to match the wall panels sat near the center of the room, while tall bookcases filled one wall. There was a window that let in light from a small garden nestled between the brownstones. An overstuffed leather couch sat against the back wall. It had been a man's room, yet Bruce decided that the room had not known a man's presence in perhaps half a century.

"Where did you find her?" Ms. Doppel asked. She had followed them to the room and was standing in the doorway.

"She was at Curtis Point," he said. "I was waiting for a delivery and just thought I'd pass the time."

"At Curtis Point." Ms. Doppel was not buying it.

"That's about it."

Ms. Doppel considered him for a few moments before she spoke. "You must be cold, mister, ah—"

"Grayson, ma'am. Gerry Grayson."

"May I offer you some coffee before you go, Mr. Grayson?"

Bruce smiled his most winning smile.

"I would like that very much, Ms. Doppel."

She backed out of the doorway, slipping back into the kitchen. "Come with me, please."

Bruce followed her. The kitchen itself was definitely old, the floor covered with white tiles, accentuated by smaller black ones. The appliances had been replaced about ten years before, by the look of them. The nurse motioned Bruce to sit at a small table with a ridiculously old-fashioned pink Formica top. The chairs looked as though they might have come from a malt shop, and the plastic on one of the cushions was split.

"What do you know of Miss Amanda, Mr. Grayson?" Ms. Doppel asked without preamble as she poured the coffee from the gleaming metal pot into two large cups on matching saucers.

"Not much, really," Bruce answered. "I'm not sure all her wiring is up to code, if you know what I mean."

Ms. Doppel almost smiled. "That is quite true, Mr. Grayson."

She picked up the cups and saucers, stepping across the kitchen and setting them on the table.

"Since we're sharing coffee, how about you just call me Gerry?"

"I'd prefer to keep things formal, Mr. Grayson," the nurse said as she sat down across from him. "Remaining impersonal will make my news easier."

"You do have a first name, though, don't you?" Bruce persisted.

She looked at him across the table, always considering what she said before she spoke. "My name is Dr. Ellen Doppel, I am—or was—a doctor of clinical psychology. I was treating Mrs. Richter and her daughter at the time of their unfortunate demise and am now barred from public practice due to inaccuracies in testimony at the inquest. However, it was the uncontested wish of both the mother and the daughter in their last wills that I inherit their house and their financial holdings. I have been a prisoner to their largess in this house ever since. Does that satisfy your curiosity, Mr. Grayson?"

"And so now you're treating the youngest daughter on your own?" Bruce asked with studied casualness.

"No, we both know that is impossible, now, don't we?"

Bruce looked up over the edge of his cup. "Pardon me?"

"Miss Amanda, as you know her, cannot possibly be Amanda Richter," Ellen Doppel continued with studied cool. "Ernst Richter died at Arkham in an accident in 1958. Marion, the elder daughter, was fifteen years old at the time. Her younger sister Amanda was eleven. Had Amanda survived, she would be over sixty years old by now."

"She looks pretty good for sixty," Bruce chuckled.

"Well, the Richter women were known to carry their age well," Nurse Doppel said.

Bruce raised his eyebrows.

"A joke," Doppel shrugged. "No, Mr. Grayson, that is not Amanda Richter."

"Well, I carried somebody into this house," Bruce said.

"But not Amanda Richter," the nurse said flatly.

"Well, she certainly believes she is Amanda," Bruce countered. "Where did she come from?"

"I don't know," the nurse answered, a troubled look creasing her brow for the first time. "She arrived on the back porch one day in the middle of a thunderstorm, soaking wet and barely able to speak."

"Where did she say she came from?"

"This house."

"But you just said—"

"I said she is not Amanda Richter," Nurse Doppel interrupted, crossing her arms. "I have tried my best to help her, but she firmly believes that whoever she once was, she is now Amanda Richter. She believes she is possessed by the ghost of Amanda and that all her father's powers to redirect men's minds are hers as well. She believes she will not be free of this ghost until Amanda has been avenged of her father's death."

"Possessed?" Bruce shook his head. "That's crazy."

"Yes," Nurse Doppel responded, sipping at her cup. "I do believe it is."

Bruce watched Doppel for a moment. There was a resigned sadness to the woman, like an animal who had been captured in the wild and whose spirit had been broken by too many years in a cage.

"She called herself Marion," Bruce offered into the silence.

Doppel looked up with sudden interest. "She did? When?"

"Just before she blacked out," Bruce said. "Who's Marion?"

"That was the elder of the Richter daughters," Nurse Doppel responded, shaking her head sadly. "This is very bad."

"Bad?" Bruce said. "I thought we were well past bad already."

"I mean worse," Nurse Doppel corrected. "She had adopted the persona of Amanda, but now it appears she is forming schisms into multiple personalities. First Amanda and now apparently Marion. Dissociative identity disorder is a setback for Amanda—a worsening of her issues. This is usually brought on by inordinate stress, but I cannot think what kind of external stress she might be under that would be a causal factor in this newly manifest disorder."

A moaning sound drifted into the kitchen from the study. Nurse Doppel set down her cup carefully on the saucer and stood up, the legs of the chair squealing against the tiles. "Excuse me, Mr. Grayson, I'll be back directly."

Nurse Doppel moved past him, careful to keep as far out of his way as possible. She opened the door to the study, closing it behind her. Bruce strained to hear, but the voices through the door were muted and muffled.

Dissociative identity is extreme. Could an alternate personality be his opponent while the Amanda personality knows nothing about it? Dual personalities . . . isn't that what I am? Or does Gerry Grayson count as three?

Nurse Doppel appeared again through the study door, closing it softly behind her. In her free hand she held a package, covered in plain brown paper and tied fast with twine. "She said I was to give this to you."

Bruce took the parcel, turning it over in his hands. "What is it?"

"I haven't the slightest idea," Nurse Doppel said, looking away and moving down the hall toward the front door. Her manner was polite, but there was a sense of accelerating farewell about her tone.

"Well, then, tell her 'thank you' for me," Bruce said, holding the object up as he passed her at the threshold. By weight and size, it appeared to be a wrapped book.

"I shall, Mr. Grayson," Doppel responded, using the door to push Bruce the rest of the way onto the stoop. The closing door nearly cut off her words. "Do call again."

He stepped down the stairs of the Brownstone on Murphy Street with a book wrapped in plain brown paper and tied with string turning over in his hands.

Bruce moved with quick steps toward the intersection with Elm Avenue—contemplating why every city in the United States seemed to have a street named after that particular tree—and descended the stairs of a subway station. He had unwrapped the book in his hands, discovering it had only a fading embossed year on its cover: 1957. Bruce opened the old diary and began reading. A security camera on the entrance ceiling recorded him reaching the bottom of the stairs but not reaching the subway platform. To the ever watching eyes of Gotham, he had vanished.

DIARY OF ERNST RICHTER (TRANSLATED FROM THE ORIGINAL GERMAN)

FRIDAY, OCTOBER 4, 1957: Regents are idiots! Shortsighted fools. Dr. Hemmingway called me a communist sympathizer! Me! And Professor Goldstein said I was calling into question the reputation of the hospital and the university.

This from a Jew, no less! After all the effort the Americans made to bring me and my family here—to give us this new life so they could have the profit of my research—now they do not want it? They cannot respect it or me? And now they accuse me of being a Stalinist—after I fled the Russians with the Americans bearing Promethean gifts! Almost thirty years of research, much of it practical, and now they want nothing to do with it? What am I doing here?

SATURDAY, OCTOBER 5, 1957: New gaggle of interns today. Goldberg had me take them in hand as punishment, no doubt, for my accent. Hate to leave Juliet and Mari on the weekend, but I cannot afford to upset the hospital bosses further. One was more promising than the rest of the dull, waddling gaggle they sent me: a young man named Thomas Wayne. He is bright and promising—and apparently very wealthy as well. He takes great interest in my research. Perhaps I should get to know this young man better . . .

CHAPTER TEN

KISMET

Thomas pushed his way toward the front of the lecture hall. The smell of the paint on the walls was still fresh. The Kane Foundation—ostensibly directed by Roddy Kane but largely influenced by the pet projects of his daughter Martha—had recently funded this new research wing of the hospital. Thomas smiled slightly at the thought, because while the building had been funded, the equipment needed to run it had not. The wing was, so far, a very public gesture struggling to find practical use. The chairs were of new, hardened plastic. The desks were of a tough new Masonite finish with gleaming surfaces. The linoleum tiles were polished to a shine. But many of the students using the facility were left to scrounge their own diagnostic tools and pool their own medical books to fill the empty shelves of the research library. This was not the fault of Martha or her father's tax-sheltered charities so much as the regents of the university, who could easily find matching funds for the construction of buildings—the literally concrete and very visible symbols of Kane's generosity. University presidents had difficulty impressing wealthy alumni or prospective star students with tours through ephemeral principles, philosophies, or concepts.

Thomas promised himself to do something about that.

He made his way down the aisle against the flow of other interns, who were exiting the hall as quickly as possible. Several of them were laughing and at least one of them called out to Thomas, but his attention was focused on the lectern at the bottom of the hall.

The doctor gathering his notes there was a slight man almost completely bald except for a closely cut swath of white, bristling hair extending from one large ear to another around the back of his head. He had eyebrows like white brushes and intense green eyes. Most striking was the long scar that extended from just above his right eye down his right cheek, cutting through the right brow. He had high and prominent cheekbones above a narrow, jutting jaw that seemed to project an air of constant defiance. He wore his doctor's smock that had been cleaned to an almost blazing white. There were razor-straight creases in his black slacks and a mirror shine on his shoes. His instructions to the new interns at the hospital had been given with a thick German accent and an almost obligatory edge of contempt.

"Dr. Richter!" Thomas called as he neared the podium. "Sir?"

The doctor looked up, puzzled to hear his name falling from the lips of an unfamiliar intern. "Yes . . . who are you? What do you want?"

"Sir, my name is Thomas Wayne."

"You are a new intern, no?"

"Yes, sir, I am."

"And why am I spending my valuable time listening to you, Dr. Wayne?"

Thomas knew he was giving Richter a stupid grin, but he plunged on anyway. "I just wanted to tell you that I am a great admirer of your work, sir. I was at your lecture at Harvard last year. Your ideas on utilizing an engineered virus as a positive carrier were groundbreaking."

Richter offered a slight, rueful smile. "I must congratulate you, Dr. Wayne. My interns usually do not have the courage to attempt flattering me until their second year."

"They should take more initiative," Thomas offered. "Perhaps have a little more vision?"

"Are you a man of such vision, then, Dr. Wayne?" Richter said, setting down his notes on the lectern and then gripping it on either side as he looked down on Thomas.

"Maybe I'm a man in search of a vision," Thomas answered, pushing his hands down into the pockets of his lab coat.

The Bowery / Gotham / 9:04 p.m. / October 8, 1957

"Good to see you, Mr. Wayne." Lewis Moxon thrust his hand out, a genuine smile splitting his face. "I was hoping to see you again. Welcome back to the Klatch."

"My pleasure, Mr. Moxon," Thomas said, matching the firm, companionable grip with his own.

"Lew to my friends," Moxon replied. "You call me Lew."

"Then I insist on being Thomas," Wayne replied. He had not quite gotten the knack of the whole beat generation's dress code. He was in an argyle patterned sweater and loafers, but at least he wore his collar open and had lost the bow tie. "Is Martha here yet?"

"Sure, sure," Moxon replied, his smile fading a bit. "She's waiting down on the floor with Celia and that Sinclair prick. Thomas, maybe you could have a word with her about him. He's bad news."

"Denholm?" Thomas laughed. "He's a bit rough around the edges, but he's a straight arrow. The guy volunteers with Celia out at the orphanage. He's helping her straighten out the books over there on his own dime."

"Yeah?" Moxon replied. "I've no doubt he's doing something with the books, but I don't think it's *his* dimes he's concerned about. Look, Mr. Wayne—"

"Thomas," he corrected. "Just Thomas, Lew."

"Right, Thomas," Moxon nodded. "Look, you seem like a nice guy. It's out of my jurisdiction, but somebody needs to pull in the reins on your friend Martha. She's got a classy chassis, don't get me wrong, but she's drivin' her life just a little too fast. Don't get me wrong, pal. She's all right in my book, but trouble just seems to follow her and she never seems to see the train coming until it's too late."

"Martha's a good egg, Lew," Thomas said, trying to keep up in Lew's wake as they moved through the liquid crowd flowing around them. "She's just like you and me, Lew: trying to survive the world our parents left us."

"Well, I'd be a lot happier if she'd slow down a little, because she's liable to total her life before she's had a chance to hold the pink slip," Lew grumbled. "Maybe we all would."

"What did you say, Lou?" Thomas asked, the noise in the café swelling just as they reached the top of the metal stairs.

Moxon turned suddenly to face Thomas. "Look, can I bend your ear a minute?"

"Lou, I really ought to be getting down to—"

There was something in the look of Moxon's eyes that made him stop; something that both warmed him and shook him to the core.

Fear and hope all at once.

"Sure, Lou . . . I can spare you a few minutes."

Lou nodded. He turned from the top of the stairs to a heavy black door set in the wall. He opened it quickly, gesturing for Thomas to follow.

They stepped into a hallway that ran back into the building.

There was a staircase and an elevator on the left. The elevator opened and out stepped one of Lew's waitresses, a tray of drinks balanced on one hand while she patted her hair back into place with the other. She nearly dropped the tray when she saw Lew, who turned to the right and opened a door with a frosted glass panel set in the top and the single word "Office" painted on the surface.

Beyond was a waiting room with two overstuffed leather chairs and a matching couch. The couch leather was stained and worn but still largely intact.

A very large, broad-shouldered man in an ill-fitting gray suit dropped the *Life* magazine he was thumbing through and stood up at once, his hand reaching without conscious thought beneath the lapel of his coat.

"Relax, Donnegan," Lew said to the gorilla in a suit. "Go get yourself a sandwich or something."

Donnegan slipped his hand out from his coat and stepped around Thomas, his steely eyes never leaving him as he stepped through the outer door.

"Public relations?" Thomas asked as the door closed.

"Just another gift from my father," Lew laughed as he opened the inner door, gesturing for Thomas to go through.

The office had too much furniture in it. The desk was finished cherrywood, as was the matching credenza behind it. Two more large leather chairs faced the desk, which had a high-backed swivel chair behind it. All of this was difficult to see beneath a thick patina of papers carefully stacked everywhere on the desk as well as the credenza. This surprised Thomas; this was a working man's office rather than a showplace. The right-hand wall was fitted with one-way mirrored glass. Thomas looked through it into the club below, his eyes fixing on Martha curled up against Denholm Sinclair.

"He should drop dead," Lew said, coming to stand next to Thomas.

"She says she's in love with him," Thomas said with practiced detachment in his voice.

"Sinclair's a shuckster, and he's takin' her for a ride in more ways than one." Lew shook his head.

"She's a big girl, Lew," Thomas said quietly. "I never could tell her what to do. And now she's all grown up."

"That she is," Lew said, nodding.

"But you didn't invite me in here just to watch Martha Kane," Thomas said, turning from the window and setting himself slowly into one of the large leather chairs.

"Right," Lew said, swallowing hard and adjusting his bow tie as though it had suddenly gotten too tight. He cleared his throat and stepped back over to the desk. The high-back chair squealed slightly as he settled into it and then leaned forward to move aside three piles of papers that were obstructing his clear view of Thomas. He took a deep breath and launched into a cascade of words. "Thomas, you know who my old man is?"

"Who hasn't heard of Julius Moxon?" Thomas said carefully as he pressed his fingertips together.

"Well, he ain't exactly *Father Knows Best*, if you know what I mean," Lew replied. "What he wants, he gets . . . and what he can't have, he takes."

"Sounds familiar enough," Thomas said, folding his hands in his lap.

"Yeah?" Lewis said, leaning forward, his own hands folded on the desk. "You're all right in my book, Thomas. Maybe we have a lot more in common than most people would think. We both come from wealthy families, and I think I know you well enough to say that we're a lot alike, you and I. I mean, sure, our daddies are rich and powerful but . . . but we don't have to be who our fathers are. Okay, maybe you had a great childhood—"

"I wouldn't count on that," Thomas whispered.

"Yeah? Well, me neither! And now I can't get away from being twelve years old my whole life," Lewis sneered. "My old man, Julie, owns me . . . still. Me, I don't like being owned. I built this club from the ground up, practically with my own hands, Wayne, and it's a successful business, too. We're in the black and making everybody good money, but that ain't enough for my old man. It ain't *enough* money, he says! He thinks I'm running a hobby here—clean enough to give him something respectable to point to when the feds or the press starts nosing about, but nothing he would consider to be a *life*. So I'm looking for the exit—not from this club, see, 'cause I love this place—but from my old man and his so-called family. Only he holds all the paper on this place, and he won't hand it over to me 'cause it makes him look good to have his name on the title."

Thomas snorted once softly. "We're both looking for the exit, friend."

"Yeah," Lewis smiled, his shaved head bobbing up and down as his smile widened. "So I have a proposition for you, Thomas . . . a business deal that's strictly on the up and up. You see your way clear of buying the Klatch, see? My old man won't see you comin' at him. Maybe offer him something else respectable in exchange."

"Then what?" Thomas said, opening his hands with the question.

"Then I work for you—pay back every dime plus interest over time," Lewis answered with quick intensity.

"Why go to all this trouble?" Thomas asked. "Why me?"

"Because you're the only boy scout I know and we got a bond between us, you and me," Lewis said. "I want out, Thomas. Out of the whole stinkin' mess of my family. I'm tired of the rackets and the dope pushers, the payoffs and the vice money. They never let it near me on account of I'm supposed to be the guy they hold up in front of the family and say what a good boy I am in the sunshine while they bleed the city dry at night. My socks may be clean, Thomas, but I'm standing in blood all the time, and there ain't enough polish in the world to get rid of it. I gotta get out before anyone notices the stains . . . and I need help to make it work. What do you say, Thomas? I'm trying to do the right thing here; you're gonna let me down, too, are ya?"

Thomas gazed at Lewis for a moment, then smiled. "Despite what you've heard, I don't control Wayne Enterprises or its money. I have to go to my own father for my living expenses."

Lewis's face reddened. "So that's the play, then?"

"No, Lew, that's not the play," Thomas said, standing up. "I don't know how, yet, but I'm going to help you find that exit."

Thomas thrust out his right hand.

Lew Moxon stood up, staring at the hand for a moment, and then reached forward, gripping it so hard that Thomas feared some of the bones might snap.

"I'll do right by you," Lewis promised. "Anytime you need a favor—anything—you just come to me."

Arkham Asylum / Gotham / 10:19 a.m. / November 14, 1957

"Welcome to Arkham, Doctor," Thomas said, thrusting his hands down into his lab coat as he stood in the center of the windowless laboratory beneath the newly installed fluorescent lights. "Will this do?"

"It is perfect, my boy," Dr. Richter answered with the first hint of a smile Thomas had ever recalled seeing on his face.

Thomas was not nearly so sure. Dr. Richter had some very peculiar requirements for his experiments, and taken all together, Arkham Asylum had been the best, if a somewhat bizarre, fit. It had been built under the direction of Elizabeth Arkham, the widow of Captain Jeremiah C. Arkham. His family had invested in a number of arms manufacturers in the previous century, and the resulting riches had catapulted them into High Society. One of Jeremiah's holdings was Winchester Arms, through which Elizabeth became acquainted with Sarah Winchester.

When Jeremiah died suddenly in a hunting accident just before the birth of their first child, Elizabeth turned to spiritualism and Sarah, her West Coast friend, for answers. Sarah believed they were both cursed by the sins of their families, and when Elizabeth became convinced of this too, she embarked on the construction of Arkham House, decreeing the building would forever offer protection against the spirits of all those who had died from the bullets on which her family had made its fortune. She chose the location for the building on Crane Island during a séance, and work began at once. The edifice rose above the low shores of the land that drove like a wedge into the Sprang River, with the Burnley District across the river to the north and the Coventry neighborhoods to the south. Its bizarre walls, angles, and ornaments were patterned after a Gothic Revival structure, but they grew wild, expanding with no clear architectural purpose. The mandate to continually build created a maze of rooms, hallways, staircases, wings, turrets, and spires that was ever expanding and never made architectural sense—in order, Elizabeth believed, to confuse the spirits that visited there. It was said in those days that to wander through the halls of the ever-burgeoning Arkham House was to walk through the mind of the mad Elizabeth herself. Workmen regularly got lost in the labyrinthine tangle of the weird halls, having to be rescued and led back into the light. Some were rumored never to have returned, with their hammering still occasionally heard in the dark recesses of the massive structure's seemingly endless foundations.

In 1921, Amadeus Arkham, Elizabeth's son, turned Arkham House into the Elizabeth Arkham Asylum, a facility he named after his late mother following her alleged suicide. The construction of Arkham had, it appeared, not allayed the family curse: Amadeus's wife, Constance, and their daughter, Harriet, were both brutally assaulted, murdered, and mutilated by an escaped inmate of Arkham Asylum, Martin "Mad Dog" Hawkins. Amadeus appeared to have dealt well with this horrific turn of events until Mad Dog was returned to his care. At the time, it was not known that Amadeus had years before actually facilitated his mother's demise and subsequently repressed the memory. While strapped down for electroshock therapy, Mad Dog unfortunately brought it all back to Amadeus. In the end, Mad Dog was dead, and Amadeus became a tenant of his own asylum, listening for the ghosts that walked the twisted, convoluted halls both in the building and within his mind.

With no living heir, Gotham City took over the estate, and though a succession of caregivers managed the facility under different names down through the decades, the Arkham family always seemed to be a part of its strange walls.

Thomas never gave any credence to the ghost stories. Arkham was strange, indeed, but understandable when one reflected on the strange twists of the human mind. And, as his investigations had discovered, it had some major benefits to Dr. Richter's proposed project.

First, it was secure. Neither of them wanted to go public with their work until they had properly tested Richter's methodology and prepared it for peer review. Richter's ideas were groundbreaking, but many an excellent researcher had been forgotten both in history and in the patent office by publishing their findings too rashly. There were a number of hidden corridors and forgotten suites that could be easily converted into laboratory space. Thomas had used his father's name in city hall and had been given access to the original construction drawing as well as the remodel. He had found exactly what he needed.

"It is something of a miracle, Dr. Wayne," Richter said, nodding in appreciation.

"It was originally a coal bin in the house," Thomas explained. "The original coal chute was enlarged into a ramp with steel doors at both ends."

"The door is huge," Richter observed. "It nearly fills the far wall."

Thomas nodded. Amadeus had intended the space for his private laboratory after the remodel, but his own fall had prevented him from ever using it. The space was forgotten in all the noise of the trial. "The ramp is large enough for a truck. We can bring in pretty much whatever you need that way. The doors are electronically activated and alarmed. I assure you they are very secure."

"What about power?"

"This was being converted into a laboratory space long before I found it," Thomas continued as he stepped into the large room. His voice echoed slightly in the open space around them. "Gotham is just finishing its new power plant across the river from here. The main power lines for the entire Uptown area go through a conduit that passes under Arkham. This room was specifically wired for high loads, so you needn't worry on that account. With the twelve-foot ceiling, you should be able to fit your equipment in here without any trouble at all."

Richter nodded in approval. "You have done well, Dr. Wayne."

"Thank you." Thomas grinned. "But there is more."

"More?" Richter replied, his white eyebrows rising precipitously. "What more is there?"

Thomas gestured into a large, darkened opening at the far
end of the laboratory space. He reached inside, found the
switch, and flipped it.

"Holding cells?" Richter said with a frown.

"Yes—or at least that's what they were intended to be,"
Thomas explained. There were five cells arranged in a semicir-
cle around the crescent of the room. Each had thick metal doors
that swung outward, each with its own electronic lock that
could only be activated from the opposite doorway. "I thought
you might use these for your laboratory animals."

"Yes . . . yes, of course." Dr. Richter was pale, sweat breaking
out on his forehead.

"Are you all right, Doctor?"

"Yes . . . I am fine, my boy," Richter said, his accent somehow
thicker than usual. "Have you any other surprises for me?"

"Why, yes," Thomas beamed. "One more."

They sat in the office. The new Formica tabletop gleamed
under the desk lamps. They could still smell the fresh paint in
the room. Richter sat at the desk in an oversized leather executive chair while Thomas sat across from him in his own leather
chair. An open bottle of champagne sat on the desk between
them as they both held aloft their filled glasses.

"Here's to our dreams," Thomas said.

"And may they remain ours for the time being," Richter cho-
rused, clinking his glass against Thomas's. "The hospital is not
that keen on my teaching as it is. If they find out about our little
arrangement before we are ready to publish things, it could go
very badly for us both."

"Then please don't tell anyone," Thomas chuckled. He sat back in his chair, sipping at the champagne for a moment before continuing. "Do you really think it will work, Doctor? I mean, I think I understand the theory, but in practical application—"

"Work?" Richter snorted. "It already has. It needs refinement, especially when it comes to the higher brain functions, but in terms of behavioral modification, it is already proven. It is the new work by Watson and Crick in the area of DNA that has really made all of this viable."

"Watson, Crick, and Franklin, you mean," Thomas said from behind his glass.

"Yeah, yeah . . . and Franklin," Richter said with a shrug. "Poor girl. Not so much as a thank-you when they handed her hat to her, and now I hear she's quite ill. Still, their research makes it possible for us to modify the DNA and use it as an information carrier on the back of a virus. We use the chemical memory techniques I've previously developed and couple them with the altered DNA carried by the viral host."

"Brings a whole new meaning to contagious thought," Thomas chuckled. "Doesn't it?"

"It is our dream, Dr. Wayne," Richter said in suddenly serious tones. "It means we can chemically and genetically alter the individual's underlying moral foundation. If we think of crime and corruption as a disease infecting the body of humanity, then we can engineer criminals to become a counter-virus to that same disease. It's like creating a sociological vaccine. Think of it, Thomas! We can turn the criminals of the world against themselves, destroying their organizations from within."

"No more bullies," Thomas sighed, taking another deep drink from his glass. "No more fear."

"A world where there is no more crime. No more war. No more injustice. For the first time, we'd have the means to correct the basic motivations of a human being—turn criminals into upstanding citizens, communists into capitalists if we choose. There would be no more prisons. No more war." Richter smiled, raising his glass. "Drink up, Dr. Wayne. You are about to end all the ills of the world."

"And that would really make me something," Thomas nodded. "Wouldn't it?"

"Are you not something now?" Richter asked.

"I'm a cipher, Doctor," Thomas answered, turning the glass as he examined the swirl of bubbles in his hand. "I'm Patrick Wayne's little boy. Nobody notices Thomas, nobody sees Thomas, nobody listens to Thomas, and that, sir, is a cipher."

"So you want to be something more?" Richter asked.

"Oh, yes," Thomas answered, draining his glass. "So much more."

"You have provided the means," Richter bowed slightly in his chair. "What shall you name our little project, then, Dr. Wayne?"

Thomas looked up at the stone ceiling overhead. "Let's call it Elysium . . . Project Elysium."

CHAPTER ELEVEN

DISILLUSION

The Batman rolled unseen beneath the city. The occasional rat that had the misfortune of entering the subterranean tunnel might, if it survived the first instant of the encounter, have been terrified by the sudden passing of a great, invisible blackness above them, the tearing sound of its wheels running against the walls of the corridor. The blackness would be gone before the creature could even register its primal fear.

The holographic displays in the cockpit gave Batman a perfect view of Gotham Power and Light trunk conduit 824LL flowing past him at tremendous speed. It was a night-vision interpretation of the GP&L tunnel, perfectly clear to Batman's eyes even though the conduit outside his craft was completely dark. He reached up with his left hand, touching a virtual display of a cascade of course turn-points that floated in the air in front of him.

Intersect at GP&L trunk M17 . . . access shaft BC418 *. . . Dillon abandoned line past station . . . Coventry service track to GP&L Trunk* AUX25 *. . .*

The analysis of the paper the invitations had been printed on had yielded an actionable clue. The paper in every instance had come from Gruidae Paper Company located in the Upper West Side manufacturing district. The company's ownership was obscure, but the word Gruidae referred to the scientific classification of the family of birds of which Cranes were a part.

Jonathan Crane, Batman thought, *better known as the Scarecrow.*

This crime fit the criminal's modus operandi well, but not perfectly. Scarecrow primarily motivated and manipulated his subjects through their deepest fears. Memory alteration or false memory implantation was on the face of it similar, but while it would have been appreciated by the Master of Fear, it also would have been a departure for the obsessive Crane.

I'll ask him when I see him.

The destination in the course window read Gruidae Paper Company.

Batman was satisfied with the computed course and pushed the graphic window further off to one side. He spoke the keyword for the computer's voice access as though it were the car's name.

"Kronos: Open file Dante one-six-two-five-one-seven," he said.

A window opened on the virtual display to his right. The frame above the display was labeled "Case File Dante: Voiceprint, Proximity Secure."

The Batmobile slowed only slightly as it came to the intersection with the main trunk line utility tunnel, riding the conduit rails fixed in the tunnels like a steel-tube roller coaster. The change in the angular momentum pressed Batman into the molded contours of his seat. The navigation program was functioning perfectly as the power conduits, gas and water pipes, and their wall mountings flashed past him at a dizzying rate on the displays. Batman focused on the new window and its glow-

ing contents, reaching out with his right hand and moving the
Dante file until it was centered in his field of vision.

He frowned at the contents scrolling down before him.

It was a compendium of information, pieces of a puzzle not
yet put in their proper places.

Richter, Ernst (PhD, virology, genetics, eugenics)

Born: 28 October 1909, Munich, Germany

Died: 2 April 1958, Gotham City

Married: Juliet Renoir (PhD, neuropsychology) 16 May 1943,
Sacré-Coeur, Montmartre, Paris (deceased: 20 November
1983 in Arkham Asylum, Gotham City, of complications
following onset of pneumonia while under treatment for
dementia)

Immigration to United States: Classified (OSS)

Batman paused for a moment as the vehicle banked sharply
and then zoomed upward through the access shaft to the abandoned subway line above. Alfred's father, Jarvis Pennyworth,
had been a member of the OSS, the Office of Strategic Services, during the Second World War. Old Jarvis had entered
service with the Wayne family shortly after the war, bringing
his wife and newborn son. That Ernst Richter had been in Paris
during the Nazi occupation of France was apparent given the
time and place of his marriage. His immigration to the United
States was smoothed over by an OSS operation. The information request on the details of the operation itself was still in
process through a series of intermediaries and would take a few
days to retrieve. The problem was the age of the information:
most of the files had not yet been converted into digital form,
and so clearance and retrieval took time. Still, it was obviously
another piece of the puzzle, a thread of a connection between
the Pennyworth and Richter families, but it did not explain why

Alfred would lie about having any knowledge of the haunted woman he had found on the grounds.

As for Amanda Richter, she was a piece of the puzzle that didn't fit no matter what he did. Batman read on.

> Children: 2
> Marion Maria Richter (born: 29 February 1944, Berlin, Germany / deceased: 16 May 1979 in Arkham Asylum)
> Amanda Dora Richter (born: 14 August 1947, Fort Bliss, Texas / deceased: 16 May 1973 in Arkham Asylum from complications resulting from drug overdose)

Batman scowled. He had long since come to believe that coincidence was only a fool's excuse for a pattern not yet understood. That all three of the Richter women would pass away within the walls of Arkham was taunting him. Both daughters passing away on their parents' wedding anniversary? That was a coincidence he heard in his mind as mocking laughter, sneering at his intellect.

The Amanda he had met claimed to be Richter's daughter, but according to the record she was dead. Even if she were alive, the birth date indicated she would be in her sixties by now. Yet Amanda appeared to have information and insights into her father—*his* father—which no one else could have known.

My father was the foundation of all that I am.

I do what I do because of my father.

Batman shook slightly to clear his head from the dark reverie that was overcoming him. He frowned in disgust at himself for losing concentration. Several screens of data had flowed past him unread and unregistered in his conscious thought. He picked up the thread of the words again.

. . . had been rumored but unproven. Richter's research applications were denied on five separate occasions by the

Gotham University Hospital Board of Directors. These applications were titled (in order of their submission):

a. Chemical Memory and Behavioral Modification: Practical Applications in Social Reform
b. Genetic Dreams: False Memories and Ancestral Influences on Behavioral Science
c. Criminal Disease: Curing Behavioral Predisposition Through Inoculation and Viral Transmission
d. Eugenics: A New Approach
e. Contagious Thought: Genetic Implementation of Subliminal and False Memory Thought

Batman considered the list of proposal topics. Behavioral modification and false memory certainly fit the symptoms from which Commissioner Gordon and a number of Gotham's leading citizens were suffering. Chemical memory and using a virus to transmit them through the invitation cards presented a host of problems, but also seemed to fit the facts. That Fay Moffit, the Spellbinder, was also operating under these same kinds of delusions meant that someone higher in the criminal food chain of Gotham was pulling everyone's strings. Whoever was behind this appeared to have gained access to Richter's research.

Research funded by my father.

Batman frowned, his voice turning to a snarl as he spoke.

"Kronos: Close file. Open file Alpha zero-zero-one-dash-zero-zero-zero-one."

The Richter file vanished, replaced at once by a new window glowing in front of him. Two achingly familiar faces stared back at him side by side from the page.

Father . . . Mother . . .

Batman's upper lip curled slightly.

The pain is always there; the demon fire that warms my soul. You have to feed hatred, feed rage; feed it daily . . .

"Heading: Background, Sinclair—"

A red, pulsing phrase appeared in the upper left corner of his vision, asking if he wished to abandon his current navigational course.

"No! *File* heading: Background, Sinclair, Denholm."

The course change notice vanished and the file display scrolled down in a blur, stopping suddenly at a line in bold type and large size.

Sinclair, Denholm
Born: 18 August 1932, Upper East Side, Gotham
Died: 16 February 1958 (REF: *Gotham Globe*)

Batman reached out with his gloved hand, tapping at the newspaper reference in the air. The window was instantly replaced with a vertical frame and a scan of a page from the *Globe* dated February 16, 1958.

FATAL ORPHANAGE FIRE DEEMED "SUSPICIOUS"

Man Held for Questioning
Accomplice Sought

GOTHAM CITY—*The disastrous fire at a Kane Foundation orphanage, where it is believed seventeen children died in the early hours of last Thursday morning in the Copper Street blaze, has been called "suspicious in nature" by investigators for the Gotham Fire Department. The fire, which completely gutted the historic former site of a Civil War hospital, engulfed the building within thirty minutes of its initial report. Unnamed sources confirmed the investigation has found evidence of the use of accelerants at multiple, simultaneous ignition points. The fire alarm within the building appears to have been pulled in advance of the fire starting, and the automatic sprinkler system appears to have been compromised.*

Most of the deaths occurred on the eighth floor in the deaf children's wing, where the fire alarms went unheeded. Staff normally assigned to the floor were suspiciously absent.

Denholm Sinclair, a man with alleged underworld ties, is being held by police for questioning in connection with the tragedy. According to police sources, Mr. Sinclair had been a person of interest in an ongoing investigation of fraud concerning recent transfers of funds through the orphanage accounts. An office worker at the orphanage in charge of those funds and an associate of Mr. Sinclair, Celia Kazantzakis, is currently also being sought by the authorities . . .

The navigation display on his left chimed, its destination pulsing with a digital readout counting down three minutes until arrival.

Batman suddenly frowned again, reaching out with his gloved hand and stopping the slowly scrolling news-article display with his index finger. He flicked it downward, the words of the archived newspaper image blurring in their rush. He arrested its movement with a jab of his finger.

. . . where it is believed seventeen children died in the early hours of last Thursday morning in the Copper Street blaze . . .

He reached over with his left hand, dragging the navigation display next to the article.

Destination in 00:45 / Gruidae Paper Company / 1628 Copper Street.

"Kronos: new search," Batman said louder than he intended. "One-six-two-eight Copper Street in Gotham City."

A third display opened.

Search: 1628 Copper Street / Gotham
1781: Street address established
1781: Erasmus Parkinson Farm
1824: Williams Bros. Greater Gotham Development
Fellowship
1827: St. Brigid's Hospital
1850: Sampson's Liver Pill Establishment
1862: Gotham War Veterans Hospital (historic site)
1915: Swensen Storage
1932: Bank of Gotham (repossessed)
1939: International Trade Building
1947: Copper Street Orphanage
1954: Kane Foundation Orphanage

The navigation display appeared again: "Autopilot disengaging in 00:10."

Batman reached forward and gripped the control yoke, gritting his teeth.

There is no such thing as coincidence . . .

Wayne Manor / Bristol / 7:37 a.m. / February 16, 1958

"Master Wayne . . . Miss Kane is . . ."

Martha pushed past Jarvis Pennyworth, nearly toppling the elder butler into the solarium. She wore a tight pink cardigan sweater with a white scarf tied around her neck and dark, pedal-pusher slacks. Her hair was pulled back into a ponytail, and she had a fresh look about her, except for her eyes, which were red, and the tears streaking down her creamy cheeks.

"Tommy! Oh, Tommy, you have to help him!"

Thomas stood up from the table at once, nearly spilling his coffee onto his breakfast plate of eggs Benedict. He laid his paper down at once, taking care to place it with the front page down against the table, hiding the headlines that had already fallen down around him. He knew why she was here, dreaded why she was here. "Martha! What is it?"

She ran toward him, brushing past the tropical plants that flourished beneath the glass roof and the walls that held the snowfall of winter at bay. She was sobbing as she ran, her shoes slapping against the inlaid stones.

Thomas barely had time to open his arms before she threw her own arms around him, pressing her head into his shoulder. Thomas flushed slightly at the feel of her firm body pressed against him, her warmth joining with his own and the smooth curve of her back suddenly somehow beneath his hands.

"Master Wayne, perhaps I may be of some assistance to Miss Kane—"

"No, Jarvis," Thomas said at once. "That will be all. Thank you."

Jarvis quickly vanished, the door to the solarium closing instantly and silently behind him.

Thomas held her.

He had dreamed of holding her, spent untold time lost in thoughts of holding her, and fantasized of this moment in a thousand different times and places and circumstances. Now the moment had come, with him standing in his open-collar shirt and slacks in the midst of palm trees, rubber plants, and orchids in the humid heat while snow fell softly beyond the glass in the cold world beyond. He knew the moment could never last; the spell would be broken in a moment when she spoke the words that would drive nails through his heart. But he held onto her, drinking the totality of her into his soul and memory so that he would at least have this one moment for his own to keep him warm when he went back into the cold of his reality.

"It's Denny!" she sobbed into his shoulder. "They've arrested him! They're saying terrible things about him!"

The moment was over.

"Yes, Martha," Thomas said, his hand reaching up to pat her on the back. "I know."

Martha pulled away, her tear-streaked face gazing up at him with searching eyes. "But it isn't true! It *can't* be true . . . all those horrible lies they're telling about him!"

"Martha, I don't know," Thomas lied.

He did know. His father had brought the news to him first, having been informed of it by the Office of the District Attorney, which was generously paid to keep Patrick Wayne informed. Thomas had vehemently denied it to his father's face that Saturday morning and, as a result, given his father the perfect opportunity to drag his son downtown and prove him wrong. The evidence compiled by the DA had been overwhelming—the recovered double ledgers from the orphanage, the various bank accounts, the matching trail of embezzlement and payoffs. Celia Kazantzakis had unquestionably been Denholm Sinclair's partner in the theft, urging Martha to provide additional donations to the orphanage and then managing to move the funds off the books. Thomas had known from Lew Moxon that Denholm had been working for the Cesar Rossetti mob, but had no idea how deeply involved he had become—or how indebted he was to Cesar's bookie operation. The payments on his debts had gotten out of hand, and the orphanage embezzlement was growing proportionately. Now Celia had fled, her Pan Am tickets were traced to Canada, where she may have purchased tickets to Spain under a different name. The police were still trying to work that out. But the authorities had caught Denholm near the orphanage shortly after the fire broke out and had subsequently discovered that he had purchased large quantities of paint thinner and kerosene earlier that previous Wednesday.

And then there was the confession he had signed.

"You've got to help him, Tommy!" Martha pleaded.

"I don't know what I can—"

"Thomas Wayne, don't you *dare* tell me you can't help Denny!" Martha said, pulling suddenly back away from him. "He is your friend! He's good and kind and . . . and . . . oh, Thomas, I know he has his rough side, and maybe he's done some things that he isn't proud of . . . but he's *good* inside and I . . . I . . ."

"You love him," Thomas said, though the words fell from his lips as cold and soft as the snowfall outside.

Martha, lost in her own pain, heard only what she wanted to hear and smiled through her tears. "You *do* understand, don't you? Oh, Tommy, please fix this for me. Please make it right."

Thomas drew in a deep breath.

Fix this for me.

Thomas nodded. "All right, Martha. I'll take care of it. You go home and I'll call you this afternoon."

Martha threw her arms around him once more. "Thank you, Tommy! You're the best!"

Holding her was not the same this time, perhaps because he knew what would follow.

Thomas watched her as she hurried away out of the solarium. As soon as he could no longer hear her footfalls, he reached down to the phone on the table. It was time to fix Martha's problem. He picked up the receiver, his finger rapidly dialing the number he had dialed so many times in the past few months.

He waited only a few minutes before the other end of the line picked up.

"Dr. Richter, please . . . Doctor? My apologies for bothering you this morning, but I needed you to take care of something at once . . . No, I'm afraid it has to be today . . . How many test subjects have you gotten reassigned from the criminal wing? Three? . . . Well, I need you to get another one transferred into our project at once. If you'll file the recommendation by two this afternoon, I think I can . . . No, right away. You'll need to make sure the cell is prepared and let me know as soon as the paperwork is filed so I can arrange for the transfer on my end."

Thomas reached down for his fork but thought better of it. His breakfast was ruined.

"His name is Sinclair. Denholm Sinclair."

CHAPTER TWELVE

THE CURE

The shadow of the Bat moved down the hall, the figure casting it barely making a rustling sound as it moved.

The darkness of the corridor was broken only with dim patches of light cast through the frosted panes in the office doors on either side, a pale continuation of the streetlamps and the outside windows beyond.

But the Batman was blind . . . and could see everything. The subsonic imaging system gave him an awareness of his surroundings that was dimensional and complete. It was now combined with a starlight night-vision technology. It was newly installed and had a limited field compared to the subsonic imager, but at least it allowed him to read signs and printing when he turned his eyes toward them. The office doors slipped by in a ghostly green texture mapped onto the subsonic 3D imaging system in his cowl. The calibration was slightly off, but if he held still he could read the painted labels on the glass panels of each office door.

It's not right . . . not yet. The next time will be better.

"Yoo-hoo!"

Batman froze at the sound echoing down the hallway. He held still, trying to determine the direction from which it came.

"Oh, help me, Mr. Batsy-watsy!" came the shrill, cackling voice. "It is such a *tragedy*. Hey, whatza matter? Ain't you the kind to appreciate a good drama when you're in one?"

"Harley Quinn," Batman muttered to himself. He flexed in the Batsuit, engaging the exomusculature systems without conscious thought. The mere sound of this schizophrenic psychopath's voice raised the hair on his arms. That she appeared completely unexpectedly was, oddly, to be expected given the entirely random nature of her shattered personality. She had been mentored by the Clown Prince of Crime himself. But everything that had happened in this investigation had been far too planned, too purposeful in meaning to have been the Joker. "What in the hell is *she* doing here?"

"You're gonna be late, Batsy!" the nasal voice screeched.

The stairwell. She's got the high ground. He moved quickly toward the open fire door but stopped short of passing through it. The door was not just propped open as he had supposed it to be; the hinges had been cut through completely and the door set leaning against the wall. He craned his head up, mapping the metal emergency stairs above him. There was an open well running up the center of the steel stairs climbing up the shaft. The space was large and, judging by its size, may once have housed a freight elevator. From the landing on which he stood, Batman could see down two floors into the basement, as well as up five more to the top of the stairwell.

"Didn't ya get yer invitation, Bats?" Harley cooed from the darkness above. "You're invited! You're invited! You're invited . . ."

The ground shook, rolling slightly beneath his feet. Batman felt the rush of hot air up the shaft before the gout of flame erupted into the stairwell, a roiling inferno rushing upward past him. He could hear the shattering of glass from the pressure all around the building, mixed with the deep thump of distant pyrotechnics igniting below.

"Boo-hoo!" The taunting voice echoed as it tumbled down the metal stairs. "Where we gonna find a *hero*, Mr. Bats-in-belfry? Oh, who shall *save* us? Hahahahaha!"

Batman snatched the grapnel gun from his Utility Belt, aiming for the lattice of steel beams at the top of the shaft. The pressure canister discharged at his touch, the grappling hook catching five stories overhead.

He could feel the heat rising behind him. It was overwhelming the starlight night vision. Batman opened his eyes. The hall was already awash with flames, spreading across the floor toward him in hungry sheets wanting to consume him.

"You're invited" . . . *Harley knows.*

At once, Batman looped the monofilament around the spool, connected the wrist hook of the Batsuit to the device, and triggered the speed winch. The exomusculature of the Batsuit stiffened, supporting his frame as it accelerated him upward along the center axis of the shaft. The dark metal stairs, lit from below by the flames, rushed past him as he rose.

Movement caught Batman's vision on the fourth-floor landing to one side of the shaft just above him. He kicked against the stairs, swinging back in the shaft even as he continued to rise. He toggled the winch once more, arresting its whining spin just as he reached the apex of his backward motion.

The shape of a woman stood on the landing, her hands on the railing as she laughed maniacally.

It was Harley Quinn . . . and yet, it wasn't.

Batman took it all in at once. There were the familiar vestiges of Harleen Frances Quinzel, the intern psychologist at Arkham

Asylum who had sought to cure the Joker and had been drawn into his madness instead. It was the same lithe, athletic shape. The large mouth and generous lips were still framed by the white clown makeup, as were her hazel eyes. The hideous voice was unmistakable, and the psychotic teasing that had become her trademark.

But she had eschewed her usual jester's jumpsuit and harlequin hat. Instead she wore a dark green, double-breasted great coat with dark stains around the collar and shoulder epaulets. Her hair, normally bleach blonde, had been hastily dyed black and fell down around her shoulders loosely rather than in the tight ponytails she had always worn before.

"Save me! Save me! Save me!" Harley chattered as she ducked back off the landing through the doorway and into the darkness beyond.

Batman pushed against the stairwell behind him, swung across the fire rising up the shaft below and released the hook. He rolled across the landing, rising to a stance just inside the doorway.

The distant sound of sirens penetrated the growing rumble of the fire below. The Gotham City Fire Department was responding to the blaze, but given the speed at which it was growing, Batman knew the building would be a loss before they got it under control. The snap and cracking sound of the supporting timbers beneath him was growing more frequent by the moment. Even though the corridor in front of him appeared sound and intact through the growing haze of smoke, Batman knew that it was an illusion; everything under their feet was being eaten away by the flames. The warehousing of the paper goods was in the basement and, no doubt, was adding to the heat growing under his feet.

Batman could feel the sweat start to build around his head

under the cowling. Heat dissipation in the exomuscular Batsuit was a problem in the best of times, but in the middle of a fire the problem was worse. The cape billowed behind him in the rising wind generated by the fire raging beneath them.

He was running out of time.

He moved quickly down the hallway. The floor under his boots was already getting soft, bouncing under his footfalls. Light was coming from a single door at the end of the corridor. It had to be Harley, leading him on, taunting him.

He reached the door. The lettering on the now-cracked glass originally read "Conference B," but someone had hastily painted over it.

It now read "Deef Orfans Ward."

Batman pulled the door open with such force that it tore free of the hinges. He launched upward, gripping the overhead girders as he prepared to take on the trap that had been so lavishly laid for him.

He stopped, dropping carefully to stand on the floor.

The flickering light of the building's fire came through the windows of the long room, reflected off the buildings on the opposite side of the street. The orange light illuminated two rows of infant cribs, eight on each side, set on the right- and left-hand sides of the room.

At the end of the rows of cribs stood Harley Quinn in her stained great coat, her hands outstretched toward him. Tears ran down her cheeks, streaking the white makeup.

"Please, Tommy," Harley begged. "Save the children! Save the children!"

Batman stepped quickly over to the first crib on his right, reaching down toward the form under the blanket. It was still, hard, cold. He pulled the blanket away.

A Scarface ventriloquist's dummy stared back at him, its features shifting with the hellish light from the windows. Between its stiff fingers it held an invitation card.

"Can you save them, Tommy?" Harley giggled. "Are you gonna save *all* your children, huh, Tommy?"

Batman moved to the next crib   and the next . . .

Each held an identical Scarface dummy staring back up at him from the crib, each with an invitation in its wooden hand.

A sudden loud crack rang through the hall. A section of the floor near the door had collapsed, the flame rushing upward in a whirlwind, spreading across the ceiling.

Batman ran over to Harley Quinn, grabbing her roughly, pinning her arms behind her. He roared at her, teetering on the edge of control. "Why are you calling me that?"

"Calling you what, Tommy?" Harley grinned. "I'm gonna call you Tommy because that's your name, and you can call me Adele."

"Adele?" Batman blinked. "Who the hell is Adele?"

"Me, you batty-bat-bat!" Harley said. "I am Adele, and I'm here to help you clean up my mess! But then you have to die . . . we all have to die, don't we?"

Batman grabbed one of the Scarface dummies and used it to smash open the far window. The building on the opposite side of the alley would have to do. If the grapnel would stick he could get them both clear before the building collapsed beneath them.

"Let's go . . . Adele," Batman said, gathering Harley to him, feeling the Batsuit compensate for the weight. There was a time when he might have managed it on his own, but that was long past.

"Where we going, Tommy?"

"You're going back to Arkham Asylum," Batman said, rigging the grapnel once more. Through the windows behind him he could see the ladders rising up from the GCFD. Soon their

hoses would be pouring water down onto and through the fal-
tering roof. Between the hoses and the fire would not be a good
place to be.

"Arkham? Ah, you're such a gentleman, taking me home,"
Harley laughed. "And such a *prude!* It's still early, Tommy."

Arkham Asylum / Gotham / 3:05 p.m. / February 16, 1958

"Dr. Wayne, this is entirely improper," Richter said, running
his hand once again back through his hair as he spoke. "There
are protocols which must be followed. Our research will be of
no use to anyone if it cannot be verified."

"I'm perfectly aware of that, Dr. Richter," Thomas replied,
standing in Richter's office, both of his fists resting on the desk-
top. "But you said yourself the genetic memory keys had performed well above the statistical curve, and that was the last step
before submitting for clinical trials."

"We've never put the entire sequence together before," Richter countered, gesturing with his hands for emphasis, the desk
lamps casing the lines in his face in stark relief. "The individual
elements, yes, they all appear to be yielding the desired results,
but in combination—"

"And what about the initial results from the test subjects you
already have?" Thomas asked, picking up the clipboard off the
top of a stack of papers scattered across the desk. "Look here
. . . Michael Smalls, a professional contract killer before shooting
up half the Tricorner Yards. Your memory replacement therapy
has worked in him. These two women— Caprice Atropos and
Adele Lafontaine—they've shown no side effects to the benign
viral carrier and have both responded to the genetic memory
triggers you engineered. You've managed to collect memories
using the viral trace therapies from both of them, and with a
degree of accuracy neither of us expected. The base motivations

are much broader in their chemical base and easier to locate than specific memories, you've proved that. All that's left is to attach the chemical memory to the genetic keys in the benign virus and the entire system is complete. In a single inoculation we can turn crime against itself . . . and rid the world of bullies, thugs, and anyone who wants to extend their domination over another human being."

"Yes, the protocols appear sound," Richter argued. "We can replace the basic motivations of these criminals, but with *what?* Whose ethics do we choose?"

Thomas thought for a moment before he spoke.

"With mine."

"Yours?" Richter said, surprised.

"Elysian is our dream, Doctor," Thomas said. "It's time to make it a reality. We have the means, quite literally, to cure crime. All we need is the will to make it happen."

Richter looked away.

"Ernst," Thomas said quietly.

Richter turned back to face him.

"We both have things in our past we want to correct," Thomas said. "We can be healed, too."

Richter cast his eyes downward but nodded.

"I've got to get back to the hospital," Thomas said. "Call me there when you're ready for me. I'll just go check on everyone before I go."

Thomas turned and stepped through the office door. The laboratory space had to be combined with the operatory, and though it was packed with equipment, there was sufficient room for what they needed. Thomas turned toward the rotunda in the back, where the cells were located.

Thomas started with the right-hand cell, looking through the four-inch square opening in the metal door. Caprice Atropos practiced yoga next to her cot, holding the lotus position perfectly still. Her flaxen hair lay across her face. She had been a sociopathic cat burglar for the Moxon mob until she decided it was more fun to kill the victims in unique ways during her thefts.

The next cell brought Michael "The Scythe" Smalls into view. The Butcher of Tricorner was a tall, wiry man with hollow cheeks. He had been a vicious hitman for the Rossetti mob who especially delighted in inflicting torturous pain on his victims before allowing them to die. He lay sleeping on his bunk—more evidence of improvement since he had not slept at all so far as anyone could determine for the prior eight months of his confinement in Arkham.

Third was Adele "Chanteuse" Lafontaine. She stood leaning with her back against the wall, reading a copy of Truman Capote's *Breakfast at Tiffany's*. Her long black hair flowed down over the double-breasted, olive-green greatcoat she had worn since her arrest and had fought violently for whenever she was parted from it. She turned her head toward the door and, seeing Dr. Wayne, smiled faintly and waved. She had been a singer once, Thomas recalled, whose husband had served in Korea. She had caught him with another woman, and the result had been two dead and a broken psyche. Eight husbands later she was known as the Black Widow of Robinson Park. The coat, it was rumored, had belonged to her first husband.

At last, Thomas came to the last cell.

"Thomas!" Denholm said, rushing to the door, his face pressed against the small opening. "Thank heaven you're here! You've got to get me out of here."

Thomas took in a shuddering breath. "But I worked so hard to get you *in* here, Denny."

Denholm blinked at this, as though the words would not register in his mind.

"I know what you've done, Denholm," Thomas continued. "The embezzlement, the lies, taking Martha for a ride—"

"No! No, Thomas, you've got it all wrong," Denholm said quickly. "I had no choice! What chance has a guy like me got? The whole game's rigged . . . so, I tried to rig a few things myself . . . but it just got outta hand."

"Out of hand?" Thomas said. "Denny, seventeen children died from the fire that *you* set."

"That wasn't supposed to happen!" Denholm whined. "I pulled the alarm . . . Me! . . . I thought there was plenty of time for them to get out. Celia said there would be plenty of time. How was I supposed to know there were deaf kids on that floor?"

"And what about Martha?" Thomas said quietly.

"Martha?" Denholm said, unsure.

"You remember Martha, don't you?"

"Oh, sure, she's a swell kid but what does she have to do with—"

"Denholm, you're not worth the gum on the bottom of her shoes," Thomas said, anger rising inside him at last. "I've known her since she was six years old, would have done anything for her if she had bothered to ask me. But now she wants *you* and some fantasy of who she thinks you are. She came to me this morning. 'Fix it,' she said. She asked me to fix it for you. It's one of the few things she's ever asked me for in all our lives. So I'm going to fix it for her, Denholm . . . and you're going to fix it for her, too."

"Great!" Denholm smiled uncertainly. "What? What do you mean?"

"You're not the man she thinks you are," Thomas said heavily. "But by the time you leave here, you *will* be."

CHAPTER THIRTEEN

SHORT LEASH ON LIFE

Utility Tunnel 57D / Gotham / 8:12 p.m. / Present Day

"You're going the wrong way, Tommy!"

Harley's whining voice echoed down the stained bricks that formed the archway of the old cellar corridor, with a maze of branching corridors leading off on either side. The Arkham sewer had been more recently encased in a large pipeline that ran down the side of the center trench of the old hall, while utility conduits as well as a number of more hastily installed cables ran down the side walls. People rarely came down here alone; it was too easy to get lost in the branching corridors. However, it was the quickest route up from the abandoned underground staging area for the old 1988 Gotham Subway Expansion Project, where he had just left the Batmobile recharging from the main power lines. The area afforded quick access to his forgotten cellar hall, and through it, to the more populated regions of Arkham above, where Gordon said he would be waiting for them both.

As for Harley, her hands were bound behind her, and Batman's grip on her arm was unyielding. The corridor was pitch dark, with Batman using the subsonic imaging in his cowl to

determine the location of the walls around them. One of the
benefits of the Batmobile having no windows was that it made
it very difficult for passengers to know where they were, and
the use of his cowl device was also part of keeping their location
secret until they stepped into the light.

So either Harley was insane or something had gone wrong.

She is insane . . . but never underestimate insanity.

"You'll be late for the party!" Harley cried. "Everyone's waiting . . . everyone . . . and here you are spoiling the surprise."

Harley stumbled slightly, and Batman tried to adjust for the
shift in weight but was too late. Harley pushed hard against him,
throwing him off balance slightly and twisting out of his grip.
In an instant she had plunged through the archway and into the
darkness beyond.

Batman roared in frustration. He should have been quicker
than that, but the years were grinding him down. He turned at
once, the Batsuit responding, drawing more power. He closed
his eyes and he dashed in after the laughing woman.

The corridor twisted and turned through several angles, a
pair of T-intersections, and a number of cross corridors. Batman
triggered the imaging recorder on his Utility Belt. The GPS
system would not function this far beneath ground—especially
with the massive bulk of Arkham overhead—but the subsonic
imaging could at least allow him to retrace his steps out of the
nightmarish belly of Elizabeth Arkham's monstrous architecture.
There was a slight heat trace in the air from her passing that
he was able to pick up from time to time in the damp, cold air
around him. He was getting closer, and the echoing taunts were
becoming more distinct with every step.

"You're invited! You're invited!"

Batman paused for a moment at a flight of stairs leading
downward but realized they ended in a stone wall. The corridors here were only three feet wide, though the ceiling was

a full fifteen feet overhead. He passed panes of Tiffany stained
glass that have never been lit by any light and looked out over
dark alcoves. The corridor turned again, inexplicably, onto a
rotting wooden veranda surrounded entirely by brick walls. A
wrought-iron circular staircase spiraled upward into a black shaft
at the far end of the veranda. Two window panes with beveled
glass were set in the stone on either side of a metal door that
exited the room to the right.

The door at the back of the veranda was still swinging, brilliant light overwhelming the thermal image. Batman opened his
eyes, his irises contracting as he pushed through the door.

Only half the old fluorescent lamp banks hanging from the
ceiling still cast their greenish pall over the room. The ballasts
of several of the lamps were failing, causing them to flicker with
occasional flash pulses. There was an enormous metal security
door large enough for trucks to move through completely filling the far end of the room, with great rust spots boiling up on
its surface where the old paint had peeled away. Set into the far
wall was a pane of laminated glass, shattered into a crystal web
in one spot from some heavy impact, a dark stain running down
the glass behind. A broken doorway lay askew in the frame leading to the dark room beyond the glass.

The floor was a jumble of ancient laboratory equipment.
Overturned metal tables lay amid shattered tempered glass,
broken beakers, and chemistry frames. Several centrifuges blue-
gray in color lay smashed on the floor among a number of incu-
bators. Massive microscopes poked up through the debris, and
many pieces of equipment defied explanation. Three refrigera-
tors, their doors open, sat against the far wall.

It looked to Batman as though a bomb had gone off in the
confined space, but the room was devoid of scorch marks or any
burning.

"Hey, Tommy!"

Batman turned at once toward the voice.

There was a large, arched opening to a circular room left of the broken door and window. Arranged around the circle of the room were five metallic cell doors. The second from the left was twisted and broken. The center door was closed with the remaining three doors hanging open.

Quinn peered out at Batman from the small window in the closed, center door. "You sure know how to show a girl a good time, Tommy! Thanks for the fun evening . . . so sorry it has to end."

Batman strode quickly over to the cell door, the glass crunching beneath his boots. He reached for the handle, moving to turn it, but it would not budge. He examined the latch more carefully.

Harley Quinn had locked herself into the cell.

She stood back from the door, throwing her hands into the air. Her white face makeup looked ghoulish in the rapidly flickering light at the top of her cell. "Welcome *home*, Tommy!"

I've spent half my life trying to put her in a cell . . . and now I need to get her out of one.

The lock was old and he thought he might have to find a way around it. Batman stepped away from the door, looking around the circular room.

Never use force to break a lock when a key will do. Where would one keep the key in a security area?

Batman turned, stepping back into the ruined laboratory space. Behind him, Harley Quinn began singing in her shrill voice, heavily colored with a Brooklyn accent to the tune of a song he vaguely remembered from World War II.

Kick Bats once, then kick Bats twice, then kick Bats once
   again . . .
It was an awful time . . .

Batman thought for a moment. The keys never would have been in the open. They would be secured as well as the inmates. Harley's voice echoed from within the cell behind him.

Past is past and dead is dead to never live again . . .
It was an awful time!

Batman stepped over a test-tube rack to the shattered office door. He pulled the remains away from the frame, feeling inside for the light switch.

The twin desk lamps came on. One of the bulbs flashed brilliantly and then died with a soft popping sound. The light flickering through the splintered laminated glass pane was barely helped by the single desk lamp's illumination. It revealed a large desk, its Formica top curling at the corners and pulling away from the wood beneath. Behind the desk stood a high-backed chair, its leather cracked and split in places, the damp stuffing spilling out through the openings. A pair of smaller leather chairs stood on the near side of the desk in similar condition.

Batman stepped carefully around the desk. A thick layer of dust covered nearly everything in the room, including the papers still resting on the curling Formica top . . . except for one volume. This single book sat squarely on top of the desk, its cover completely free of dust and well kept.

It was an old-style composition book, the hand lettering on its cover distinctly readable as "Project Elysium—Dr. Ernst Richter."

A single, yellowed envelope stuck out from between the book pages.

You'll never know the schemes they've weaved around you . . .
To call in all your father's debts that are way past due . . .

Batman reached down, opening the book to the marked page, but was stopped at once by the envelope.

It was more of his father's old stationery. The typewriter lettering across its face said, "From Dr. Thomas Wayne to his son."

As he turned the envelope in his hand, his gloved thumb ran across its face, smearing the type. He looked down at the facing page of the book and could see the faint impression where the ink had transferred from the envelope over onto the page.

The ink from the typewriter is still fresh!

In the distance, through the shattered office door, Harley Quinn warbled at the top of her lungs.

> *Kick Bats once, then kick Bats twice, then kick Bats once*
> *again . . .*
> *Here comes an awful time!*

The words at the top of the page caught Batman's attention. Harley Quinn faded from his thoughts, as did his promise to deliver her to Commissioner Gordon up in the lobby of Arkham above them.

Batman began to read . . .

Project Elysium Observation Log

17 FEB 1958 / 0835 HRS: Standard breakfast served to all subjects at 0810 hrs. All subjects awake. Subject 3 appears agitated and nervous—responds abusively to questions. All other subjects conversational and calm. New subject added yesterday: subject 4, male, approx. 28 years of age, excellent physical condition, evidencing antisocial and borderline sociopathic symptoms. Introduced into the program yesterday at 1700 hrs by Dr. Wayne. Simultaneous with arrival of subject 4, Dr. Wayne directed that I advance the program to

Phase VI protocols, integrating both the mirror ethics chemical extraction with the genetic memory integration and the viral delivery systems. The most promising carrier appears to be a Group 1 dsDNA in the Caudovirales Myoviridae family coupled with an Escherichia coli carrier. This makes the transmission waterborne and therefore more manageable. The modified genetic memories we then imbed through chemical alteration of the Myoviridae strands, and the system should be complete. I would prefer additional tests, but as our initial behavioral modifications will be only at the basic ethics levels, the risks are minimal.

20 FEB 1958 / 2245 HRS: The chemical alteration of the DNA is not binding to subject 4's DNA properly through the Myoviridae. We can match the dsDNA directly to the subjects as was done in Subjects 1 and 3, but ultimately for the protocol to work properly the carrier will need to be self-modifying in order to match the subject's DNA for binding. We will need to modify the Myoviridae to adapt to the host, making the delivery more dynamic.

11 MARCH 1958 / 1640 HRS: The dynamic mutation modifications to the Group 1 dsDNA have proven ideal carriers. All four subjects have shown remarkable improvement in their mental acuity and base motivations. The new memory-channeling additions to the genetic memory have made the ethics implantations more stable and permanent. Even the physical appearance of each of the subjects seems to have improved, although that is strictly a personal observation. I shall institute some limited freedom on the grounds next week for each of the subjects if their improvements continue at this pace. Must get home on time tonight. The girls miss me.

17 MARCH 1958 / 2135 HRS: The dynamic mutation components in the Myoviridae are transforming outside their original parameters. Subjects 1, 2, and 4 are each showing

signs of physical alteration brought on by the dynamic genetic restructuring. I am instituting the counter-virus protocol to halt the spread of the mutation until this aberrant result
can be investigated. Personal note: The Americans' Vanguard
missile finally launched successfully into orbit today. I trust
my old friend Werner will not begrudge them that much
success.

25 MARCH 1958 / 0300 HRS: The counter-virus has
not proved effective. The ethics redirection of the subjects
appears to be deepening as intended, but more apparent
physical changes in all subjects continue. Each is manifest
differently: Subjects 1 and 4 are showing signs of greater
strength. The female subjects 2 and 3 are demonstrating
greatly enhanced agility. All of the subjects demonstrate advanced mental acuity. I cannot keep up with their request for
books and reading material. All subjects also are demonstrating hyper-emotional states and manic-depressive emotional
swings. Unfortunately this appears to be coupled with a
deepening sense of superiority and a reinforcement of their
original sociopathic issues.

29 MARCH 1958 / 0100 HRS: All four subjects have
begun questioning me about my past. I can see how they
look at me—what they are thinking about me. We have made
them and now they will unmake us. They are the monsters
and we are the monsters for making them. I have called
Thomas but his father passed away on the 26th and it has
been impossible for him to get away. He says that now he
will be in charge of the family's assets and can properly fund
this research—but no amount of money will fix what we have
done.

31 MARCH 1958 / 1130 HRS: We must put an end to this
for our sakes and for the sake of all four subjects. Thomas is
unavailable as he has been dealing with both his father's fu-

neral and issues regarding his father's company. Meeting now scheduled for Thursday the 3rd.

2 APRIL . . . They have gotten out. The phone does not work. I am in the office and they are at the door. I see them grinning at me through the glass. They are at the door. They are

The page was splattered with dark splotches.

Batman looked up from the open book. The spiderweb of the smashed laminated glass shone brightly in the light from the green fluorescent lamps in the room beyond, colored only by a dark stain running down the glass and the wall beneath it to the floor. There was another group of stains to the left of the impact point in the window. It was barely visible, but Batman realized it was writing.

He stepped toward it to get a better look at the faded word scrawled there, his father's envelope still in his hand.

CHAPTER FOURTEEN

BLOODY MESS

Thomas took a step back. He could not stop shaking. He blinked, staring at the word scrawled in blood across the window next to the shining radius smashed into the glass.

Nazi

Dr. Ernst Richter lay like a broken doll beneath the splintered laminated glass, his blood extending downward from the impact point. The bones of his face had been crushed from the force that propelled him across his desk, its features swollen and discolored. A part of Thomas's mind catalogued the various injuries quickly, his medical training running at the back of his head almost with a will of its own. There were probably broken vertebrae at the C5 or C6 by the canting of the head on the neck. He suspected skull fractures as well in the frontal and parietal regions, given the odd shape of the head. The clavicle was probably snapped on the left side, along with several ribs. There was a compound fracture of the radius in the left forearm and quite likely breaks in both legs, too. The temporal lacerations from the impact as well as the laceration of the external carotid artery on the right side had been the cause of most of the bleeding, and judging by the amount of blood spread across the desk and pooled on the floor, the artery had been severed before Dr. Richter had been thrown into the glass.

While he was still alive.

Thomas shivered as he backed against the filing cabinets. He was finding it hard to think.

He had been feeling bad about putting off his meeting with Dr. Richter and decided to visit him in the research laboratory that night. Patrick Wayne's sudden death by heart attack almost two weeks ago had overtaken Thomas's life. It had seemed as if his father's cold hands had also stopped the heart at the center of Thomas's life, dragging his son down into the grave with him. The funeral arrangements, the various incarnations and machinations of his father's convoluted will, and the demands from the estate and empire that Thomas show leadership and strength for the sake of the market and the stockholders—all these had robbed him of the life he had chosen for himself.

But this was a different kind of death that lay staining the linoleum tile on the far side of the large desk. It was not the cold, quiet numbing imagined sleep but a violent, crimson rage and fury. It was an uncaged thing that somehow spoke to Thomas's center, calling to a beast that he kept carefully locked within, never listening to its howl. He feared that beast, and the fact that the carnage all around him urged it to awaken within him chilled him all the more.

Thomas stumbled over the broken office door and back into the wrecked laboratory. The equipment and tables tossed in a jumble about the room had been his first shock on entering through the maze passage door. He had rushed to the office at once upon seeing the damaged glass. But now he was becoming more aware of his surroundings and the danger they implied.

His body was still flush with adrenaline as he turned to the cell alcove on his right.

The doors to all the cells were open. Their occupants had fled.

"Denholm," Thomas breathed.

A gentle, chill breeze scattered papers at his feet. Thomas turned his face toward the freshening breeze.

The great vault doors were partially open to the long ramp rising beyond.

Thomas dashed through the gap between the doors, rushing up the ramp. The outer doors were open as well, and he at once found himself standing on the grounds behind Arkham Asylum. Somewhere in his mind he thought about finding Denholm and the other subjects of their study—yes, that was the word for it, wasn't it, *study*—and for a time he wandered frantically in search of them.

It was some time later—how long he quite suddenly could not recall—that he fell through the doors of a Bell Telephone booth, closing it behind him. The light came on overhead as he pulled the handset off of its chrome cradle. His hand shook so badly coming out of his slacks pocket that he spilled dimes and nickels across the metal floor. He picked up a few, jamming them into the slot and then quickly dialing the only number he could remember.

The speaker bleated in his ear as the phone rang, seemingly a million miles away.

"Good evening," the tin voice said with the practiced disdain of a London accent. "Wayne residence."

"Jarvis!" Thomas spoke the word as though the name itself were a life preserver thrown to him in a tempestuous sea. "Help . . . please . . ."

"Dr. Wayne? What is it, sir? May I be of assistance?"

"Please, Jarvis . . . I need you."

"Where are you, sir? I can send a car at once—"

"NO!" Thomas shouted into the receiver. "Don't send anyone . . . I don't want anyone . . . I mean, I need *you*, Jarvis."

"Calmly, Dr. Wayne." Jarvis's voice changed subtly. The deference was gone and there was a commanding edge to the tone. "Tell me your location."

"I . . . I don't . . ." Thomas stammered.

"Look around you," the quiet, demanding voice said over the phone. "What do you see?"

"There's . . . there's a park across the avenue," Thomas said, swallowing hard. "And a river beyond. I'm on a street with brownstones . . . I was at Arkham but . . . but . . ."

"Did you cross a footbridge?"

"Yes . . . yes, I did. I think I'm on the south side of Burnley by the Riverside Parkway."

"Do you see a street sign?" The voice was insistent.

"Oh, no, Jarvis . . . I don't know what to do."

"Street sign, Doctor! Do you see one?"

"What? Yes . . . yes," Thomas peered through the dirty glass of the booth. "It says Cronk Street . . . One Hundred Fourteenth Avenue, I think."

"You are to wait right there for me, Dr. Wayne," Jarvis said, his voice defying contradiction or question. "You are to leave the receiver off. You are not to call anyone—anyone, you understand?"

"Jarvis, what about—"

"Do you understand me, Dr. Wayne?"

"Yes . . . yes, I understand."

"I'll be there inside of fifteen minutes," Jarvis instructed. "Do nothing until I arrive."

"But I . . ."

"Nothing, you understand! Do NOTHING! I'm coming now . . ."

The grandfather clock in the front hall was just spooling up to strike three when Thomas heard the steps coming up the front steps of the mansion. Light from the rising moon cascaded over his shoulders from the two-story windows behind him as he sat on the grand staircase in the main foyer. He had managed to change out of his bloodstained shirt and slacks, his hands shaking throughout the process, and had tried to cleanse his body and his soul in a long, hot shower. He felt calmer, but sleep was impossible. He wondered if it would ever be possible again.

Thomas stood up as the latch on the great front doors was released, swinging them wide.

Thomas caught his breath.

No detectives. No police. No condemning witnesses.

It was Jarvis—alone.

"Dr. Wayne, you should be in bed," Jarvis said, his elegant English accent once again dominant.

Thomas breathed out a shudder. "But, Jarvis, what about the escaped subjects? They are loose in the city now and . . . Dr. Richter lying . . . lying there in his . . . in his own . . ."

"Everything has been taken care of, Dr. Wayne," Jarvis said smoothly. "I have taken the liberty of seeing to it personally."

"Seeing to it . . . personally?" Thomas parroted. "But, Jarvis, a man is dead . . ."

"Yes, Dr. Wayne," Jarvis pulled off his white cotton gloves with an almost casual boredom. "It is a tragedy, but I serve this family, Dr. Wayne . . . and I assure you that everything has been taken care of *personally.*"

"But, Jarvis, how could you possibly—"

Jarvis interrupted Thomas. "Did your father ever tell you about my earlier profession, Dr. Wayne?"

Thomas, taken aback, shook his head slowly. "No, Jarvis. We weren't much on speaking terms."

"As you are the master of Wayne Manor and, it would seem, most obviously in need of my services, perhaps I might enlighten you," Jarvis continued, setting his gloves down on the side table. I was born in 1908 in a little village outside of London. My father was in service, although he fancied himself a bit of an actor. I trod the boards myself for a time in my youth but proved myself a bit of an adept with a gun. I was in my late twenties, as you say, when war was brought home to my beloved England. And I answered her call, Dr. Wayne . . . I answered most emphatically."

"Jarvis, I don't see what this has to do with—"

"What do you know about the SOE, Dr. Wayne?"

"I don't think I'm familiar with it." Thomas sighed.

"It was the Special Operations Executive, although the few who knew of us often referred to us as the Baker Street Irregulars, after they moved us to 64 Baker Street." Jarvis stepped toward the base of the grand staircase, his eyes fixed on Thomas. "You might be more familiar with our American counterparts—the OSS?"

"You were a . . . spy?" Thomas blinked. He considered for a moment whether the shock of the evening's events had driven him mad, or if perhaps it was Jarvis who had gone around the bend.

"That's far too broad a term, Dr. Wayne," Jarvis continued, moving toward where Thomas stood. "In fact, I was trained as a medic. Our specific purpose was to conduct sabotage operations and guerilla warfare, as well as train and support resistance units behind Nazi lines. I was part of SO2—conducting operations in Telemark, Norway, against a heavy-water production plant. It was part of our training to be far past the front lines, Dr. Wayne, and it was often helpful to us while we were there to make sure we cleaned up after ourselves. Sometimes it was just better for the living if the dead were found somewhere other than where they died—or, in most cases, not at all."

"What have you done with Dr. Richter?" Thomas asked, both dreading and desperately needing the answer.

"As I have said, Dr. Wayne," Jarvis replied, looking up at Thomas with his placid face. "You need not concern yourself. Do not return to the laboratory. I have secured it. This incident will not be traced to you. Things will look better in the morning."

"Jarvis, how can I—"

"Come, let me help you to bed. I have a special drink for you to help you rest." Jarvis took Thomas's arm and turned him, guiding him back up to the second landing. "It is what I do, Dr. Wayne. I clean things up."

Arkham Asylum / Gotham / 8:31 p.m. / Present Day

Batman carefully folded the pages of his father's stationery. They were on different paper than the pages he had discovered waiting for him in the hands of the dead Dr. Moon and, in this case, appeared to start in the middle, as the first page was number seven. He had not yet read half of them, but he had read enough.

Batman looked up from the pages to glare again at the faint stain on the glass.

Nazi.

He glanced back at the book and then all around him. Something here was not right. He felt as if . . .

I'm being watched.

Whoever was behind this had controlled every situation very carefully; it made sense they would not leave anything to chance. They would want to watch the mouse struggle beneath their paws. Someone had baited the trap—this Manipulist, as he had begun to call the person in his mind—and he had taken the bait.

No . . . I haven't taken it yet.

He glanced at the open logbook on the table.

They wanted me to see this, but me alone. If they had wanted it to be public knowledge, then it would be on every news outlet nationwide by now. No . . . They want me to take it, but what if I don't? What if I don't spring their trap but set another trap inside their own?

Batman bagged the envelope and its contents, securing it in a belt pouch at his waste. Then he reached over with his gloved hand, slowly closing the logbook and adjusting it squarely on the table. He closed his eyes.

The room was instantly replaced in his mind with the ghostly, three-dimensional image.

"Contrast thermal overlay," he muttered quietly.

The room in his mind was colored in a spectrum of heat signature. He could see his own footprints, the warming of the book on the desk from his opening it, and the far brighter signatures of his hands and fingers on the book itself.

It's not there yet . . . almost but not quite.

"IR shift," he whispered into the silence.

The cowl heard and the image in his mind shifted the thermal and light readings into the infrared band.

"Hold!" he commanded with quiet firmness.

I own the dark. The darkness is my strength.

Pinpoints of brilliant light in the IR band. Tiny, fiber-optic cameras—the type often used in medical procedures—had been placed throughout the wrecked office and laboratory beyond. He could not see the holding cells from where he stood, but Batman did not doubt they were being watched as well. Each had a coupled IR emitter that would enable the cameras to function with or without the lights on in the room.

Batman smiled. Whoever he was fighting was not perfect . . . They were good, but they could make mistakes.

He then stepped over the broken door of the office, searching about the scattered, smashed remnants of the laboratory. There were several pieces of equipment that still looked serviceable; a microscope, a pair of centrifuges. There was an operatory table with motor drives that appeared functional. Finally he found what he needed: an infrared spectrometer still in good condition.

Batman smiled beneath his cowl. He would have preferred to use his own equipment, but he could not risk the time it would take to go to his lair and return.

He stooped down and picked up a centrifuge, examining it carefully.

Take your time.

He discarded that and picked up a microscope, examining it with infinite care for several minutes.

Patience is part of the illusion.

He walked casually toward the spectrometer, saw that the crude emitter was still intact, and that the device was still connected to power from the wall. He knelt down next to it and flipped the switch on the emitter.

The IR image went suddenly blank in his mind.

Batman opened his eyes, standing in a rush and moving to the overturned operating table. He pulled his collapsible tool set from his Utility Belt and started to remove components from the bed, first taking its motors and then stripping the adjusting cables clear.

It all took shape in his mind. He loved to work with his hands.

A few minutes later, the infrared emitter died. The IR image in Batman's mind cleared, showing him once again to be kneeling in almost the identical position he had been in when he had turned on the emitter in the first place. Batman continued to play with the instrument for a while and then moved to another broken piece of equipment.

"*Hey, Batsy!*" Harley called out from her cell. "When are you gonna take me to the dance? I *never* get asked to the dance!"

Batman stood up amid the ruin in the lab. "Right now, Harley. We're going right now."

"**A**nd just where the hell have you been?"

James Gordon stood on the secure receiving dock on the south side of Arkham. It had been placed in an awkward location—like so many things in Arkham—but it was well suited for prisoner transfers. It sat off a narrow alley across from the guards' block, with great flying buttresses arching overhead against the wall of the old chapel. The stars could be seen brightly through the band of open sky directly overhead.

"Nice to see you, too, Commissioner," the Batman growled. "Sorry I'm late for the party, but I did bring you a present."

The Caped Crusader pushed forward the still bound Harley Quinn, who was unusually quiet. James Gordon motioned to the four armored SWAT police behind him to come forward and take the woman into custody.

"You told me to meet you here over an hour ago," Gordon replied. "You've made me cool my heels here—along with the High Security Team—all this time. That's not like you."

Batman waited as the guards walked Harley back into the dark maw of Arkham. Only when he heard the security door clang shut did he turn away and speak. "I've got to go."

"No! Just hold on a moment," Gordon said. "There's something going down tonight. Harley's just the tip of the iceberg on this."

"On what?" There was impatience in his voice.

"Aren't you supposed to tell me?" Gordon shot back. "I've got reports from every precinct of vigilante actions going down all over the city. It's like a sudden outbreak of do-it-yourself justice. We found one of Falcone's goons hanging upside down from the West Side Bridge, dropped there by some unknown citizens—a tailor, his son, and two businessmen from the Diamond District. The 125th Precinct down on Moench Row had to hold back a mob trying to lynch a mugger, for Pete's sake! And don't try to tell me this is just some random coincidence, either, because I know better!"

"Why?" Batman turned, glaring at the commissioner. "What do you know?"

Gordon rarely had the advantage on Batman and was enjoying it. "You don't know, do you? I think I'm going to just take a moment and savor this. I know that all this happened once before—decades back—and if there's something that has to do with taking a shortcut to law in this town, it has to do with *you*. So what's going on, Batman? Let me in on the joke."

"Your job is to hold them," Batman said simply. "Mine is to catch them."

"Damn it, that's no answer!" Gordon shouted. "What are you hiding?"

"You've got your job to do," Batman said as he turned away, stalking into the darkness. "And I'm late to do mine."

CHAPTER FIFTEEN

DON'T SHOOT THE MESSENGER

The ruined long-forgotten laboratory was dark and silent once again. The space felt relieved, as though it preferred to be a sealed tomb of dreams and death hidden from the world.

But the world was not yet finished with it.

The rusted handles of the great steel doors at the end of the laboratory slowly rotated, groaning with the effort. The gears attached to them pulled at the closing rods, which squealed as they slowly withdrew. At last the sound stopped with the motion.

Batman quietly watched it all through his closed eyes, as he had for the past three hours. The world around him was canted slightly from the angle of the telepresence device he had left lying atop the debris in the laboratory. It worked on the same principle as his cowl—using sonic imaging—but could transmit remotely over short distances directly into his cowl, thereby allowing him to "be" in the room while his physical presence was actually a few dozen feet away.

Maybe the press will call it the Bat-Ghost device, he thought wryly from his perch above the door he had used earlier to enter the room. He had dropped the telepresence transmitter just before returning to the spectrograph and switching off the emitter that had masked his movements about the room. Then he retrieved Harley Quinn, turned her over to Gordon, and returned here as soon as possible.

Whoever put the book and envelope in that lab expected them to leave with me. If they had wanted the book public, it would be by now. So that means they'll come back for it.

There were only two entrances to the room, and he was over one of them. The other was opening as he watched from his remote device and that, too, he knew, was covered.

A figure passed between the steel doors at the far end of the room. He sensed the outline although not the features through the sonic imager. Whoever had been monitoring the room with the IR cameras had decided to kill those feeds and the emitters as well, so he had to rely on the hazier imaging from the sonic system. From the narrow opening between the steel doors, the figure moved cautiously into the room, picking its way through the darkness. It hesitated for a moment, made a careful step, and then proceeded toward the broken door of the office. It appeared to be holding something in its hand.

Batman switched off the link to the ghost, his own immediate surroundings coming to him. He slid silently from his perch, opened the laboratory door without a sound, and slipped inside.

The silhouette had a flashlight, its circular beam shifting across the fallen office door. It took one more step . . .

Click . . . whirrrrr . . .

The figure swung around, its light flashing along the wall, but it was too late. The tripwire had already done its job, keying the electric motors that had been liberated from the operatory table and pulling down a pair of heavy rods against the door.

The great steel doors swung closed with a tremendous, ringing finality as the second motor coiled up the cabling and spun the latching mechanism closed before the silhouette could escape.

"You wanted to see me?" Batman rumbled as he stepped out into the rubble behind the dark figure at the doors.

The figure spun around at the sound in a panic, the flashlight glaring in Batman's eyes. The figure drew one hand up to defend itself, but Batman could already see the flashlight shaking with fear.

"No! Wait!" It was a woman's voice, panicked and quivering. "You don't understand! Let me explain!"

She tripped, falling backward onto the debris.

Batman rushed over to her, the beam of the flashlight now canted across the woman's suddenly recognizable face. He caught himself, ever mindful of the many different faces he was required to wear, remembering from moment to moment which of them he presently was.

"Who are you?"

"Dr. Doppel," the woman gasped out. "I mean, Nurse Doppel." *Play the game. Play the part.*

"Why are you here?" he growled into the woman's face.

"I work here . . . I mean, I used to work here."

He curled his left gloved hand around the back of her neck, pulling her face closer to his own. His voice raged, "Why are you here?"

The woman shook beneath his fists, but her eyes remained fixed on the blank visage of the cowl. "I came for a book."

"This book?" Batman held the stained, old-style composition book up with his right hand, turning her head to look at it with his left.

"Yes . . . maybe . . . It looks like the one she described."

"Who?" Batman shook the back of her neck slightly. "Who described it?"

"Amanda!" Doppel blurted out, tears welling in her eyes. "She told me to come here and get this book. She called me. I didn't know she'd left the house. I don't know how long she might have been gone. She said I'd never find her again if I didn't . . . if I didn't . . ."

"If you didn't what?" He shook her neck again.

"If I didn't follow her instructions and retrieve this book out of Arkham," Doppel choked out. "She said I wasn't to call the police, that everything would be all right if I would just come here, get that book off the desk in her father's old research laboratory, and bring it to an address in Midtown."

"What address?"

"Please, I just want to—"

"What address?"

"Fifteen-two-forty-seven Moldoff Avenue," Doppel blurted out.

Batman stood up slowly, raising the nurse up as he did, bringing her to her feet. "How did you know about this place?"

"I didn't," Doppel replied, trying to get her balance amid the broken equipment strewn over the floor. "Amanda told me where the outside doors were located and how to get through them. I worked for years in this facility and never knew this was down here. Look, I'm just trying to find a woman. Her name is Amanda Richter, she's a severely disturbed individual, and I think she's being manipulated into doing things against her will. You're apparently the Caped Crusader all the news channels rave about. What are you going to do about this?"

"I'm going to do what I must," Batman replied with a wicked grin. "And *you* are going to deliver this book."

Utility Tunnel 57D / Gotham / 9:17 p.m. / Present Day

Batman climbed into the pilot's seat of the Batmobile and powered up the vehicle.

Amanda Richter, he thought. *There are no coincidences.*

He pulled out the envelope and letter he had recovered and bagged earlier. There would be chemical testing on it later, but for now the contents were what interested him. He switched on a map light overhead—which he never used for maps—and pulled out the letter.

Batman paused.

My father was a saint. My father was the perfect man.

He wondered if any of it could be true. His father using the wealth and power of Wayne Enterprises to finance eugenics research . . . the idea was beyond belief. His father was . . . his father was . . .

It was not until this moment that Bruce Wayne realized he really knew nothing of his father beyond the belief that he was a noble and good man who had died senselessly in the arms of his son. Thomas and Martha Wayne had always been marble statues, the ideal of perfection, and the paragon of all virtues. Yet now he was being confronted by the stark reality of their past, which, in that moment, he was loath to know.

Batman opened the pages. He scanned over the sections he had read so quickly in the laboratory—his father's discovery of Richter in the lab and his calling in Jarvis to help.

Something caught his eye.

. . . just keep quiet. I did not know what else to do except follow Jarvis's advice. There was an item the next day in the *Gotham Gazette* about Dr. Richter's death—short and below the fold—describing how he had died as the result of an accident in the secure wing of Arkham Asylum, but nothing else. I was left alone to carry the guilty knowledge that he had died as a result of our behavioral modification studies.

And it was with terrible irony that our work began to bear fruit. The four subjects of our experiments had escaped into the city, and soon the papers were filled with reports of criminals and underworld mobsters being suddenly dealt with in ways that had the criminal elements in the city afraid for the first time in a long while. I began to have hope that the terrible sacrifice of Dr. Richter might actually achieve the dream of a crime-free Gotham that we had labored with such diligence to create.

The papers and television began calling our four escaped subjects "the Apocalypse"—a reference perhaps to the Four Horsemen of the Apocalypse. I believe they took this appellation from the criminals who had been confronted by them in the streets . . .

Batman spoke out loud. "Kronos: new search. Circa 1958, Gotham, Apocalypse."

The display opened to his right in midair. Much to his dismay, the first item coming up was from Wikipedia. He touched it with his gloved finger, and the page opened.

APOCALYPSE, THE

This article is about Gotham history. For specific Apocalypses, see Apocalypse (disambiguation).

The Apocalypse were four vigilantes who waged a war on criminal and mafia groups in Gotham City beginning in mid-1958 through winter of 1968. Initially heralded as heroes by both the public and the press, they soon proved themselves violent and extreme in punishments, and unstable in their narrow interpretation of what constituted a crime.

There were four members of the Apocalypse, known by four sensational names given to them by the popular press. They had notorious criminal backgrounds and used their knowledge of crime against their targets during their vigilante spree. Their actual identities were not initially known, but they were subsequently identified:

- FATE: Caprice Atropos, formerly a cat burglar and murderess with alleged ties to the Moxon crime family. Fate was recognizable by her slender build and long, light blond hair. She wore a black mask and a black knit body suit with fitted black gloves and special-soled, black suede boots. The only two victims who escaped death at her hands reported that they only saw her hair as she attacked. She often traversed rooftops and scaled walls, and could circumvent any lock in her pursuit of her victims. She largely pursued criminals engaged in extortion, bribery, and theft.

- REAPER: Michael "The Scythe" Smalls had been a professional contract killer for the Rossetti mob. Reaper was a tall man with a narrow build that belied his unusual strength and agility. Like Fate, he was known for stalking his victims and was always seen wearing black—in his case, a dark, hooded cloak. His weapons of choice were all blade-edged weapons—including scythes—and dismemberment was a signature of his attacks. Several reports claimed he flew down on his victims like a bird of prey (needs citation). He often targeted bullies, murderers, hitmen, and authority figures.

- CHANTEUSE: Adele Lafontaine, known formerly as the Black Widow of Robinson Park, was the most subtle member of the Apocalypse. She had long, raven-black hair and, regardless of whatever else she wore, was always seen in a military green wool greatcoat. The sole surviving victim of one of her attacks claimed he heard the pleading voice of his sister calling for his help just before Chanteuse attempted to cut his throat. Many others who found themselves in her vicinity reported having heard voices of recognized associates calling to them, and having felt compelled to respond. Her victims were primarily pedophiles, prostitutes, and drug traffickers, although she later expanded to include banking executives, stockbrokers, lawyers, and judges.

• DISCIPLE: Denholm Sinclair, an embezzler implicated in the Kane Orphanage Fire. While pictures of Sinclair abound prior to his initial arrest, afterward, no consistent description was given by any surviving victims or witnesses. All accounts agreed he had tremendous physical strength and fanatical determination in pursuit of his prey. Many reports claimed he wore disguises so as to strike his victims from close range while they were unaware. Disciple was noted not only for killing his victims, but also for doing so in such a manner as to humiliate them in death. His primary targets appeared to be mobsters, racketeers, and city officials he deemed "corrupt."

All four had been committed to Arkham Asylum prior to their escape and subsequent coordinated efforts. While rumors have persisted of additional members belonging to this group, no substantial evidence has been offered to confirm any additional individuals associated with these four.

HISTORY

While the newspapers did not apply the moniker "The Apocalypse" until Sunday, May 18, 1958 (Gotham Gazette), the first incident involving the Apocalypse has been traced to Saturday, April 5, 1958, when Mr. Joseph "The Irish" Donohough was discovered dead, hanging upside down from the West Side Bridge with the word "mob fixer" pinned to the back of his shirt. Donohough was a known associate of the Julius Moxon mob at the time. The following Tuesday, the 8th, three Rossetti gangsters—James "Jimmie" Noonan, Maurice "Mort" Arbuckle, and Percival "The Purse" Vernandez—were pulled out of the Gotham River in a car belonging to mobster Cezar Rossetti, each with the word "thug" carved into his forehead. The following day, Anthony "Tony" Falcone, a nephew of Brutus Falcone who had tried to bring his operation into Gotham from Chicago earlier that spring, was found hung from a lamppost on Moench Row with the word "racketeer" pinned to his chest . . .

Batman stared at the display for a moment, the engine of the Batmobile thrumming behind him.

"Kronos: correlate police records circa 1958 and Apocalypse to police records this month."

There was a momentary pause before the cascade of data began.

"Damn," Batman muttered to himself. "We're being haunted."

Every Apocalypse incident from 1958 was being reenacted throughout Gotham in the present.

"Kronos: autonav fifteen-two-forty-seven Moldoff Avenue," Batman spoke to the interface.

"Destination set," came the voice response. The three-dimensional map of Gotham erupted in a colorful display floating before him, the surface streets appearing closer than the subsurface routes he would be taking. "Confirm?"

Batman knew the destination well. He had known the address the moment Nurse Doppel had uttered it.

"Confirmed. Move out."

The vehicle moved from its hidden cove and began its head-long rush beneath the streets of Gotham, southward beneath the Schwartz Bypass and under the streets of Coventry. The East Side District would soon follow.

Amanda had asked her nurse to deliver the incriminating

book to a house Bruce Wayne had often visited as a boy. His mother had brought him to play with the little girl who lived here. That girl had grown into the last woman he now expected ever to see again.

It was the home address of Mallory Moxon and her crippled father, Lewis.

CHAPTER SIXTEEN

MOXON

15247 Moldoff Avenue / Gotham / 9:36 p.m. / Present Day

Watching Ellen Doppel from the stairwell of the corner brownstone townhouse as she walked down the darkened street, Bruce Wayne again considered his options.

Moldoff Avenue was in a quiet, upscale area called the Upper East Side. Some of the trees lining the wide street were almost a hundred years old. Where they were lit by the streetlamps, each was ablaze in autumnal colors with leaves that, given the cleanliness of the street, one might believe dared not fall to the ground. An earlier rain had left the asphalt shining. There were very few cars parked on the street itself, and those few that came rarely stayed for long. It was a quiet and peaceful night.

No doubt, Bruce acknowledged to himself, because Mallory Moxon had decreed it would be so.

The Moxon muscle enforcing this peace was subtle but all too evident to Wayne's trained eye, even in the darkness. There were three broad-shouldered men chatting near the entrance of 15247—two polos and a turtleneck, all of which were covered with loose windbreakers that barely warranted the concealed weapons permits each had been issued. Two more goons lounged across the street—one on the wide stone steps to a townhouse and the other leaning not too heavily against one of the trees. There were more at the far end of the block, and a pair so close to Bruce he could hear them chatting about the Knights game last night, how Bounous had ended the eighth inning by trying to extend a single into a double and how Rising's pitching nowhere near justified his salary.

Look up. Always look up.

There were more of them poking their heads above or leaning over the low crenellation running along the top fifth stories of the townhouses. They were trying hard not to disturb the illusion of tranquility below them, but to Bruce the atmosphere was charged with the feeling of a sleeping hornet's nest.

I love kicking over the nest. I'm the exterminator.

Bruce drew in a long, silent breath. Under other circumstances, wrapped in his cowl and cape, he would have enjoyed taking this street on, sweeping the thugs into the gutter and off the rooftops until the apparent tranquility had been made real. But as he had approached the East Side sanctuary and secured the Batmobile in its hidden cove, he realized fists and fear would not get him what he wanted tonight.

What was needed was Bruce Wayne.

He waited in stillness as Nurse Doppel walked stiffly down the street, the bound book gripped tightly to her chest. He would have to wait until Doppel left before he could move—it would not do to have Mr. Grayson appear unexpectedly, especially for what he had in mind.

As he knew they would, turtleneck and the two polo boys watched her carefully as she climbed the steps to the front door. She pushed the buzzer and then spoke something into the intercom. Doppel stood waiting on the stoop for less than a minute before the door opened.

They had not met in person in more than two decades, but

Bruce still knew the shape of the face and the set of her eyes. Even cut short, there was no mistaking the rust-red hair or her strong shoulders.

Mallory Moxon had answered the door.

Bruce watched as Mallory took the book from Nurse Doppel. They exchanged a few words on the porch, with the nurse looking more panicked by the moment. Bruce could see the three muscle men at the curb standing a little taller as they watched, their hands reaching automatically inside their jackets. However, in a moment, Mallory nodded and closed the door, leaving Nurse Doppel to walk back down the steps with her shoulders slumped forward—and without the book.

Bruce waited until Doppel turned the corner and then gave one last check of the position of the guards, making sure his appearance on the street would not startle any of them. When he was satisfied, he stepped up out of the stairwell and onto the sidewalk. It was getting chill in the evening, and he almost wished he had the Batsuit on just for the warmth.

It's not just the chill. He smiled to himself.

He was completely aware of the turtleneck and his two pals as he passed them and mounted the stairs, but he studiously gave no indication of even acknowledging their existence. He stepped up and pushed the buzzer on the intercom.

"Who is it?" came the gruff, baritone voice through the tinny speaker.

Definitely not Mallory's voice.

"Barabbas," Bruce said. "Tell Mallory Barabbas wants to see her."

More than a minute passed. Bruce was aware of the three men moving listlessly behind him near the curb but stood still on the stone stairs facing the closed door.

Steel core and frame. Mallory's living in a safe.

The intercom cracked. "Who is this?"

The sound and tone still takes me back. It might have worked . . . It could never have worked . . .

"Come on, Malice, it's Barabbas. It's cold out here, and I need to come in."

The thugs at the bottom of the steps behind him moved back, relaxing slightly. Bruce heard the electric buzz as several security bolts slammed back at the same time.

Getting in is easy . . . It's getting out that's going to be hard.

Bruce grabbed the handle and swung the heavy door open.

"It's been too long, Mallory," Bruce said, settling back into the overstuffed leather chair. It was uncomfortable, and he felt as though he were going to slide out of it at any moment.

The library was on the second floor of the residence. The dark wood paneling between the towering bookcases extended upward into a surrounding balcony on the third floor. Several oxblood leather chairs and a matching couch were set about the room, with a large desk at one end. The desk was a heavy hardwood, stained to complement the paneling. The kickboard panel on the front of the desk featured a carved relief of the head of Janus—a man whose twin faces looked both to the past and the future. It had a definite "manly" feel to its construction and had probably been her father's at some point in the past. The desk's surface was cluttered with papers, but Bruce could easily make out the book Ellen Doppel had just dropped off sitting in a cleared space in the center.

"It's been fifteen years too long, but who's counting," Mallory replied from where she sat on the edge of the desk, her arms folded across her chest. She wore jeans and a scoop-neck sweater that fell slightly off her left shoulder. Her feet were bare and her short hair had been quickly brushed out. There

was a hint of makeup about her eyes, above her prominent cheekbones, and a touch of rouge on her pouting lips. She slipped down from the desk to stand in front of it. "Can I get you a drink? Scotch and soda, I think, was always your first choice."

She casually pushed the wrapped book behind her, out of sight.

"No, thank you, Mal," he replied. "That's not why I've come."

"Indeed?" Mallory leaned back against the desk, a smile playing on her lips. "Don't tell me that Gotham's most reclusive son has come to pick up where we left off."

"Mallory, please," Bruce continued. "I need your help with something."

"Really?" Mallory snorted in derision. "For that you can go help yourself . . . or I'm sure that butler of yours would be happy to call any of a number of services."

"Not that kind of help."

"Oh."

"I've got trouble with the SEC." It was a story, a tale full of just enough truth to make it palatable. The question for Bruce was whether the book he had just seen delivered was enough to make her believe his lie. "After the subprime scandal, they're smelling blood in the water. They're even saying they may go after us under the Racketeer Influenced and Corrupt Organizations Act."

Mallory genuinely smiled at that with the same radiance he remembered being so winning when they had met years before. "RICO? Now *that's* ironic, Bruce. Even you have to admit that's funny."

"They're serious, Mal," Bruce asserted with as much authority as he could muster. "It could force a breakup. It could mean the end of Wayne Enterprises worldwide."

"You want me to do something about the SEC?" Mallory asked in earnest, her long, elegant hands curling around the edge of the desk behind her. "I think I could arrange that."

"No, Mal, that's not why I'm here."

"It would be expensive," Mallory mused, not really hearing him as her mind worked through the logistics of the problem. "But given your revenues worldwide it would give you a good return as an investment."

"No, Mal," Bruce stopped her. "I don't need any fix put in at the SEC."

"You always talked a good game," Mallory sighed, disappointment evident in her voice. "But underneath you were always such a boy scout, Bruce. I knew it when we met up at the Du Lac Resorts when we were kids. It was a good thing Mama was on your side . . . Papa couldn't stand the sight of you. So what *do* you want?"

Bruce drew in a breath. "I want to talk to your father."

Mallory stood up. The smile was gone. "You can't be serious."

Bruce knew the Moxon house actually occupied what looked from the outside to be six separate townhomes. It was effectively a mansion in the middle of the city. Moreover, the Moxons controlled all of the surrounding blocks. Bruce had walked into the center of the Moxon criminal organization—a hidden fortress in the center of the city—but there were answers he had to have from Lew Moxon, and Mallory was the key to getting them.

"Someone has been sending me old things . . . diaries, book, letters," Bruce pressed on. "They don't make much sense to me, but they're about dealings my father had with your father. I'm trying to keep a lid on them. If the SEC gets hold of them it could be bad for both of our families."

"You've got these diaries? You have the tapes?" Mallory asked a little too anxiously.

Tapes? What tapes?

"Not yet," Bruce continued, "but I think I can get them."

Mallory unclenched, her smile a bit easier now. "Well, that should be something of a relief."

She is nervous. She is making mistakes. That's not like any Moxon . . . especially Mallory. She's anxious about me being here. Keep her talking . . . stumbling . . . stalling . . .

"It would be if I could just keep the attorney general off my back until they're safe," Bruce went on. "What had you heard about this business, Mallory? You know me, I'm not all that up to speed on the—"

The phone rang too loudly in the room.

Mallory started visibly, nearly jumping from the desk at the sound. Her words came too quickly. "Hold that thought, Bruce. I've got to take this."

Mallory picked up the phone handset from the desk and jabbed at the answer button. "Yes?"

She turned her face away from Bruce.

"Yes, it's here," she said into the phone. "She left it about ten minutes ago. What? . . . Look, I've done what you asked, and I've gotten what you wanted. You can pick it up at eleven tonight, and then we're finished, you understand? Don't ever call this number again."

Mallory hung up, her hand shaking slightly.

Bruce watched her carefully as he spoke. "Mallory, it's no big deal; I just need to ask your father about something called the Apocalypse."

Mallory stiffened. "That's one word you are *never* to use in front of my father. Ever."

125th Avenue and Broad Street / Gotham / 9:37 a.m. / October 17, 1958

Thomas had not chosen the place.

The Brass Ring Diner was reasonably clean for a dive on the

edge of the theater district. It was on Broad Street, after all, and did look out on the oddly named Diamond Square, the heart of Gotham's nightlife. But as he sat in the booth, Thomas could almost smell the decay with the rising sun. Theater had been big in Gotham during the early part of the century, rivaling New York for the big first-run shows. But that was before two world wars and Korea. Now it was movies or, increasingly, television taking over the attention of the public. It seemed to bleed the life out of the theaters and the entire district had a gritty, run-down feeling to it.

In that respect, the Brass Ring Diner was exemplary of the times. It had originally been fashioned in the art deco style, bordering on Streamline Moderne, with long stainless steel panels in parallel lines, layered and curved. Even those panels were now tarnished and stained. The inlaid wood was cracking and had lost its luster. The Bakelite lamp fixtures were largely cracked. There seemed to be a film coating the rounded-cornered windows that looked out on the square. Thomas was certain the Formica tabletop was permanently lacquered in unimaginable layers of maple syrup, gravy, and spilled sodas—all polished to a dull shine.

It was Lew Moxon's idea they meet here over breakfast. It was on the way for Thomas, as he crossed the Robert Kane Memorial Bridge from the mansion in Bristol while traveling toward his continuing residency at the university hospital. He was not due on rounds for another hour and a half, so it seemed as good a place to meet as any.

Thomas leaned back into the corner of the booth, the vinyl cushions crinkling slightly as he moved, trying to cling to his coat. He snapped the newspaper open to page one. He already had seen the headline and was dreading the article. He reached down, took a sip of his coffee, and forced himself to read.

Apocalypse Murders in Financial District

Three Bank Managers Killed for Alleged Mob Ties

GOTHAM CITY / VIRGINIA VALE / AP WIRE: *Managers of three banking institutions were found murdered in their offices last night in the latest in a series of assassinations by a gang of vigilantes styling themselves as "the Apocalypse." The victims appear to have been targeted due to their alleged connections with the Rossetti, Moxon, and smaller Falcone mobs. Each died "through extraordinary means," according to sources inside the investigation.*

Dead are Marvin J. Collings, manager of the Gotham First Federal Savings, residing in Bristol; Jerome P. Montague, manager of the Bank of Gotham, residing in Coventry; and Lawrence N. Marconi, president of Bristol Bank, also residing in Bristol.

According to unnamed sources inside the police department, all three murders took place at approximately the same time: 11:11 p.m. Mr. Collings was found bound to his office chair, suffocated by a tightly rolled stack of one-hundred-dollar bills and other currency pressed into his mouth. Mr. Montague was discovered by Leonard Murphy, night watchman of the Bank of Gotham, with his throat cut. Mr. Marconi's headless body was discovered at his desk by the cleaning woman. A search for the head is currently in progress.

The police are pursuing several clues, including a report of a blond woman briefly seen fleeing the rooftop of the Bank of Gotham at that approximate time, and a tarot card found clutched in Mr. Montague's hand. No arrests have been made.

The three deaths are the latest in a series of high-profile murders of alleged criminals throughout the city. According to Police Commissioner Gillian B. Loeb, these murders are "increasing in frequency" and targeting subjects accused of less serious criminal offenses.

The first killings by the Apocalypse took place in April, when Joseph "The Irish" Donohough was discovered hanging upside down from the West Side Bridge. Since that time fifteen additional deaths have been investigated as being associated with the Apocalypse.

Concurrent with the vigilante action, and discounting the deaths attributed
to the Apocalypse, the crime rate in Gotham has fallen by 69.5 percent.
When asked whether the drop in crime could be attributed to the actions of the
Apocalypse, Commissioner Loeb responded, "Where do these monsters stop?
How will the public feel about them when they start killing jaywalkers?"

The newspaper rustled slightly under Thomas's shaking
hands.

I did this. I wanted to cure crime and now the cure is worse than the
disease. Jarvis did his job well . . . perhaps too well. It's been months now
since Richter died and no one has said a thing. Crime is dropping—and
don't we cure cancer by killing it? And now Richter's virus is out there in
the world—killing crime one life at a time. How can I live with that kind
of cure?

"Hey, Dr. Wayne!"

Thomas looked up, startled, from the newspaper.

Lew Moxon seemed not to notice, his broad face beaming beneath his bristle-cut dark hair. His bow tie was slightly
crooked and his sports jacket fit him a little tightly. "Thanks for
coming . . . crazy news in the papers, huh? Everybody in the
family is sweating bullets. I can't tell these days whether my old
man is spitting nails or just ready to piss himself."

"Julius isn't taking all this Apocalypse nonsense seriously, is
he?" Wayne said, pushing the newspaper down next to him in
the booth.

"Serious?" Moxon chuckled and then leaned forward across
the table. "I'll tell you how serious he is: last night between
drinks he told me at this rate, my Koffee Klatch may be the *only*
family business still running by the end of the year! Can you
beat that? The old man's seeing red. He thinks Rossetti's behind
it, but Rossetti's sweating in his socks just as bad and points the
finger at that punk greaser Falcone, but Falcone hasn't got a clue
either. They're gonna start doing the DA a favor pretty soon and

start plugging each other if these Apocalypse clowns aren't put down."

That was the plan, wasn't it? That's what Richter and I wanted for the city . . . wasn't it?

"Sounds like a gang war," Wayne spoke into his coffee, hoping it would make him appear calmer than he felt. "Do you think it's going to come to that?"

"Nah!" Moxon replied, leaning back comfortably in the booth. "My old man says one way or the other, he's going to put these clowns down permanently—but you didn't hear it from me. All that is good news for us both, Thomas."

"Good news? How?"

"The families in this town have never been weaker! I make my break now, it makes sense to everybody and I don't get hurt. So, you got my financials and you know the place. How about it, Wayne? Can you and me be partners?"

Thomas looked at Moxon. "I'm going to help you, Lew, but you have to keep your nose clean."

"No sweat, Dr. Wayne!"

"I mean it, Lew," Wayne insisted. "You can't be involved in anything or I'll never be able to get approval from the board, you understand?"

"Absolutely, Wayne," Moxon said, reaching across the table and nearly crushing Thomas's hand with his grip. "I'll be clean as the driven snow, just you wait and see! The only one around here lookin' at an Apocalypse is my old man, Julius!"

15247 Moldoff Avenue / Gotham / 9:44 p.m. / Present Day

"Look, Mal," Bruce looked confused. "I'm in the dark here about what's going—"

"It was that old goon Salvatore who tipped you, wasn't it?"

Mallory seethed. She snatched the wrapped book from the desk, clutching it with both hands. "That son of a bitch was there that night, and he decided he could tap you for a few grand, didn't he?"

Salvatore? Arnold Salvatore worked the Robbinsville and Eastside rackets under Julius in the '60s, but he was Moxon's muscle before his promotion. And just what night was Mallory talking about?

"No, Mal, nobody tipped me." Bruce stood up. "I just came here because I thought you might help an old friend. I'm up to my ass in federal alligators, and all you want to do is toss crocodiles at me."

Mallory stared at him for a moment and then laughed, the stormy mask of her face softening back into the beautiful woman he remembered. "Well, no matter how it works out, it would be fun to watch. Sorry, Barabbas, it's an old wound and a deep one. I can't tell you anything about this Apocalypse and seriously, there's no way I'll let anyone bring that up in front of Father."

Bruce nodded, setting down his drink. "That's all right, Mal. It was a long shot anyway."

"I still think I can help with that SEC nuisance," Mallory offered. "I own a guy or two down there who could probably make this go away."

"Great," Bruce answered, extending his hand. "Thanks, Mal."

Mallory looked at Bruce's hand for a moment with a wry smile, shaking her head slightly before she reached forward and took it. "You're welcome, Barabbas."

Bruce took his hand back. "Say, Malice, why did you start calling me Barabbas?"

"I didn't," Mallory shrugged, her bangs falling over her eyes. She flipped her head out so that they fell out of the way, a move Bruce found familiar and comforting. "I used to call you all kinds

of nicknames. Bwain, Wayno, Beeswax and, as I recall, one particularly difficult summer, Coxswain."

"So where did Barabbas come from?" Bruce asked.

"That was Father," Mallory said, stepping toward the door
with the wrapped book held with studied casualness in her
hand. "He used to call you that all the time."

"All the time?"

"Well, no," Mallory said from the door, appearing thoughtful.
"I guess it was after your parents died. Look, I'm sorry, but I've
got a lot to do today—do you mind?"

"Here's your hat and what's your hurry, eh?"

Mallory smiled again. "But it was good seeing you again,
Bruce. I'm glad you haven't turned into the horror-show picture
the papers keep printing of you."

"Not yet, Malice," Bruce chided, his hands in his pockets as
he rocked slightly on his heels. "Go ahead, I'll just let myself
out."

She flashed her smile once more and was gone.

As the door closure clicked, Bruce turned at once to the
phone on the desk, pulling a cloth out of his pocket. With an
eye on the door, he picked up the receiver, waited a moment for
the dial tone, and then punched the call-back button.

Someone answered on the fourth ring.

"Good evening, Wayne residence . . ."

Bruce stared at the phone for a moment.

"May I help you?"

Alfred's voice!

"Yes," he said, "this is Bruce. I'm in the city."

"Indeed, Master Bruce?" Alfred's voice was always affected
calm, but Bruce thought he heard a strain in his words. "So you
informed me earlier, sir."

The caller ID! He knows where I am.

"Well, I'm going to be longer than I thought," Bruce said casually. "I've found a lead here at Moxon's that is going to require some surveillance in lower Gotham. I won't be home until around one in the morning. Don't wait up for me."

"As you wish, Master Bruce," Alfred replied. "I shall leave the lights on for you."

"Thank you, Alfred," Bruce said quietly. He hung up the phone and rushed from the room.

Utility Tunnel System / Gotham / 9:58 p.m. / Present Day

Barabbas. According to tradition he was the criminal who was set free so that Jesus would be crucified. Why would Julius Moxon insist on calling him by that name?

Bruce moved quickly down through the access tunnel, pushed through the hidden panel in a tiled side wall, and entered the abandoned subway tunnel. His cross-trainers rustled the gravel between the old ties as he hurried toward the concealed maintenance siding where he had secured the Batmobile. His chest worked with the exertion of dragging air into his lungs. He had told Alfred he would not be home before one in the morning—but someone at Wayne Manor had made arrangements to meet Mallory about the book at ten that evening. Alfred had answered the callback, and now Bruce was determined to return to the Manor in time to join that little party. Alfred was certainly mixed up in this twisted business. It was not until this moment that Bruce considered it quite possible that Alfred was behind all of it. He knew it all—every Wayne secret—and had access to all of Batman's resources to pull it off.

Keep your friends close . . . and your enemies even closer.

Bruce's call had an unplanned-for benefit: it would force

Alfred to act. Now, if he moved quickly enough, he could expose Alfred and get to the bottom of his father's past.

Bruce rounded the corner and stopped, astonished even as he instinctively ducked into the shadows.

A large group of traffic policemen were helping winch the Batmobile up onto a flatbed railcar attached to an electric service engine.

He was being *towed?*

CHAPTER SEVENTEEN

THE JOKE'S ON HIM

Utility Tunnel System / Gotham / 10:04 p.m. / Present Day

Bruce considered his options as he stood with his back against the abandoned subway wall, hidden for the time being in the shadows behind a supporting arch. The vehicle looked intact and secure—there would have been a rather large crater under Gotham had the security somehow been breached—but the question remained in his mind how they had found it in the first place.

Bruce crouched down, carefully looking around the corner once more. The uniforms were definitely the light blue shirts with dark ties, caps, and slacks of Gotham traffic police, ornamented with shields and full-duty belts decked with extendable batons, cuffs, magazine holders, and gun holsters.

The authenticity, however, was spoiled by the latex clown masks each of them wore.

A wry smile crossed Bruce's face. He counted eighteen of them, which looked like a pleasant challenge . . .

Until he remembered his exomuscular Batsuit and all of its associated tools of his trade were inside the vehicle. He felt suddenly awkward, as though he had shown up to a formal dance wearing only his underwear. He was still Bruce Wayne . . . and what had been an asset was now a liability.

Voices from the ersatz police echoed down the siding toward him. It was impossible to distinguish one voice from another.

"What does he want done with it?"

"We're supposed to get it out of here before he comes back and take it down to Sixty-one."

"What if we don't?"

"You really wanna risk that?"

"Come on, tie that down good and tight—you want to scratch the paint?"

"Do you think I *can*, Joey?"

Bruce looked around him for something, anything he might use. When his eye saw it, he smiled. A quick check of the sight-lines of his enemy, and he crossed to the far side of the tunnel, silently swept up the old paint can, and fled back into the tunnel.

"Hey, Joey, what's that?"

One of the clown police looked away from the flatbed railcar. They had almost wrapped up the Batman's car. A couple more minutes and the thing would be ready to bring back to the boss with a ribbon on it. "What's what?"

"I hear something down the tunnel. What is it?"

The Joey Clown raised his head. The latex mask bothered him, but you wore the face the boss told you to wear or you could end up not wearing any face at all. "I don't hear nothin', Saul."

"Just listen, man, I'm tellin' ya."

Joey Clown stepped back around the flatbed toward the entrance to the maintenance siding. The old subway ran into the black in both directions.

Now he heard it, too.

"Aw, jeez, Saul," Joey Clown griped. "It's just some water running. We've been livin' in these tunnels for, like, a year, and you ain't heard water before?"

The sound of the water stream suddenly stopped.

Joey Clown reached down for his holstered 9 mm and drew the gun.

From the darkness, the sound of streaming water resumed.

"What the hell?" Joey Clown muttered to himself, his weapon held ready in front of him by his right hand as he fumbled to pull the flashlight off the duty belt with his other. The beam of light flashed down the dark tunnel as he stepped cautiously forward.

"Oh, you gotta be kidding me," he muttered to himself as the beam came to rest on a water tap protruding from the tunnel wall. Water streamed out of it, splashing onto the gravel beneath it. Joey Clown stepped forward quickly, holstered the gun, and began quickly to turn the knob, closing down the valve. The rushing water was beginning to make him uncomfortable. He had been down in the tunnel longer than expected. The stream of water stopped.

"I got it—nothing here," Joey Clown said as he turned around.

The water started again.

He turned quickly, the beam of his flashlight falling back at once on the water tap.

No water was coming out . . . but he could hear the sound of a thin stream of water somewhere further down the tunnel. It was an all too familiar sound that made him more anxious by the moment. Nature was beginning to call to him.

The sound stopped . . . then resumed.

Joey Clown peered down the shifting beam of light, but try

as he might, he could not discover the source of the sound—a sound that was calling to his bladder with rising urgency.

The sound stopped again, but the urgency remained. Joey Clown waited as long as he could manage, judging the sound to be just another leaking pipe among a million others.

As for himself, he was in urgent need of relief. The tunnel was dark and seemed as good a place to him as any. Joey Clown tucked the flashlight under his latex chin as he quickly unzipped the regulation police pants and reached down. This time the sound of water against the tunnel wall was a tremendous relief to Joey Clown.

When he was finished at last, he started to zip up . . . but was unconscious before he could button his slacks.

"Hey, Joey! What took you so long?" shouted Saul Clown.

Joey Clown just shrugged.

"Well, thanks for nothing," said the Muscle Clown. "While you been chasin' boogeymen, we got the job done."

"Hey, can we get out of here now before the Bat shows up?" said the Nervous Clown.

"Yeah," said Joey Clown, climbing up onto the flatbed. "Let's ride with it."

"You don't think the boss will mind?" asked Nervous Clown.

"Him?" Joey Clown answered. "He'd be *glad* to see us."

Bruce sweated under the latex mask. The clothes had been a close enough fit, and as long as he slumped slightly and did not talk too much, he could manage a fair impression of Joey.

Poor Joey. I'll go back for him and turn him over to the police when we're done here. He can manage a few hours gagged and naked in the dark.

The flatbed pushed along through the old subway tunnel. Bruce knew the subway system well, but there were parts of it that had escaped mapping. During World War II there were a number of tunnels build by the War Department that were never catalogued. Bruce had heard stories of Platform Sixty-one, a special underground siding that allowed President Roosevelt unheralded access to the city. There was an identical platform in New York, but its location remained a secret in both cities.

And now, if these goons were to be believed, they were headed off the official map of Gotham's underground.

He thought they might be somewhere under Old Gotham on a sublevel never used anymore. They might be near Central Station—perhaps under it, for all he knew—and in the light of the switcher engine pushing the flatbed railcar down the old track, the walls of the tunnel were growing increasingly bizarre. Enormous cutouts from amusement parks began to decorate the walls, each one only partial and cut up into individual features—ears, eyes, gaping mouths, and even then never whole, never complete. They were random hieroglyphs that promised and tantalized with the hope of meaning and remained elusive.

Bruce touched the Batmobile lightly with his hand. Its surface gave way slightly at his touch. It was reassuring and was achingly close at hand. He longed for the power it represented and to be a part of that power once more.

Restraint is power. Knowledge is more important than strength. Wait to strike when the time is right.

The wheels beneath the flatbed railcar began to squeal. Brilliant light spilled into the tunnel as they rounded a turn from an archway ahead of them. The railcar holding the Batmobile slid to a halt at a platform next to an enormous vaulted room nearly three stories tall. Enormous dynamos stood in rows across the floor, coupled to engines over a half century old. At the far end of the mechanical space, a metal staircase rose to a second level of walkway that ran around the perimeter of the square room. All about the main floor of the room and lining the walkway above stood clowns in similar dress and masks, all cheering one man standing on an elaborate throne at the top of the metal stairs. His greasepaint was smeared and the makeup uneven, but his wild hair was pulled uncharacteristically back and bound behind his head. The lines on his face had always been hideous, but now they sagged with age, the skin beneath his chin loose and waddlelike. He still gestured theatrically, but the old spring had gone out of the motions. The suit was the same stained purple. He held an enormous Magnum revolver in his right hand. But it was, above all, the eyes—the terrible eyes—and the voice like gravel carving across a chalkboard that confirmed to Bruce it could be only one person in the entire world.

Joker . . .

"That's right, children!" Joker screeched from his perch. "They stole it all from you for your own good! What a bedtime story: rob from the poor and give to the rich, 'cause *they* know what to do with it. We've never had any money—better let those who have handled it before take care of it before we do something *useful* with it! But I've got a better idea, kiddies! I say we take it *back*! Take from the rich and give to *ourselves*! And when I'm elected—any minute now by my watch—that's exactly what we're going to do!"

Cheers erupted again from the clown police, including those on the railcar. Bruce cheered with them.

"And so"—Joker bowed low, his hand holding his .44 Magnum across his heart tenderly—"it is with deepest humility and a sense of awe-inspiring hollow promises"—his voice rose to a crescendo—"that I announce my unopposed candidacy for emperor of the United States of America!"

The cheering was deafening. The yard engine that had brought them here was uncoupling from the flatbed railcar and backing out into the tunnel again.

Joker raised up the Magnum. The gun roared in his hand, throwing him backward with such force that he nearly pushed the throne over. Clown police tried to scatter out of the way, but one caught the projectile full in the chest and was slammed back against an electrical panel. It exploded in sparks when he hit it, but that was incidental so far as the clown policeman was concerned. He was dead before he hit the panel.

"A terrorist!" Joker declared. "He's dead so he *must* be a terrorist. He infiltrated our safe and secure home, and now, you see, I have made you all safe from him once more! Bad terrorist! We have to stop them . . . We have to stop them from making us do what we don't want to do!"

Making us do what we don't want to do? What is he saying?

"We want to be free," Joker said, slumping onto his throne. "They are making us do what they want . . . and we want to be FREE, DAMN IT!"

Joker's last words echoed through the room, falling into an uneasy silence.

The clown police looked at each other uneasily as Joker sat unmoving upon the throne.

"PRESS CONFERENCE!" Joker shouted, pushing himself to his feet at the top of the stairs.

The clown police shifted uneasily.

"I'm the emperor, and I've called a press conference!" Joker demanded. "The press pool will assemble here before the throne, and we will magnanimously answer your questions about our new domestic policy of a one hundred twenty percent flat tax on everyone who has more money than we do, as well as my ever-popular find-the-bastard-who-did-this-to-me-and-kill-him security policy. Questions, people! I need questions!"

"Sir," Muscle Clown asked tentatively from the railcar. He was standing next to Bruce. "What do you want us to do?"

The Joker raised his head as though considering the question. "I'm glad you asked that. Actually, no one is ever glad they're asked such a question, but that's what people who rule things always say, don't they? But in your case, because we are all men of action, damn the torpedoes and into the valley of death, I'll answer that question."

The clown police listened carefully.

Joker leaned forward.

"We . . . are . . . going . . . to . . . WAIT!"

"Wait?" Muscle Clown blurted out.

"That's right! You win the prize, Bongo!" Joker laughed hideously. "We're going to sit on our fat asses . . . pardon me, *your* fat ass . . . because . . . it's a brand-new car! That's right, Bongo . . . It's a brand-new Batmobile with bucket seats, fine Corinthian leather, CB radio, eight-track player, AND more armament than any third-world country you can spell! And as long as WE hold the pink slip to this lovely prize, the Bat has his wings clipped here in the city. He's not going to call a cab, because with all those wonderful toys on his belt he never thought to carry a wallet. He can't hitchhike, because just look at the freakish way he dresses! His pal Gordon is under glass and . . . and . . . it's too far for him to walk in time so . . . he will miss his date at the ball and I'll be FREE!"

Joker screamed, howling with his hands on his temples.

"I cannot STAND these thoughts . . . these poisonous, OR-GANIZED thoughts, ordered in neat little rows full of purpose and . . . meaning!" Joker shook with rage. "I want them out of my head . . . I want myself back!"

Joker's breath was ragged. "He'll come . . . He'll come for his car, because he won't want to report it stolen or his insurance premiums would go up. But mostly he'll come because it's HIS . . . and he won't let ME have it. We're old friends, you know . . . and getting older by the minute. And when he arrives we have to throw him a party and *keep him here* until morning so that those terrible, orderly, REASONABLE voices they've put in my head cannot have him. Then I'll be free of purpose again. Then I'll be myself."

Joker's breath was ragged, but then he smiled, his horrific face rising up as those eyes burned bright again.

"Hello-o-o-o," Joker purred. "I think our guest may have already arrived unannounced."

CHAPTER EIGHTEEN

GAUNTLET

"Come out, come out wherever you are," Joker sang softly in a reedy falsetto voice as he descended the metal stairs, a poor imitation of Billie Burke from *The Wizard of Oz*, "and meet the young Batman who gave me this scar."

Bruce stood still with the other clown police on the flatbed railcar next to the Batmobile. The latex clown mask clung to the sweating skin on his face. Salvation was tantalizingly close. The Batmobile lay under his fingertips, but the security access panel, hidden within the malleable skin of the vehicle, was just out of his reach to the right. He would have to locate the panel, key the access sequence, and dive through the hatch before the Joker's clown police could stop him. Nervous Clown stood in his way, and he couldn't manage it without attracting attention from the Joker and his sentry of armed thugs. He could deal with the Joker—but not as Bruce Wayne . . .

Not with only this flimsy mask.

"He fell from afar to give me this scar," Joker continued singing as he pranced to the bottom of the staircase, waving the revolver over his head, "and Batman, he says, wants to repo this car. Batman, he says, has a fetish bizarre."

Bruce glanced at Muscle Clown on his left. His stance was casual. The timing would have to be right . . . and time was the issue. He was desperate to get back to the mansion, and every moment he remained here meant giving Alfred—or whoever was involved—more time to cover his tracks. Bruce slowly shifted his weight to his right foot.

"You see, it's really quite simple," the Joker said in what passed for a rational tone of voice, belied by his pointing the .44 Magnum randomly around him for emphasis. "There are one hundred and fifteen of the finest Gotham police uniforms money can buy in the room, but there are only one hundred and fourteen ID transponders. Now, if I were balancing my check-book, I might be tempted to just ignore minor discrepancies"— his voice suddenly rose in anger—"but I'm trying to run a BUSINESS here! And while I know . . . I KNOW you won't appreciate the gesture, I'm trying to actually preserve our bat-obsessed friend from doing himself AND me terrible harm. So, I say it's time for a little honesty between friends. *I* say we should ALL be special today. Now that the gang's all here, *I* say we should end the charade, take off our masks, and let our mystery guest sign in, please!"

I wear the mask to terrify others. How strange that a lack of a mask should terrify me.

Bracing his hands against the Batmobile, Bruce gave a quick kick to the back of the knee of the Muscle Clown on his left. The thug's leg folded forward, tipping the Muscle Clown off balance. Instinctively, the Clown next to Bruce tried to recover, but there was not enough room on the crowded railcar. With a short cry, the Muscle Clown tumbled off the edge of the flat-bed, falling flat on his back between the tracks and the wall of the tunnel, the air rushing out of his lungs from the impact.

The Joker leaped forward as most of the clown police in the

room drew their weapons. "Don't kill him! That's *my* job! Get out of the way!"

The clown police parted in front of the charging Joker. Two of them did not get out of his way fast enough. Joker lowered his weapon, shooting one of them in the back. The recoil threw Joker's arm back behind him, but he kept running forward.

"Fair warning," Joker shouted as he jumped over the shot clown's body bleeding out onto the painted cement floor.

The other clown police on the railcar turned their drawn weapons toward the fallen Muscle Clown struggling to get up. Several clown police who had stood near him on the railcar, dove onto the Muscle Clown, pinning him to the ground. With the distraction complete, Bruce slipped slightly to his right, brushed his hand over the hatch pad, and quickly keyed the sequence.

"Hold him steady!" Joker shouted as he bounded off Platform Sixty-one. He landed on the tracks in front of the railcar and crossed to the other side, where the Muscle Clown was being smothered under his restraining thugs. "It's about time we had a nice face-to-face chat!"

The Joker knelt down and ripped the mask off the Muscle Clown.

A whooshing noise sounded behind him. The Joker turned to see a gull-winged door open between the binding chains over the Batmobile . . . and one of his clown police diving through the opening.

"Hahahahaha!" the Joker exclaimed, raising the .44 Magnum. "How I *love* initiative!"

The gull-door slammed shut, sealing seamlessly into the gleaming body.

"New game! New game!" Joker screamed, doing a strange

shuffling dance next to the rail way. "Kick the can! I'll provide the kick and Batman is in the can!"

"How do we get him out, boss?" the Muscle Clown gasped between painful breaths, still pinned down by his compatriots.

"Out?" Joker sneered. "I don't want him *out*! I want his spam to stay in that can! I want him to sit in his toy car until the party is completely over!"

The chains across the vehicle started to groan. Joker raised his eyebrows.

Bruce tore the clown mask off his face, throwing it forcefully over the back of the command seat to the passenger compartment behind. He was sprawled awkwardly in the space, having jumped head first into the cockpit while calling for the hatch to secure. He knew that the reactive armor of the vehicle had passive qualities, but Bruce wondered why he could not hear the sound of projectiles striking the body.

He tried to right himself, but realized he had left the Batsuit he had shed earlier draped over the seat he was now trying to sit on. The Batsuit shifted under him, bunching up in places, and the Utility Belt was making it impossible for him to sit properly in the space.

What else can go wrong?

"Kronos: activate!" Bruce said, squirming as he tried to shift the Utility Belt away from his seat.

The security system did not answer. The Batsuit was present in the vehicle—a required security precaution—but the biometrics were not registering him properly out of the Batsuit.

"Kronos: activate!" he said again.

"Activated." The console answered this time, but Bruce realized the sound was indistinct and muffled, as it was coming from beneath him. "Systems online. Main bus charge level sixty-nine percent."

The cowl . . . the sound is routed through the cowl.

"Kronos: audio to panel and exterior view to panel," Bruce barked. The visual displays would all be two-dimensional without the cowl, and he would have limited tactical awareness. The vehicle was chained down to the railcar, so the drive wheels would be useless. Time was slipping away from Bruce Wayne.

The eye-level displays lit up instantly. Bruce could see the clown police milling about the car with their weapons drawn but none of them firing. The Joker stood next to the rails pointing up at him and doing a little dance.

I've got to get out of here. I've got to know who is behind all this.

"Kronos: increase physical profile twenty-five percent," he said, pulling at the safety restraints. He managed to find and straighten them out, though each needed adjustment to fit him without the bulk of his Batsuit, which still sat under him.

The vehicle responded to his command. The exterior shell of the car, charged with electric current, pushed outward, inflating its size against the restraining chains, which creaked and groaned under the pressure but held strong.

"External resistance approaching stress limits," the car responded. "Fuel stable at eighty-six percent. Power reserves dropping to fifty-three percent."

"Kronos: reset physical profile," Bruce said.

I have to move! There's no time . . .

"**D**id you ever wonder how long a bat will keep?" the Joker asked the Nervous Clown, his gun arm draped over the quivering thug's shoulder. "I mean without refrigeration. Normally I would never advocate leaving a bat inside a car, say, on a hot day while going into a grocery store or embarking on a protracted cruise. However, we have an opportunity now to—"

Short gouts of flame exploded from ports suddenly appearing in the car's body, rocking the railcar from side to side. The clown police leaped off of the railcar, scattering from the jet's blast.

"Oh, pardon me!" Joker exclaimed. "Was that me?"

Suddenly, four columns of flame and smoke erupted from the back of the chained-down Batmobile, their exhaust merging into one. The roar filled the enormous space with a sound that forced many of the clown police to their knees, hands slammed against their ears.

The railcar groaned . . . and then started to roll down the track.

"NO!" the Joker screamed, his words swallowed up in the deafening sound of the rocket motor. "You'll ruin everything!"

The railcar and its chained, raging cargo, rumbled faster and faster down the rails together, picking up speed as it vanished into the subway tunnel beneath the city.

"Stop him, you morons! Arrest him!" the Joker yelled. "What's happened to law and order in this city? Bring him back!"

The clown police were galvanized into action. Those left standing on the tracks rushed back into the tunnel and down a maintenance side tunnel. They soon reappeared in pairs astride ATVs, their drivers hunched down over the handle bars while their passengers were readying weapons ranging from assault rifles to rocket-propelled grenades. They plunged into pursuit of the rocketing railcar, the high-pitched keening of their engines changing to an echoed pitch as they followed the smoke trail into the subway tunnel.

The Joker clambered quickly back onto Platform Sixty-one, smoke from the rocket engine still choking the room.

"Well, that might have gone better." The Joker sniffed, and he climbed back up the stairs to his throne. "But you know, whenever I get discouraged or think life is getting me down, there's one thing that always cheers me up."

He sat down, picking up a laptop. An Ethernet cable connected it into a port on one of the routers rack-mounted in a stack on one wall. He opened the laptop. The screen sprang to life, displaying "Gotham Transit Authority Rail Service."

"I relax by playing with my trains," the Joker said, cracking his knuckles before pressing the keys.

The displays were giving Bruce a clear night-vision view of the tunnel as it moved past him at an increasing rate. A digital counter in the corner continued counting down the seconds to the four PAM rockets shut down.

Twenty-five . . . twenty-four . . . twenty-three . . .

It cannot happen too soon.

The PAMs were propelled by solid fuel. It was efficient and relatively stable as propellants went, but once ignited, it could not be stopped—it had to burn its full duration. Each alone would have been sufficient to thrust the Batmobile forward significantly in normal conditions, but the enormous weight of the railcar might have slowed his exit enough to allow the Joker and his henchmen to toss something large in front of him and completely block his escape. So he had ignited all four at once. Even then, he was only guessing at the mass and resistance of the old railcar and, for a moment, was concerned the thrust would not be adequate. Then the flatbed started to slide down the rails propelled by the vehicle, straining against its restraining chains and leaving the platform and the underground control room behind.

Bruce now saw that he had leaped from the Joker's frying pan into a different line of fire; the transformation of the railcar into a rocket sled. The speed may not have been great compared to the normal operating limits of the Batmobile in these tunnels, but for a rolling stock railcar attached to the rails only by its weight and the strength of its open wheels, the velocity was beyond dangerous. They were a top-heavy, rocket-driven sled . . .

And they were rapidly approaching a bend in the track.

"Kronos: plot track forward and display!" Bruce said quickly.

"Three hundred meters to intersection with Diamond District line."

Bruce glanced again at the PAM countdown to end of thrust. *Fifteen seconds. At this speed, the corner is four seconds away.*

"Kronos!" The stress Bruce was feeling was reflected in his voice. "RCS control to manual. Status?"

"RCS manual and online."

Bruce gripped the controllers on either side of the pilot seat, drawing in a breath as the railcar entered the left curve.

The railcar pushed hard to the right with inertial force, tipping precariously. Bruce slammed the lateral control hard to the left. The reaction rocket motors fired both front and back, pushing against the tipping mass. He held the thrust constant, watching the heat indicators on the thrusters climb dangerously high but knowing the alternative to melt down was an uncontrolled crash. The thrusters kept the railcar held through the curve, and the left wheels of the carriage slammed down with a terrible squeal as the rail tunnel straightened out before them.

Bruce shook from side to side in the still-too-loose restraints, sweat beading on his brow. The turn had robbed some of their speed, but the continued burning of the PAM motors was quickly increasing the acceleration once more.

"Kronos: track green to Diamond District Line!" Bruce called.

"Track green," the computer answered.

Wayne Enterprises had computerized the subway routing system back in 2004. Bruce had made sure that he knew the back door into the control system precisely for this purpose: so that he could manipulate the subway traffic and allow this version of the Batmobile to traverse beneath the city. It was normally a sophisticated system that subtly delayed or advanced the subway trains in such a way that commuters never knew that the Caped Crusader was moving through the same tunnels they used to commute to work and home again.

Now is not the time for subtlety.

The red light on the line switched to green, the points ahead having been switched. Suddenly the light went red again.

Joker! He's using my own system against me!

"Kronos: track green to Diamond District Line!" Bruce shouted, though he knew the only difference it would make to the audio interpreter was possibly to confuse it.

"Track green," the computer answered as the light turned green once more.

It was barely in time. The railcar hit the rail points hard in another left turn into the main subway line. Bruce again slammed the translational controller all the way to the left, firing the side-thrusters at full throttle. He could feel the carriage under him shudder under the contradicting forces. The flatbed railcar again fell hard against the track, but it was now on the main commuter line running around the city. Bruce knew that they were traveling west now on the southern circuit—a straight run for at least a mile before it turned northward. He glanced to his right as the rockets continued to press him into his seat. The Geilla Park Station flew past in a bright blur, its platform filled with the gaping faces of commuters before the rocketing sled and its chained Batmobile cargo again plunged into the darkness.

Then he saw the light ahead of him.

The headlight of an oncoming train.

That's impossible. The trains on this route always run clockwise around the city.

"Kronos: magnify ahead times fifty for two seconds."

The image of the subway train ahead of him suddenly leaped forward.

Empty! What's the matter with Joker . . . couldn't he find a full commuter train in time?

"PAM cutoff in three seconds," the console announced.

"Kronos: start main drive," Bruce said, pulling the straps on his restraining harness as tight as he could make them. The engine behind him spun up. He could feel the rumble through the seat.

"Kronos: prepare to execute on my command," Bruce continued as he settled his hands on the steering and drive controls, his feet resting in an awkward position because of the Batsuit still under him. "Minimize profile smooth. Standby?"

"Ready," the console confirmed. "PAM cutoff in three . . ."

The train was closing quickly with the rocketing flatbed.

"Two . . ."

Bruce held down the clutch, revving up the engine in anticipation.

"One . . . Cutoff."

Bruce felt the release from the acceleration pressure of the rockets.

"Execute!" he yelled as he released the clutch.

The reactive armor shell of the vehicle suddenly collapsed inward, tightening to its smallest size and smoothing itself out. The chains that had bound it suddenly hung slack. They would still rake the car and possibly damage the adaptive armor, but Bruce hoped it would be enough to slip the bonds.

The wheels of the Batmobile squealed against the rough surface of the flatbed railcar. The Batmobile lurched rearward. The chains tore at the car but with the Batmobile's exterior minimized, the restraints could find no real purchase in the smooth surface. The Batmobile suddenly sprang free of the chains, its wheels pushing the still-careening railcar from under it as it shot backward.

Bruce shoved the clutch back in, standing on the brakes at the same time. The Batmobile landed astride one of the rails skidding to a stop.

The flatbed, shot forward toward the oncoming train, derailing it as it jammed under the front wheels. The subway train began to pile up in the tunnel, folding on itself in a rolling wreck that filled the passage ahead before it ground to a stop.

Bruce engaged the drive forward, skidding the Batmobile on the tracks and pointing it back toward Geilla Park Station.

"Kronos: plot course home, then display—"

An explosion rocked the Batmobile.

"Combat mode!" Bruce called out as he threw the throttle forward and released the clutch. The displays inside the cockpit of the Batmobile suddenly changed. Weapons systems were coming online in the far right display while the left-hand display showed the car's exterior shifting from transport optimization to adaptive armor. Heads-up targeting and maneuver displays sprang to life in front of him, although without the Batsuit he had lost some of the dimensional imaging.

It's not perfect . . . but it will have to do.

The Batmobile shot forward over the rails. Bruce could now see the Clown Police's ATVs charging down after him in the tunnel.

Small arms and RPGs. They've come to play.

In the night-vision display he saw the flare of an RPG ignition from the back of one of the ATVs. Bruce reacted instinctively, turning the Batmobile into the path of the ATV that had fired on him. The rocket-propelled grenade slid past the Batmobile, exploding against the wall and kicking Bruce's vehicle sideways.

Bruce drove on. The ATV driver wavered for a moment, uncertain as to whether he should drive into the wall or cross in front of the Batmobile.

It was hesitation enough for Bruce. He clipped the front of the ATV, sending both its occupants sprawling into the tunnel. Then he turned slightly back into the center back onto the tracks and accelerated.

Bowling for clowns. Bruce smiled to himself.

The Batmobile plowed through the ATVs on the track, crushing two of them beneath its wheels. Four more bounded off the reactive armor, slamming into other ATVs and tumbling them all savagely across the tracks and against the walls of the enclosed tunnel. The remaining ATVs scattered out of the Batmobile's way as it powered through them, turning as quickly as they could to continue their pursuit.

Bruce now saw the Geilla Park Station platform on his left, still filled with commuters. He could make out their astonished faces as they watched the Batmobile roar past them a second time—now free of the railcar—pursued by what looked like traffic patrolmen in clown masks on ATVs.

With that commuter train blocking the westbound tunnel, it's going to be a long commute home for them. I wonder if anyone will believe their story?

The Batmobile roared down the tunnel, its wheels straddling the rails. The tunnel curved through the bowels of Gotham, snaking to the right and then turning hard to the north.

Fashion District coming up next. That track runs parallel with the City, Financial, and the Sommerset Express lines under the old Cotton Station.

Another explosion shook the vehicle, sending its back end momentarily into the air. The wheels rebounded as the chassis crashed back toward the tracks, skidding slightly.

Bruce glanced at the rear display. The remaining ATVs were still behind him, though they were falling further behind.

He could clearly see the bright area of the Cotton Station platforms ahead through the night-vision displays . . . and the burning headlight of the scheduled commuter train closing with him directly ahead.

The regular Diamond District commuter. It has a stop here. I'll swing to the other track before we reach the platform and lead these clowns down the abandoned Harbor line.

Bruce's eyes widened.

The Diamond commuter train was not slowing down to stop at the station. He could see the panicked engineer frantically trying to work the suddenly ineffective controls.

Bruce pitched the throttle full forward. The Batmobile responded immediately, surging forward down the track toward the rapidly approaching train. The Cotton Station had platforms on both sides of the track, but only one of them was now in use. There would only be commuters on the western platform, Bruce thought. The east side platform should be deserted. He *hoped* it was deserted.

Never play chicken with a train . . .

The Batmobile cleared the tunnel moments before the train. Bruce kicked the thrusters again, to the right this time, shoving the Batmobile off the tracks and up onto the east side platform. The back of the Batmobile shattered tiles covering the subway wall.

Bruce slammed the brake pedal to the floor. The tires of the Batmobile squealed on the cement of the platform. The concrete wall at the north end of the platform was looming ahead of him. To his left, the Diamond District train was still roaring through the station, its cars still filling the tunnel at the northern end of the station, leaving him nowhere to turn.

The Batmobile continued its skid against the right-hand wall, the all-too-solid end of the platform rushing toward Bruce.

How long can this train be?

Suddenly, the last car cleared the tunnel and Bruce kicked the thrusters to the left. The Batmobile responded, slammed sideways by the thrusters back onto the barely cleared tracks and vaulting back into the darkness of the subway tunnel.

"Now *that's* what I call railroading!" the Joker howled. "I say it's time we all enjoyed a little mass transit."

An empty train pulled onto Platform Sixty-one, its doors opening. More trains could be heard approaching behind it. The Clown Police grabbed their weapons, piling into the open subway cars.

"All aboard!" Joker screamed. "It's coupon day and everybody rides the ride!"

Bruce gulped down a breath. The external optics had taken a beating and their clarity had suffered. Some of the feeds were blurry from the right side of the car.

Through the blur, however, he could see something quite clearly: another train, paralleling him on a second set of tracks, its doors open and filled with heavily armed clown police.

Bruce throttled back suddenly. The train on the parallel track continued forward, its breaks squealing in reaction. The Clown Train could not brake fast enough. Bruce wheeled the Batmobile around the end of the train, falling in behind the last car. He could see through the smudged cameras that the clown police

were gathering quickly in the rear car, working to open the
access door so they could fire the rocket-propelled grenades.
The momentum of the train continued to carry them forward
into the tunnel of the old Harbor line.

Wait for it . . . Wait for it . . .

The breaking train shifted slightly as it crossed the switcher
points to the old Coventry line and veered to the right.

Bruce nudged the steering to the left. The Batmobile disappeared into the forgotten crosstown tunnel to Coventry as the
clown train ground to a halt down the side tunnel.

A train was stalled on the crossing ahead of him. Another
was roaring after him from behind. The red control lights
were burning bright in unheeded warning. Bruce dropped the
Batmobile precipitously down through an access conduit, the
sounds of the grinding collision of the trains fading behind
him as the Batmobile fell onto the Westside University line
below.

The entire subway system had become a deadly gauntlet.

It's time for this mouse to leave the maze.

He roared past the University Station up the Coventry line
only to find yet another pair of subway cars—both packed with
clown police—converging with the northbound rail and falling
in behind him once again.

The old subway train rushed up behind him. The clowns'
small-arms fire pinged off the walls and the reactive armor of the
vehicle shell.

Bruce swung the car off of the main Coventry line and into
an abandoned tunnel. Just behind him, the points of the rail line
suddenly shifted, and the pursuing railcars careened into the
abandoned tunnel after him.

He's got me. Joker knows I've gone down a dead-end spur, and he's sure he's won.

The fuel gauges were hovering just above empty and the power reserves had dwindled to eight percent. When they went, the armor would be ineffective and everything could come apart.

Ahead of him he could see the barricade at the end of the line. Beyond that, the tunnel ended in an opening beneath the Westside Bridge.

"Kronos: surface," Bruce said, his voice weary.

The train was nearly on him, the RPGs, no doubt, at the ready.

Near the end of the track, a pair of steel ramps dropped down onto the tracks. The Batmobile roared up the ramp on its wheels just before it cleared the end-of-line barricade.

The careening subway train full of clown police did not.

Driving beneath the Westside Bridge, Bruce closed his eyes.

Joker had tried to stop him. Bruce wondered if something far more sinister awaited him at home.

CHAPTER NINETEEN

NO LONGER REQUIRED

The servants' entrance door rattled slightly from the key working the deadbolt.

He always complained about it but never got around to fixing it.

The deadbolt gave way and the door handle toggled the latch. The old man's silhouette was framed in the panes fitted into the upper panel of the door, obscured by the Wayne Family crest etched in the frosted glass.

I've waited in the dark. I've been in the dark so long . . .

The door swung wide. The silhouette was clear now; stark and sharp against the brightly lit stoop. The outline of the overcoat and the slight gleam off the hatless, balding pate were both so familiar to him. There was something small and rectangular clutched in his left hand as he entered the dark space of the servants' hall, closing the door behind him. The balding man reached for the light switch . . .

But the lights came on before he could reach the toggle.

"A little early Christmas shopping, Alfred?" Bruce said quietly from the adjoining servants' dining area. He was still dressed in the faux police uniform, his shoes crossed atop the edge of the long table as he leaned back in the chair. His hand slowly with-drew from the light switch on the wall behind him as he eyed his manservant with detachment.

Alfred Pennyworth caught his breath, startled for the moment but recovering quickly. He crossed his hands behind him, taking a parade rest stance that allowed him to hide the package in his hand from site. "Master Bruce! My apologies; I understood you were to be out for the evening."

"Plans change, Alfred," Bruce said with his calm voice about ten degrees colder than normal. He shifted slightly in his chair as he folded his arms across his chest. "So, I see you've picked up a little something . . . What is it?"

"Nothing, sir, really," Alfred's complexion blanched as he shrugged. "Just a little something I picked up for a friend."

"So am I your friend, Alfred?" Bruce asked.

Alfred drew in a considered breath. "You are as much a friend to me as I could have ever hoped."

"Well, then, my dear old friend," Bruce said through a sad smile, "let me see what you're hiding behind your back."

"It's really nothing, sir. A nasty little joke really." Alfred moved suddenly toward the kitchen door. "Could I interest you in a little something, Master Bruce? Some sandwiches perhaps or some chamomile tea? It won't take but a few—"

Bruce rocked forward suddenly, bolting from the chair. His arm crossed the kitchen door, barring Alfred's way. Bruce could feel the fire behind his eyes. His voice was barely controlled when he spoke. "No, Alfred! Master Bruce does *not* want his cookies or his milk! Master Bruce does *not* want to be coddled or put to bed. I've been asleep far too long. What I want is for you to explain that book you're holding behind your back!"

Alfred took a step back, bumping into the heavy dining table, causing its legs to squeal across the stone tile floor.

"No, Master Bruce," the old retainer answered. "This you must not do . . . I beg of you."

"You *beg* of me?" Bruce seethed.

"I've never asked anything of you before, Master Wayne," Alfred said, desperation rising in his voice. "I've done everything that was required of me—of the family and of you even when . . ."

Bruce took a step toward his former butler. "Even when . . . *what?*"

"Even . . . even when you embarked on your mad crusade," Alfred replied.

"My mad crusade?" Bruce shouted. "*Our* mad crusade, Alfred! You've been a *part* of this mad crusade from the very beginning! Is that what this is all about? Does the faithful retainer suddenly have cold feet and want to pretend the past never happened?

"I didn't know it would come to this, Master Bruce. I certainly never thought it would go this *far.* But the criminals were taking apart the city, and you were always setting things to rights. And I came to believe in what you were trying to do. I've dragged you broken and bleeding back to that black cavern of yours and patched you up more times than I care to count . . . and through it all I've kept the secrets of this family safe. Now, I beg you, Master Bruce, leave this alone and let me handle it for you. That's part of my job as a press agent, isn't it . . . to handle messes for you? Just think of this as a mess from which you need some distance. Walk away from this investigation right now and let me handle it for you."

"Handle this for me?" Bruce was shaking, fighting for control of himself.

"Yes, Master Bruce! Please!"

"Like your father handled my father's messes?"

Alfred's face fell. "No, Bruce. Don't speak of it!"

"But you see, Alfred, I've already *read* the book," Bruce said. "In fact, I've been doing a lot of interesting reading lately. Your father was not just OSS in the Second World War. I've checked his file. He was original SOE—Special Operations Executive for the British Secret Service. He was a guerilla warfare expert trained to fight the Nazis in their own backyard. It wasn't until late in the war that he was attached to the OSS. He was a spy, trained to operate in extreme conditions, tend his own wounds, kill without question, and, most importantly, clean up after himself so no one could suspect he had ever even been there at all."

"How dare you!" Alfred stared back in indignation. "My father was a hero!"

"So was mine," Bruce sneered, stepping up until his face was within inches of the former butler. "That's what you've always told me. But someone's been pointing out the cracks in the marble statues we've built of them, my good man. Your father was enough of a hero to clean up my father's mess at the Arkham Asylum back in 1958."

"What?" Alfred squeaked. "How did you know?"

Bruce snatched the book from behind the elder man's back. "Because I've already *read* the book, Alfred—and the letters from my father."

"What letters?" Alfred snapped back. "There were no letters!"

"In my father's hand and on his stationery," Bruce countered, waving the book menacingly in Alfred's face. "I'm relatively new at this, old bean. When did you find out about it?"

"Please, sir, this isn't going to help any."

"WHEN?" Bruce shouted.

"1967," Alfred replied. "Just before my father died."

Bruce drew in a shuddering breath. "Go on."

"It was a heart attack, but then he was sixty-nine at the time," Alfred continued, pulling himself up to sit on the table. He was bent forward now, the paper-wrapped book turning in his hands. "It was right after his first mild episode in the spring that he called me in. He told me everything just as Dr. Wayne had told it to him: the vision he had of using science to rid the city of crime by turning the criminals against themselves, Richter's bold ideas and the behavioral virus and how everything had come apart so quickly. He told me he had cleaned up everything 'spic-and-span,' as he used to say. My father said that he had done things in his life he wasn't proud of, but that he was hoping to make it right when he recovered. Then he had his massive attack a month afterward and left it all in my hands."

"That must have made it easy to get your father's position," Bruce rumbled. "All you had to do was hint at your newly acquired wisdom to my father and make sure the facts were kept off the written résumé."

"How dare you!"

"So that's what this is all about?" Bruce seethed. "Your father covers up a brutal murder and now you're covering up for him?"

"*My* father?" Alfred yelled back. "My father kept the secrets of this family to his last breath! *My* father covered up for *your* father's complicity in setting the stage for a spree of murders at the end of the '50s and took that secret to the grave with him. And his *son* has been keeping those same secrets for the benefit of this family and its only heir for most of his adult life! It was all under lock and key before the Richter woman showed up."

"Amanda?"

"Who else would it be?" Alfred grumbled. "I knew she was trouble when she first showed up on the grounds. Now it's missing . . . the files, the films, the tapes."

"Tapes?" Bruce demanded. "What tapes?"

"Your father's recorded diary," Alfred said. "The reels have all gone missing."

"So you've known about this my entire life," Bruce breathed, his eyes narrowing. "But that's not all, is it, Alfred, old friend?"

Alfred's breathing became suddenly shallow and fast.

"There's more to this than my father's funded experiments having gone wrong," Bruce prompted. "Something you're not telling me."

"Bruce, I've taken care of you your entire life," Alfred said, his voice quivering despite his obvious effort at control. "You are as much a son to me as my own flesh and blood could have been. I am telling you for all our sakes that you must let me handle this for you. You must stay out of it entirely, and if you do this, I promise you everything will be all right."

"Why the hell would you think that?" Bruce snapped. "All these years fighting the darkest souls of humanity . . . why would you *ever* be so stupid as to think you could bargain with a blackmailer?"

"Because it's always worked before," Alfred yelped. "This isn't the first time I've heard from the Richters. Their requests have never been unmanageable, and it was your father's wish that they be taken care of. I've always quietly taken care of the problem and they've always gone away, but this time—"

"Things got out of hand," Bruce growled.

The wall phone in the hall rang loudly.

Bruce and Alfred stared at each other.

The phone rang a second and third time.

"Answer it," Bruce demanded.

"I . . . I don't—"

"Now," Bruce insisted.

Alfred stepped sideways around Bruce and walked briskly toward the phone. Bruce followed uncomfortably close at his heels.

"Wayne Manor, how may I help you?" Alfred said.

"Do you have the item?" It was a woman's voice, muffled and indistinct.

Alfred looked at Bruce. Bruce nodded.

"Yes, I have it."

"Then I have what you want in return," the voice said. "You'll know where to bring it. Let the party begin."

The receiver clicked and went dead.

"She has the tapes," Alfred said to Bruce. "She'll exchange them for the book, but she has not yet told me where to make the delivery."

"Like hell," Bruce shook his head. His smile had a vicious edge to it. "I've been chasing that book across the city. Even the Joker took an interest in keeping me from getting back here tonight as I followed that book . . . a book that led me right back to you. And when I got back here, do you know what I found?"

Alfred shook his head. "No, sir, how could I . . . I just got in myself."

Bruce held up an invitation envelope.

"It's identical to the one delivered to everyone in the city," Bruce said, turning the envelope through the fingertips of his right hand. "It was waiting on the table—this table here in the servants' hall—when I came in. There was no name on it, so I opened it."

Always proper. Alfred always taught me to be proper.

"But I locked the house," Alfred sputtered. "The security system was engaged."

"The same security system that allowed Amanda access to my mother's garden?" Bruce asked. "Well, I see we'll need to take a look at upgrading the system—or at least changing it up a bit." He pulled the plain invitation card out of the envelope, holding it up in front of Alfred's face so that he could read it.

. . . TO A GALA IN YOUR HONOR.

KANE MANSION

MIDNIGHT TONIGHT

"Kane Mansion?" Alfred sputtered. "That residence has been boarded up for two decades!"

"How convenient that it's right next door," Bruce said. "I think I'll accept."

"No, Bruce, you must not go there," Alfred said quickly, grabbing his master's wrist with a surprisingly strong grip. "You have no idea where this hole leads nor where the darkness ends. Your parents are dead . . . The past is buried with them. *Let them rest!* I've taken care of this family my entire life; it's all I have and all I ever wanted. Leave it alone, Master Bruce. Stay here and everything will be all right."

"So I'm back in short pants again, am I, Alfred?" Bruce took in a shuddering breath. "You'll clean up this mess and I should just go on with my life? *What life?* I cannot rest because of the life I live. I run after some elusive dream . . ."

Joe Chill ran down the alley. I cannot catch him. I can never catch him.

" . . . and every time I think it's in my grasp, it vanishes and is replaced by some new threat to the city. Gotham balances on the edge of an abyss, and I alone feel the weight of holding it precariously there. What kind of a life is that?"

"An important life," Alfred urged. "A necessary life. A life given so that others might live theirs."

I'm the guardian. Who guards the guardian?

Bruce snatched his arm out of Alfred's grasp. "I'm not that boy in the alley anymore, Alfred! It's time to put an end to these games."

"No, Bruce," Alfred said sternly. "You must not go over there. There are some things that need to stay buried. I won't let you."

Bruce turned. "Alfred, you're fired."

The old retainer blinked. "What, sir?"

"I said you're fired, dismissed, downsized, or whatever you prefer to call it."

"You . . . you *can't* do that!" Alfred sputtered.

"The hell I can't," Bruce said rushing up menacingly once more. "You crossed a line. You're standing between me and my prey."

"What prey?"

"The truth!"

"The truth can be a terrible beast, Master Bruce," Alfred said more calmly than he felt. "Sometimes the truth hunts you."

"Get out," Bruce snapped. "Out of the manor, off the grounds, and out of my life."

"No! Sir!"

"Get out while you can, Alfred, because this is the only parachute you're going to get," Bruce growled. "Cheer up. You're about to get a very nice severance package—including medical, which I sincerely hope will not be needed in the near future. But don't bother packing, it will all be mailed to you. Just take the Bentley and consider it a bonus."

"Sir! Please—"

"GET OUT!" Bruce screamed, his face purple with rage.

Alfred, his face flush, turned on his heels and vanished out the servants' door. Bruce waited a few moments until he heard the motor of the Bentley come to life and the hush of the wheels diminishing across the gravel driveway.

Bruce choked back a single sob. Alfred had lied in order to hide something from him—had been hiding it from him his entire life. It was a betrayal that Bruce could not accept . . . and it left him more alone than he could recall feeling in all his life.

"It's time to put an end to the game," Bruce said, looking at the invitation once more.

CHAPTER TWENTY

MISDIRECTION

Amusement Mile / Gotham / 10:55 p.m. / October 25, 1958

"What do we do NOW, boss?"

"Shut up, Salvatore! I gotta think," Julius Moxon said through a grimace. The slug in his right shoulder had lodged in the joint and was excruciating. He gripped it with his left hand, trying to stop the blood and keep his arm from moving at the same time. He leaned heavily against the wall in a narrow alley between the milk-bottle throw and the balloon dart game booths. There were fifteen more of his boys jammed in the tight space around him, each packing everything from Thompson SMGs to pump shotguns. The lights of the midway beyond the alley were bright and harsh, swaying overhead in the October wind. They cast heavy, shifting shadows across the faces around Julius, and despite packing serious heat, their faces reflected the fear that was threatening to close around the mobster's heart. "Who we got left?"

"Hard to say, boss," Salvatore answered, pushing up the brim of his hat with the muzzle of his Thompson as he tried to see down the midway. "Ricky and his boys are all hanging from the Ferris wheel like they was Christmas ornaments or somethin'.

Somebody oughta go over there and stop that thing from turning . . . It ain't decent them swingin' like that."

"*You* do it, Salvatore," one of the thin hitmen said through
chattering teeth.

"Like hell, Jonesy!" Salvatore barked back. "I ain't walking out
for no guys that's already *dead*."

"I thought that was the whole point of robbing the Gotham
National in the first place." The fat killer called Kelly the Kel-
vinator was sweating despite the cold. "Lure these Apocalypse
jerks here with the bait and then whack 'em with heat from all
the mobs at the same time. Bye-bye Apocalypse and back to
business as usual."

The corrugated steel roofing gave a light rattle from above.
Everyone in the alley ducked at the sound.

"Yeah," Salvatore countered, "well, it looks like the Apocalypse isn't following the plan."

"Quit flapping your gums and reload," Julius barked. He was
beginning to feel a little light-headed. "We gotta find a way
outta here."

"Who done that to you, boss?" Salvatore asked, nodding at
the damaged shoulder.

"That Disciple jerk . . . I think," Julius moaned, then grinned.
"I put a slug in him, though, before he took my Browning and
turned it on me. If I hadn't taken a dive off the roof into that
dumpster, my number might have been up."

"It might be yet, boss, if we don't get that taken care of,"
Jonesy said. "You're leakin' like a sieve. Still, you're lucky: that
Disciple don't ever let anyone walk away in one piece—literally."

"That one they call Chanteuse," said Mikey, a weasel-faced
thug. "I heard she leaves like a Tarot card on each guy she kills."

"Nah, that's that Fate chick," Salvatore snapped. "Chanteuse
is the one with the murderous voice. "She's, like, one of them
Greek sirens or something."

"Listen to you guys," Julius spat, his spittle tinged with a streak of his blood. "A bunch of mama's boys scared of their shadows. There's only *four* of them, you dumb apes. You can't whack four creeps? Two of them are *broads*, for hell's sake!"

"What's the name of that other mug?" Kelly asked.

"Let's see," the weasel sniffed. "Disciple, Chanteuse, Fate, and . . . what's his name—"

Suddenly, a long scythe tore through the darkness from above, the blade impaling the fat killer through the chest and against the wooden wall of the milk-bottle booth. Impossibly, the blade dragged the fat Kelly upward over the edge of the roof, where the black robes and dark hood of death incarnate stood.

"REAPER!" The weasel shouted, his shotgun suddenly raised and barking into the darkness above. A ragged chorus of machine-gun fire joined in, but there was nothing there to shoot.

The fat killer was gone.

"Get me outta here!" Julius shouted and then coughed. More blood came into his mouth and he spit it out. He tried to run across the midway, but his legs felt loose and rubbery beneath him. Salvatore grabbed his boss, throwing his shoulder under his arm and dragging him toward the fun house across the way. Julius heard the sounds of the machine guns following behind him. A high-pitched scream tore above the sound of the gunfire as Joey flew past Julius, slamming into the wall next to the entrance.

Salvatore busted down the entrance door with a single kick and dragged Julius inside. The remaining Moxon hitmen pushed their way through the door after them . . . tumbling into a mirror maze.

Guns raised, all they could see around them were reflections of themselves seemingly going into forever. The stark light of the overhead bulb was repeating in all directions.

"May . . . maybe we should go back, boss," Salvatore stammered.

"Out *there?*" Julius snorted. "It's just a kid's maze, Sal! We'll go out the back and blow this whole scene."

They plunged into the maze together, threatened on all sides by their own reflections. The shifting images with the raised weapons they saw were themselves, but now and then a face would appear that was not their own, vanishing so quickly it was impossible to tell if the image had been real or an illusion of their own fears.

"Hey, boss?" whispered the weasel.

"What is it, Mikey?" Julius asked.

"You hear that?"

"Hear what?"

He *did* hear something. A high, reedy voice was echoing through the mirrors.

"Michael! Please help me!" the voice pleaded. "I'm so afraid! What do they want, Michael? I don't know what they want!"

"Ma?" Mikey the Weasel asked. "Boss! They got Ma!"

"What are you talkin' about?" Julius stared at the slim thug. "What would your ma be doing in this nuthouse?"

"MA!" Mikey shouted. "It's my ma, boss! They got her. I'm coming, Ma! Don't you worry, Ma, I'm coming!"

Mikey plunged down a side corridor in the maze, his reflection scattering in all directions. In a moment, he vanished.

"You want I should get him, boss?" said the thin man with chattering teeth.

A deathly scream suddenly rattled among the mirrors.

"I don't think so," Julius answered.

A gunshot rang out, followed by the sound of shattering glass. Then a burst of machine-gun fire rang out.

The man with the chattering teeth lurched forward, bloody patches exploding across his back. He fell into the mirror, smashing it as it scattered at his feet.

Guns suddenly began firing everywhere. Julius dropped painfully to the ground as Salvatore shielded him. Several bodies fell through the collapsing mirrors in front of them.

"Knock it off!" Julius shouted to his own men, but it took them several more rounds before they were able to stop.

"Hey, boss, check this out," Salvatore said.

Julius stared at the bodies on the floor in front of him. "Who are these guys?"

"They're Falcone's boys," Salvatore said, biting his lip. "And that one over there is one of Rossetti's. Looks like we got company, boss."

"We've been set up—all of us," Julius seethed. "Those Apocalypse creeps have us butchering each other for them! Well, I'm tired of this game and I don't want to play anymore!"

Julius staggered to his feet.

"Everybody out there—down!" he shouted. "Sal, our luck can't get no worse. Break me a few mirrors!"

Salvatore grinned, raising up his drum-fed Thompson. It started to spray bullets and mirror shards began to fall like rain.

Salvatore eased Julius into the back of the Cadillac Fleetwood Sixty Special. Julius knew the upholstery in the back would be ruined by his blood, but he could afford it.

If I live that long.

He had a terrible headache and was having trouble concentrating. Salvatore was saying something to him, but it was hard for him to hear. He desperately wanted to sleep but knew somehow that if he did, it would be for the last time.

"You want we should take you to Gotham Hospital, boss?" Salvatore repeated in his face as though Julius were deaf.

"No! We might as well walk into the DA's office and start singing!" Julius snapped. The pain was overwhelming. "Who's that
doctor Lewis is always going on about? That rich friend of his?"

"Rains . . . Bains . . ." Salvatore stammered.

"Wayne!" Julius said. "Dr. Thomas Wayne, old Pat Wayne's
kid. He can patch me up and we can keep one step ahead of the
bulls."

"But, where we gonna find him, boss?" Salvatore shrugged.

"That party," Julius said, grabbing Salvatore by the collar.
"Lewis was going to some big-shot fancy party at the Kane
Mansion tonight. Wayne will be there—along with every other
money-spoiled snob of Gotham. That's where we'll find him.
How many boys we got left?"

"Counting us?" Salvatore glanced around outside the car. "Ten
. . . maybe fifteen here now. They're all piled into a couple of
cars behind us like clowns in a circus."

"That's enough to handle the Hoi polloi," Moxon smiled. "Tell
the boys we're going to crash a party over at the Kane Mansion."

"You want me to go out *there*?" Salvatore gaped.

"Am I talkin' to myself?" Moxon barked through the pain. "I'm
bleeding here! Just do it!"

Salvatore jerked on the handle, shoving the door open as fast
as he could manage. It rebounded, but the big thug was already
clear of it, running back toward the next sedan. He shouted at
the third car idling behind and was glad to see the windows of
both cars roll down slightly to hear him. He did not want to
have to stand out in the open and say it twice.

"Moxon says we're going to the party at the Kane Mansion!"
he shouted, glancing at the dark midway buildings that seemed
too close for comfort.

"Where's this Kane place?" called the driver of the third car.
His voice sounded a staccato, like his teeth were chattering.

"It's in Bristol," Salvatore shouted back. This was taking too long for his liking. "Read the map, knucklehead, and stay on our bumper!"

"But why this Kane place?" the driver persisted.

"There's a doc there by the name of Wayne who's gonna patch up the boss," Salvatore answered over his shoulder as he rushed back to Moxon's car. "Or else we're gonna make a few new openings available among the kings of High Society."

From a hidden spot nearly twenty feet away, the entire conversation had been overheard.

Wayne Manor / Bristol / 11:30 p.m. / October 25, 1958

Thomas examined the costume that had been carefully laid out on the divan in the dressing room of his east-wing suite. It had been his parents' inviolate territory when he was growing up, and he still felt like an intruder for moving into the rooms. He had finished showering and had shaved once more for the evening. He wore a towel wrapped around his waist and considered just what one could do to make his attire for the evening less ridiculous.

Thomas was uncomfortable with costumes in the first place and had asked Jarvis to secure one for him to wear to the party. The servant had assured him that the character was extremely popular, but Thomas only knew it as coming from an old 1920 silent movie that his father used to make him watch now and then when Thomas was a boy. It was about the only activity Thomas remembered doing with his father that did not involve an argument or a beating. Unfortunately, this costume had been assembled incorrectly, with tights and trunks rather than the proper leggings and with a cape that looked more like something Dracula might wear than a caballero. Unlike everyone else, Thomas didn't have much time for television but he knew everyone at the hospital liked to talk about Westerns. The mask was a hooded cowl in the style of the old Fairbanks films. To Thomas's dismay, the outfit had no cowboy hat. Worse, whoever had assembled the costume seemed to have done a rushed job of it, tossing in tall black boots and a wide leather belt more suited to a buccaneer. By the time the costume had arrived, it was too late to do anything about changing it. Perhaps, Thomas thought, he could find something more suitable than the tights and the trunks to wear under his costume.

Thomas turned back to the mirror over the sink. There was still Burma-Shave on his face despite the new Gillette safety razor having done a much smoother job on his face. He began to sing to himself as he splashed water from the basin, rubbing off the shaving cream.

"Good evening, Thomas" came the quiet, familiar voice.

Thomas looked up into the mirror with a start.

"It's been a long, long time," the man said, leaning on the back of the divan.

"Denholm!" Thomas breathed, his eyes wide. He wondered how Denholm Sinclair had managed to get into the mansion . . . and whether he had managed to do so unnoticed.

"Denholm? Yes, I suppose I will allow that I was Denholm Sinclair," he said. "It pains me to admit it, though . . . pains me terribly. It was a pain that *you* gave me, Thomas. Remember? I wasn't the man you thought I should be . . . and you were going to *fix* me, weren't you? And you *did* fix me, Thomas . . . you fixed me better than you could have hoped. I couldn't be old Denny Sinclair any longer because Denny was a liar and a cheat, a guy who burned up little orphans in their beds just to cover up his extensive fraud. So I've become what you wanted me to be, Thomas, and I'm bringing justice down on the very vermin and predators among whom I once numbered. Denholm Sinclair is dead—I buried everything he ever was—and now I'm the man Martha Kane asked that I become. And I have you to thank for it, my dear friend. I am . . . so very grateful."

"Denholm—"

"That's not who I am!" the man roared, his voice startling Thomas.

"Okay." Thomas drew in a slow, controlled breath, holding both his palms forward and acutely aware that he was only dressed in a towel. "What should I call you, then?"

"They call me the Disciple," he replied, his left hand pressing against his abdomen. Thomas could see blood seeping out between his fingers.

"The Disciple?" Wayne asked.

"*Your* Disciple, Thomas," he replied evenly. "You made me strong. You made me wise. You made me see the purpose of my existence."

I've got to get the authorities. I've got to buy some time.

"What . . . what purpose?" Thomas asked.

"To be the cure, Doctor!" Disciple smiled, his eyes bright. "We are the antibody of Gotham—my companions and I. We flow through the lifeblood of the city, searching for the antigens of crime and corruption, of intimidation and greed. Fate finds them, Chanteuse calls them home, and the Reaper . . . Well, he is always busy."

"And you?"

Disciple smiled again. "Me? Why, I am the judge, the jury, and sometimes the executioner all in one."

Keep him talking. There's got to be a way to get help.

"You've been very busy," Thomas continued. "Too busy if the newspaper reports are true."

"It's a living," Disciple chuckled darkly. "But it's all been nothing compared to what's coming tonight. Moxon, Rossetti, and even Falcone all set aside their differences tonight so they could face their common enemy, but the laugh was on them. We were ready for them. Now Moxon's got a few slugs in him, and he's on his way up to the Kane Mansion with what remains of his goon squad."

"The Kanes'?" Thomas's mind raced. "Why would he go there?"

"Last time I saw him he didn't look too good," Disciple shrugged. "I guess his little boy bragged you up to his old man. He needs a doctor who knows how to keep his mouth shut . . . so he's looking for *you*."

"Oh, no," Thomas breathed.

"You needn't worry, Thomas. I'll take care of them; I'll put them out of their misery," Disciple said, rubbing his large powerful hands together. Blood stained his palms, fingers, and forearms. Thomas realized those stains had not all come from Denholm's wounds. "We're a lot alike, you and I: it's just that my surgery is a good deal messier than yours in the end. And come to think of it, while I'm cleaning out the Moxon cancer at the Kanes' ball, there are a few among the upper crust I think could use my attention, too . . . a few of them who could use a good cleaning as well."

The line of his moral judgment is shifting more and more toward the perfect and the ideal. If this continues, everyone at the ball could be in mortal danger—simply by not being perfect. I've got to stop him.

"You . . . you're hurt," Thomas observed, pointing to the wound.

"Can you help me, old friend?" Disciple asked in a pleading voice as he sat down on the divan next to the costume. "I seem to be in need of your help."

Thomas nodded. "I'll . . . need to get my bag."

"Your bag?"

"My medical bag. It's downstairs. It will only take me—"

"No," Disciple said, shaking his head. "That's not the help I need."

"But it will only take—"

"NO!" Disciple screamed, his face suddenly purple with rage.

Thomas shook off a chill at the dreadful sound of Disciple's voice. The man was manic and possibly schizophrenic. Moreover, he appeared far stronger than Thomas remembered him. "All right . . . what do you need?"

Disciple stood up, moving carefully toward Thomas. "I need your help to exact justice on those who are unjust."

"How?"

"I need to be *you*," Disciple said through a Denholm Sinclair smile . . . and then knocked Thomas Wayne cold with a single, perfectly placed punch.

Batcave / Wayne Manor / Bristol / 11:39 p.m. / Present Day

Bruce stepped up to the Batmobile on its service platform, where it was recharging. He considered fueling it but decided there was not time, and besides, the distance he had to go was not that far.

He opened the gull-wing doors and started pulling out the components of his Batsuit. The capacitors were somewhat discharged from the previous night's activities, but he gauged them sufficient for his needs.

He began assembling the Batsuit around him as a knight might have donned his armor, connecting its components until it was a seamless whole. He ended with the cowl, completing his costume.

He had a party to stop by at the abandoned Kane Mansion next door.

CHAPTER TWENTY-ONE

MASQUERADES

Batman passed as a shadow beneath the porte-cochère that dominated the main entrance to Kane Mansion and moved silently up the broad, deserted steps. The main doors, long since barred, were open wide, inviting him into the dark foyer beyond.

He slipped into the enveloping shadows, closing his eyes to get his bearings. The old foyer sprang into three-dimensional relief in his mind, a place at once familiar and alien.

I played here as a boy. My mother would stand at the bottom of this stair-case and call me down from the landing above. I always tried to slide down the wide banister, and Mother would always warn me it was too dangerous. It was a game we always played . . . here on these steps . . .

Batman frowned in the shadows, too dark to be seen.

That was before Grandma Kane died and Mother sold the property to Kane Corp in '65. The entire estate had gone into receivership following my mother's murder. The company folded not long afterward and locked the doors, and the estate has been in litigation ever since. Gotham Bank acquired the paper on the grounds twenty years ago and locked the doors on a prop-erty it could not maintain and for which it never gave a damn.

The faint sound of music drifted into his ears from the back of the foyer. He switched to night-vision mode and a brilliant rectangle of spilling light sprang into view outlining the double doors at the back of the foyer.

Batman moved toward the doors, opened his eyes and pushed them open.

Kane Mansion / Bristol / 11:44 p.m. / October 26, 1958

"Ladies and gentlemen!" the doorman announced to the hall, banging down his ornate staff. Bertie had been dressed as an Elizabethan footman and was all too pleased to maintain the appearance for his part.

The band stopped playing at the far end of the ballroom. Brightly costumed oddities stopped their gyrations on the dance floor to look, while those crowding the edges of the floor turned in curiosity. Several of the guests on the patio beyond the French doors squeezed back inside to gawk.

Harold Ryder shifted his Bell and Howell 70D 16 mm newsreel camera toward the entrance and pressed the shutter trigger. He was dressed as a cowboy for the occasion, taking for a costume what he considered to be the path of least ridiculousness. The camera held to his face required that his cowboy hat be pushed back on his head. The party was a bore: he preferred to be working the crime beat, but crime was down. He had heard about some action going down on Amusement Mile earlier in the evening, but by then he was stuck out here covering the cotillion crowd.

Still, only a certain few of the guests rated this kind of general introduction, and their entrance was worth a few feet of film for the news broadcasts later in the evening. He had only a few feet of film left on this reel anyway and this would give him an excuse to run out the film before putting in a new one.

"Who is it this time?" asked Virginia Vale, reporter for the *Gotham Gazette*. She was in her Little Bopeep outfit, complete with bonnet, but the illusion was spoiled by the cigarette bouncing at the corner of her lower lip as she spoke.

"Don't know," Harold replied, checking the focus as the camera whirred on. "Number five hundred and one of the five hundred, I supposed."

Bertie straightened up in his costume, giving all eyes in the crowded ballroom opportunity to pay proper attention.

"Dr. Thomas Wayne!" Bertie announced.

The costumed figure stepped into the doorway to the applause of the packed ballroom. The clockwork camera drive whirred on.

"Dr. Wayne looks like he's been exercising," Virginia sniffed.

"But get a load of that costume," Harold breathed. He had not bothered with the balky and bulky sound equipment and could say whatever he pleased, so long as he said it in a way that would not shake the camera. "Who's he supposed to be?"

"The Kane press release says he's coming as Douglas Fairbanks," Virginia said, looking down at his folded sheet.

"Fairbanks?" Harold said. "Then what's with the tights and the trunks?"

"If that's Douglas Fairbanks, then I'm Bettie Page," Virginia snorted.

"Don't get my hopes up," Harold chided. He released the shudder trigger, pulling the camera down in front of him. Without thinking, he flipped out the winding key, holding it steady in his right hand while twisting the body of the camera with his left. It was an old habit from his days as a war photographer in the South Pacific, making sure the camera was wound quickly and always ready. "I'll tell you what, though . . . He looks more like a bat than a hero in that getup."

"Well, it seems to be working for someone," Virginia said, pointing.

Martha Kane, in her flapper dress and wearing a sequined white domino mask above her dazzling smile, crossed the floor and took her new guest by the arm.

Kane Mansion / Bristol / 11:47 p.m. / Present Day

The air smelled strongly of burning dust and lavender.

Batman's eyes narrowed behind his cowl, his lips stretching thin against his teeth as he drew back from the assault on his senses and pushed through the double doors.

The ballroom was enormous, and its extents were difficult to see. Everything was in motion, the room filled with dizzy, sweeping dance.

Long, red silk streamers cascaded downward from the cracked dome ceiling overhead, suspended from a complex of horizontal metal rods, motors, and more rods—an enormous mechanical mobile that nearly filled the hall. Between the silk bolts, several dozen life-sized mannequin couples swung inches above the floor. The figures, suspended from the mobile above, swayed and whirled in their poses, each costumed for a masquerade.

The noise of an old phonograph echoed from the distant end of the ballroom, a scratching version of a big band song.

Batman stepped gingerly into the hall.

Let's see if we can crash this party.

The walls seemed to writhe beneath shifting shadows of the silk cascades and suspended figures. Gaudy chandeliers glowed too brightly overhead beneath their cheap linen coverings. Thin smoke drifted up from where the old light bulbs touched cobwebs. Each of the enormous fixtures twisted and swung as the silk brushed them in passing, their hanging crystals sounding with painful brightness in his ears. The cracking paint and golden gilding of the plaster wall ornaments lay dulled beneath two decades of neglect. The soap-coated French doors obscured any view of the terrace.

A pair of suspended marionette figures swung into view. One was dressed in what looked like a bad imitation of some of his early Batsuits. A female figure hung limp in a matching dance pose, suspended from the ever-shifting rods overhead. This one clothed in a flapper dress with the head lolled backward, jaw hanging open.

Amanda Richter!

Amanda swung almost at once out of view, wheeling into revolutions of the shifting figures suspended from the ceiling and disappearing among the red silk drapes that also swung in arcs through the hall.

He reached down without looking to his Utility Belt. The Teflon-bladed Batarang snapped open in his hand. He checked the Batsuit power levels and discovered they were at 38 percent. There had been no time to recharge the Batsuit since its last use earlier that day. It would have to be enough.

The figures jerked slightly. The recording made a ripping sound, as though the needle had been pushed across the grooves. Then another sound filled the room, hollow, echoing, and vaguely distorted. It sent a chill down Batman's spine like none he had experienced before.

"My name is Dr. Thomas Wayne . . . I suppose this is my testimony . . . or, perhaps, my confession regarding the events of October 26, 1958 at the Kane Charity Ball. I've kept silent far too long."

Batman stepped in among the costumed mannequins swinging between the silk cloth, his index finger set along the curved back edge of the Batarang, prepared to cut the cables should the

life-sized marionettes get in his way. He could see the red flapper
dress of Amanda ahead of him through the maze of shifting forms.

*"I could not rest until I had left a record for my sons, both of whom are
dear to me. I could not bear the thought that they might be confronted by my
past without hearing from me the reasons for what happened, how it had all
gone wrong despite my most noble intentions . . ."*

One of the mannequins to his right moved.

Batman ducked low and pushed under the arm of the Confederate soldier, shoving the Uzi in his hand upward as it sprayed a
stuttering stream from its muzzle. The Marie Antoinette mannequin in front of him jumped from the impact of the bullets,
the head exploding into plaster shards that clattered onto the
warping hardwood floor.

A series of popping cracks sounded all around him. A number
of mannequins dropped into a crouch on the floor.

*Real and unreal. Living and dead. Some of these costumes hold plaster,
and some hold breathing killers. Which is which?*

Musketeers, ninjas, cavaliers, pirates, and shoguns rose against
him, but they had one thing in common: they held identical
kukri tanto machete blades.

*" . . . So I make this record for their sakes and for the sake of my own
soul's peace."*

"The music's changed but it's still the same song," Batman
growled. "It's time to dance."

Kane Mansion / Bristol / 11:53 p.m. / October 26, 1958

Lew Moxon stood in his gray cowboy costume with his
domino mask, sipping a martini at the side of the dance floor
and watching his friend in the ridiculous bat costume dance
with the flapper hostess. It looked as though Bruce Wayne was
finally making some progress with Martha after all.

Lew had heard rumblings around the Koffee Klatch about something big going down tonight. His father and his old way of running the town was going the way of the dodo. They were all running scared of this Apocalypse boogeyman and were getting desperate.

Let 'em sweat. Lew smiled, raising his glass to the bat as he swung past him on the ballroom floor. *I've got my ticket out . . . Thank you, Dr. Wayne!*

In that moment, the double doors at the end of the ballroom slammed open. Salvatore, followed by six more from the Moxon gang, pushed their way into the room. Big Eddie drew up his Thompson, firing a burst into plastered ceiling over the screams of several women and not a few men. The band lost the beat to their song and stumbled to a halt.

"Everybody! Down on the ground!" Salvatore shouted over the continued cries. "Play nice and nobody gets hurt!"

Lew slowly sat down along with the fear-stricken partygoers.

"We're just lookin' for a doctor who can make a house call," Salvatore shouted. "Where's Dr. Wayne?"

Kane Mansion / Bristol / 11:53 p.m. / Present Day

" . . . had every intention of attending the event until Denholm Sinclair— then calling himself the Disciple—appeared in my rooms here in Wayne Manor. He assaulted me, rendering me unconscious, and then, using my costume, was able to enter the Kane Mansion under the guise of being me . . ."

Batman picked up the Confederate soldier, continuing to use his momentum against his assailant. He wrapped his arms around the soldier, who continued to flail with his free arm, trying to maneuver the Uzi into a firing angle on his target. But the Batman pushed against him, swinging them both on the suspending cables. This launched them into an arc, rising higher

off the ground as they both cleared a pair of pirates ducking out
of the way.

Batman swung with the Confederate, slamming his back into
the mirrored wall of the ballroom. He heard the breath of the
soldier rush out of his lungs with a satisfying "whuh" as the man
went limp beneath him. The Caped Crusader tore the Uzi out
of the man's hand, breaking the soldier's trigger finger in the
process. The automatic came apart in Batman's practiced hands
as he dropped to the floor, rolling to a fighting stance.

*"I was unconscious. As soon as I came to my senses, I knew I had to get
over to the Kane Mansion and stop Denholm. Martha was there. I had no
idea what he might be driven to do . . ."*

Two pirates attempted to flank Batman at once, while the
cavalier tried to distract him from the front. Batman trapped
the thrusting arm of the first pirate on his left, using his body
mass to add weight to the thrust-kick against the pirate charging him on the right. His boot drove deep into the second
pirate's gut, and he cocked the leg again at the knee, raising
the second kick higher to the side of the head. The power-
armor reacted at once, driving into the second pirate's head
with such force that his feet left the ground, pivoting him in
the air.

But during the second kick, the cavalier had made a quick ad-
vancing step, slashing across the Batsuit's extended leg. Batman
felt the Batsuit stiffen suddenly as the reactive armor engaged,
and he pulled the leg back behind him and twisted around,
still trapping the first pirate's arm. He felt the pirate's shoulder
joint slip with a satisfying snap as he turned, pushing his body
backward and flipping the pirate over him directly toward the
cavalier.

Amanda and her red flapper dress flashed past him among
the long red silk drapes and the still-circling mannequins. The

shoguns, ninjas, and musketeers were shifting around him, their blades raised as they looked for their opportunity.

Batman became aware of an alarm chiming in his cowl. He glanced down at his right leg. A long gash ran across the thigh of his Batsuit. Black liquid trickled from the cut.

What kind of blades are they using?

The Dark Knight chose his target—a Union cavalry officer just to his left. He feigned into the man, who swung his blade too soon. Batman dodged, then body-kicked the man in the chest, sending him flying backward and scattering the suspended mannequins. Batman followed him into the thicket of costumed figures and leaped on him almost at once. He drove his left knee into the man's wrist, smashing it against the floor and causing him to release the blade at once. His right hand drew up to take the Union officer out of the fight for good.

His fist did not come down.

An acrobatic blond woman in a dark green leotard had bound his hand in one of the long bolts of silk suspended from the ceiling. A second woman—a brunette—spun down a second bolt from the ceiling with deadly grace.

Query and Echo? Riddler's henchwomen in on this, too? It's as though every criminal in the city is being played!

The musketeer and the ninjas closed in, with Batman's wrist hopelessly tangled in the silk. He gripped the cloth with both hands, trying to climb it, but Echo was shifting around him, wrapping the second bolt of silk around his swinging feet. Batman kicked hard, sending Echo spinning away, but she steadied the spin, swinging back toward him. Query drew in a third bolt of the silk, swinging it around the Batman's torso, under his arms, pinning down the cape.

The swordsmen below began slashing at the Batsuit above them. Batman swung his legs upward, wrapping his feet around the silk above him. This pulled him up out of the way of the slashing blades just as Query swung in again, trailing the long silk behind her. Batman pushed against the cloth with his feet, using his mass for leverage. He struck Query with a solid backhand blow, sending her into a fast spin, but Echo had wrapped his left hand from behind. Batman pulled hard against the fabric—the weave was supple enough that it would not break or sheer.

Guns, knives, explosives . . . I survived them all only to be immobilized by a web of silk?

Batman howled, raging against the bonds, but he had nothing solid off which he could push or have any leverage.

Batman could feel the life bleeding out of the Batsuit.

Below him, Amanda Richter swung past, suspended in the arms of a mannequin while his father's dead voice continued to ring through the hall.

"I came to the Kane Mansion, but I was too late . . ."

CHAPTER TWENTY-TWO

SECRET IDENTITY

Kane Mansion / Bristol / 11:57 p.m. / October 26, 1958

"Tommy!" whispered the woman in the red flapper dress, shaking as she sat on the ballroom floor. "Please! What do we do?"

The man in the mask and the cape took her shoulders in his hands. His voice was deeper than usual—she would remember it as being affected with the emotion of the moment. "Martha, I'm going to take care of you . . . I'm going to take care of all of us."

The caped man stood up and stepped away from the red-dressed flapper. The mob gang at the door swung the muzzles of their guns in his direction.

"I'm Thomas Wayne," the caped man said gruffly. "What do you want?"

Thomas staggered up the servants' driveway behind the Kane Mansion, his medical bag in hand. He had clung to it like a life preserver when he first spotted it on the sideboard of the Wayne dining room. He had the horrible idea that he would need it.

His head was still pounding from the blow Disciple had given him. His dressing room had come back to him as though from a distant place, and it was a few minutes before the awfulness of what had happened was fully realized in his thoughts. He dressed quickly in jeans and a collared shirt, slipping on his shoes without bothering about socks.

Thomas could see the closed French doors off the ballroom. There were figures inside the glass, but the band was not playing, nor could he hear any other sounds. He was momentarily confused as to whether he should try to enter the ballroom directly from the patio or find another way in.

His eye caught movement through the glass on his left.

Through another set of French doors, Thomas saw two large men lay a third on the couch in the library. He recognized the man at once from the pictures in the paper.

It was Julius Moxon.

Thomas stepped onto the patio, peering through the glass of the doors. The two large men had left. Julius lay alone on the couch. Even from this distance it was obvious his breathing was labored and a shoulder wound was still bleeding badly.

Moxon's men are already here. Denholm must be somewhere about. Lewis must be around. If I can get the elder Moxon patched up before anything happens, then maybe Lewis can help me get these guys out of here before Denholm makes a mess of everything.

Thomas tried the handle on the door. It opened easily and he moved quietly into the library, opening his medical bag.

He had to fix this.

"Psst! Wayne!" Lewis tried to get the caped man's attention. "Stop it, man! You don't know what you're doing!"

The man turned to face Lewis.

Lewis's buzzed haircut was glistening with sweat as he stood up, pulling off his cowboy hat and patting his head with the bandana from around his neck.

"It's okay, folks," he said loudly through a forced grin. "Just a little Halloween joke is all. Haha! These boys really had us all fooled. Right out of a Cagney movie, right?"

A few isolated spurts of nervous laughter drifted over the ballroom but nobody else moved.

"Just relax, folks . . . the joke's about over," Lewis said as he stepped over to the caped figure. He leaned in close and spoke in a quiet, *sotto voce* voice for the masked man's ears only. "Play along with me, Thomas, and nobody will be the wiser."

"You think this is a *game*, Moxon!" the caped man shouted, reaching up suddenly and grabbing Lewis by the throat. "The Moxons have been draining the life from Gotham for too long, bullying and muscling their way into every decent life and laughing at the society on which they feed. Your family is a cancer on the city—a cancer I intend to remove with my bare hands if necessary!"

"Thomas," Moxon croaked from under the man's grip. "It don't have to go down this way."

"Saulie!" one of the pale-faced mobsters with a Thompson in his hands said. "What do we do?"

"Do we blast 'em?" growled another.

"And make hamburger out of the boss's kid?" Salvatore snapped. "Are you nuts?"

Lewis reached up, trying to pry the hand away from his neck, but the grip was like a vise. It was dragging him backward, his heels squeaking across the polished floor.

"Thomas, stop," Lewis pleaded, tears welling up in his eyes. "You'll ruin everything!"

"You getting this, Ryder?" Virginia breathed with barely contained excitement in the cameraman's ear.

"Shut up, Vi!" the cowboy whispered. "I'm busy here."

The Bell and Howell 70D whirred on. Harold ticked down the seconds in his mind. He had just reloaded the film in the case and had nearly a hundred feet available to him. At twenty-four frames per second that was about three minutes worth, but the clockwork drive was never good for more than thirty seconds a shot before it required rewinding. He knew with unerring instinct that he would have to stop and wind the camera in a few seconds.

This upper-crust Wayne had Julius Moxon's brat by the throat and was actually dragging the guy the length of the ballroom toward the armed goons at the entrance.

Twenty-four . . . twenty-five . . . twenty-six . . . damn it!

Harold released the trigger, flipping open the winding key and twisting the camera for all it was worth. He rotated the turret at the front of the camera so the wide-angle lens was over the aperture, and he raised the camera up.

"Lower your weapons or I snap his neck," the caped man bellowed as he dragged Lewis Moxon almost the length of the floor.

"Sure, Doc." Salvatore watched him with steely eyes. "You heard the man, boys . . . Relax a little."

The man in the cape shoved Lewis backward into the group of thugs as he passed between Salvatore and Big Eddie.

Big Eddie was long on moxie but short on brains. He had been pushed around all night and wanted some payback.

He raised his 9 mm Browning out of his coat pocket thinking he was fast enough to take some pansy doctor.

He was wrong.

Harold's camera missed it.

The gunshot went off just as the camera was coming up to his eye. Harold swore as he jammed his finger down on the trigger and the Bell and Howell began to whir once more.

"Damn!" Ryder exclaimed. "That's Thomas Wayne!"

Here was the bat-costumed socialite driving Edward "Big Eddie" Cronkle down to his knees. The man's forearm was bent at an impossible angle, the radius and the ulna both snapping as Wayne held the arm with both hands and broke it over his knee. A semiautomatic handgun tumbled from the big thug's hand, clattering across the floor.

Through the camera's lens, Harold saw Salvatore grabbing the bat costume from behind and trying to pin his arms, but the masked and caped figure was a demon unleashed. He planted both feet on the ground and kicked so hard that Salvatore bent backward. They both fell hard against the floor. The remaining hitmen of the Moxon gang reached in for the manic doctor, trying to drag him off Salvatore.

One flew upward from the pack, his head snapped back as he fell like a broken doll to the floor. Suddenly it appeared the costume-clad dervish was standing upright, surrounded by the gangsters, his fists engaging the circle of them in a frantic melee. The panicked mobsters were scrambling in the brawl. The masked vigilante blocked a punch while ducking another. He drove his booted foot down the length of one man's chin, who howled in pain just before the costumed bat slammed his fist down like a hammer across the man's jaw, sending him sprawling in silence.

The camera continued to whir . . .

The human bat caught Lewis Moxon as he was trying to open the doors. He turned him around as he struck. The back of Lewis's head bounded off the door behind him and he slumped to the ground.

Twenty-six . . . twenty-seven . . . twenty-eight.

Click. Ryder released the camera trigger.

He watched the man he knew was Thomas Wayne open the doors of the ballroom, the breeze from the hall billowing his cape behind him as he stepped through. Harold cursed again, because he was still winding the camera.

But he managed to twist the close-up lens into place on the turret in time to catch the reaction of Miss Martha Kane in her red flapper dress as she stood among her stunned guests and watched the caped hero depart. It was adoration and wonder.

He released the trigger. The camera stopped with a sudden click.

"Now *that's* news!" he sighed.

Thomas Wayne looked up from his work. Julius Moxon was out cold on the couch—gratefully—but Thomas had taken care of most of the critical damage and managed to stabilize him.

"He's mine, Thomas," said the familiar voice behind him.

Thomas turned, looking up from where he knelt in the library.

"You might have just asked me to borrow the costume," Thomas said casually. "It looks terrible on you."

"Step out of the way, Thomas," Disciple said. "You're not the problem that needs fixing."

"And just how are you going to fix this . . . problem, Denholm?" Thomas asked, standing up and facing the man in his costume. The wound from earlier was bleeding again, and he was limping slightly from a second, fresh wound. His blood was dripping onto the carpet.

"You don't fix cancer," Disciple sneered. "You destroy it."

"You kill it," Thomas amended.

"That's right," Denholm smiled beneath the old-fashioned mask.

"And what about Dr. Richter?" Thomas asked. "Is that why he died?"

"He was a Nazi, Thomas!" Disciple snarled. "He worked the experimental medical branch for the SS. He did the most unspeakable things imaginable to other human beings, all under the cover of discredited science and a society darker than hell itself. Then when justice was about to fall on him, he made a deal with our government—our military intelligence—to be repatriated to these good ol' United States under some secret deal called 'Paperclip.' Now all the torture, the hideous pain, the drawn-out murders he oversaw are supposed to be forgiven and forgotten because he might have carried some piece of knowledge with him to a well-deserved grave? We watched him—Fate, Chanteuse, the Reaper, and I—and we heard his excuses and his lies, but we knew him for who he was at his heart, Thomas . . . We knew who he had been and that he would never change."

"He was trying to help you," Thomas said quietly.

"He was trying to get *published*," Disciple spat the words. "He was trying to erase his past by burying the stinking, rotting corpses and who he really was under a pretty linoleum floor bathed in Spic and Span and polished with Aerowax!"

"He had a family," Thomas shouted back. "A wife and daughters who cared about him."

"And what of the men he tortured to death in his experiments?" Disciple shot back. "Did they not also have wives and little kiddies? And don't tell me that he was only following orders or that he just didn't *know* what he was doing was destroying civilization because . . . because . . ."

Disciple looked up, his eyes bright and shining behind the mask and rapture reflected in his sudden smile.

"I see it clearly now," Disciple muttered. "You're so right,

Thomas. It's not just the Julius Moxons, but those who empower him . . . They, too, are guilty. Moxon has to die, of course, but now I see it's not enough. They all have to die . . . every last one of them . . . before the city will be clean. Why, I'll bet half the people at this party alone are profiting from Julius Moxon's deals. They'll have to die, too, the corrupt upper class. Then the city will be clean, then—"

"What about Martha?" Thomas asked quietly.

"It would be better for her to be cured just as I have been cured."

"What about me, Denholm?" Thomas said, standing up and backing slowly toward the open French doors.

"You? You're the one who opened my eyes, Thomas," the Disciple said. "I'm your disciple."

"But I'm the worst of them all," Thomas goaded. He had reached the door, the cool evening breeze cooling the sweat that pooled at his back. "I *paid* Richter's bills. I gave him the money that allowed him to do his experiments. And I've just operated on Julius Moxon here—willingly aided and abetted a known criminal, I think they call it. And now I'm going to *fix* you . . . Take away your purpose and your specialness and make you *common* once more. And when I do, I'll have *beaten* you, Denholm Sinclair . . . and the Disciple will be no more."

Denholm howled in rage, lunging for him, but Thomas was prepared and leaped back onto the terrace.

Thomas started running. He could hear the Disciple charging after him as he crossed the lawn and bounded down into the ravine that lay between the two estates. He knew his old friend had been badly wounded in the gun battles earlier in the evening, but it did not appear to be slowing him down as much as Thomas had hoped.

What was I hoping for? That I could lead him away from Martha and the others? That I might find the forgiveness that Richter could never have?

He had headed in the direction of the house, but now he knew he would never make it that far. Denholm would catch him climbing up the hill and that would be the end of him.

There was only one other place he could go where he might find a weapon against the monster he had helped create.

He hoped it was still there.

He hoped it still worked.

CHAPTER TWENTY-THREE

THE ABYSS

Kane Mansion / Bristol / 11:58 p.m. / Present Day

Batman could feel the life draining from the Batsuit. The response was getting more sluggish and there was more resistance to his own movement than there should have been. He could not break his bonds, nor could he manage to untangle himself from the bolts of silk, whose flexibility and strength caused his own weight to work against him.

He had to go up.

Batman gripped the silk and pulled with all his strength, moving upward from the slashing blades below that continued to put gashes in his Batsuit, shredding its integrity. Echo and Query continued their aerial dance around him, swooping in and trying to further wrap him up in their silken web. Batman backhanded Query on her next approach, sending her spinning and rolling downward until the silk wrapped around her waist arrested her tumbling fall. Batman continued to climb, dragging the crimson silk up with him as he did. He could see the long, black streaks of the Batsuit fluid staining the cloth that trailed down below him.

Automatic weapon fire erupted below, and bullets sprayed the ceiling just above him. He looked around quickly and found what was needed: the motorized hub of the mobile. Everything turned on this large mechanism bolted to the ceiling. Batman reached one of the crossbars of the mobile and pulled himself up. Echo grabbed hold of his booted foot, trying to drag him off the beam, but he kicked hard, sending her spinning off, too.

His father's voice continued through the hall.

"... the guests had no idea what had actually happened. They all believed that I had been the one in the costume ... that I had been the heroic figure who had defeated the Moxon gang and gone to apprehend Julius Moxon ..."

Batman reached the central mechanism, pulling several small C-4 balls and remote detonators from his Utility Belt. He began pressing them next to the eight bolts that mounted the mechanism to the ceiling.

He had five of them in place when Echo and Query both pounced on him at once. Echo had his neck in a vice grip with her right arm. Query had attached herself to one of his legs and was trying to pry him free of his foothold on the crossbeam.

It will just have to be enough.

Batman looked away and triggered the explosives.

The small devices sheared off the bolt heads, peppering the front of his Batsuit. The reactive armor engaged but he could feel the impacts. The Batsuit was failing. The force had caused the plate to partially pull away from the ceiling. The sudden jolt and noise of the explosions took both Echo and Query by surprise, each loosening her grip. It was all Batman needed. He shook both the women off him and sent them tumbling down into the silk wrapped around their waists. When it grew taut, they rebounded slightly almost fifteen feet below the ceiling.

"... the man I knew as Denholm Sinclair was now lost to me ... certainly lost to Martha. He had become this abhorrent monster calling himself the Disciple and naming me as his inspiration and creator ..."

Batman pulled himself up, gripping the bar with both hands. The Batsuit alarms were pinging in his ear. He swung his legs upward around the crossbar, planting his feet against the ceiling on either side of the damaged mount in an inverted squat, and then held tight to the bar as he pushed with his legs.

"I knew he was going to kill Julius Moxon and once he was done with that he would return to the party and kill again . . . in my costume and in my guise . . ."

The mounting bracket groaned with the sudden load. The Batsuit alarm became more insistent.

Suddenly, the mount gave way, pulling a large plaster part of the ceiling down with it. The mobile, its multiple crossbeams, long silk bolts, Amanda, Echo, Query, and all the suspended mannequins came crashing downward onto the ballroom floor.

Batman barely managed to roll as he hit the floor, allowing the remaining power in his Batsuit to dissipate the energy of his fall. He turned on his feet only to find Query, Echo, and their swordsmen struggling to escape their own web. He stepped in among them, binding each where he found them in his zip ties and, when necessary, using his fist to explain why they shouldn't resist. All the while his father's voice resounded in the hall.

" . . . So I made myself his next target. I could think of nothing else that might lure him away from the Kane Mansion. My original thought . . . so far as it went . . . was to lead him away from the Kane household and back to my own estate. Heaven knows there were plenty of weapons left behind by my father . . . but even with him badly wounded I could not get far enough ahead . . ."

He found Amanda among the mannequins. He pulled out a knife, cut her cables, and wrapped her in one of the red silks so that the Batsuit's fluid would not stain her. He picked her up, draped her over his shoulder, and turned to follow the sound of his father's voice.

It led him to the bandstand. There was a vintage Wollensak 1515 reel-to-reel tape recorder running seven-inch reels in long-play mode. A stack of weathered Scotch audio tape boxes were stacked next to the recorder, the top-most box open and empty. The tape machine itself was connected to a large speaker that was still sounding throughout the hall.

"I ran down Peterson's Ravine. I could hear him close at my heels. I was panicked and uncertain as to just what . . ."

Batman reached forward, pressing the stop button on the far right-hand side.

The tape reels stopped moving. The sound died in the hall.

Batman looked down at the tape reel. The clear plastic was yellowing, as was the label, but it was still legible.

T. Wayne—Apocalypse Observations / #3 of 12.

There were seven boxes next to the tape machine . . . including the empty one.

Batman pushed the rewind lever to the left. The tape spooled backward onto the reel. Batman pushed the selector back into the middle just as the tape cleared the recording/playback heads, slapping freely only a few revolutions before stopping. He removed the reel from the spindle and set it back in the empty box, closing the lid. Then he stepped over to one of the unconscious Confederate soldiers lying bound on the floor of the ruined ballroom and took his map bag from him. He returned to the record, Amanda still over his shoulder, and stuffed the tapes into the bag.

His hands were shaking the entire time.

He walked toward the soaped pane of the French doors, opened them, and walked into the chill night. With Amanda and the tapes, he walked across the weed-choked grounds into the bordering woods and down into Peterson's Ravine, and its cave.

Cave / Wayne Manor / Bristol / 11:59 p.m. / October 26, 1958

Thomas was soaked to the skin.

The old underground lake that had created the caverns in the first place had long since shifted. The cavern entrance itself became the drainage point for the lake, a river flowing out into the ravine beyond. The entrance was easy enough to find simply by following the river, though, and being in the untamed area of the Wayne Estate, only a few had discovered it. Thomas hated the place with his soul but was desperate. He plunged blindly into its maw, splashing noisily up the waterway and into the darkness.

"You cannot escape yourself, Thomas!" Disciple's voice echoed slightly as it came into the cavern from behind Dr. Wayne. "I've grown beyond you now . . . become something greater than you had hoped or knew possible."

Thomas knew that was, unfortunately, partially true. He had seen the carnage in the laboratory and read the reports. The virus he and Richter had unleashed had unpredictable results in its genetic reprogramming, but in general, the results were consistent: they enhanced and magnified a number of set characteristics. Those infected seemed to be more flamboyant, taking on extreme dress, uniforms, or costumes as an outward expression of their inner vision of themselves. Certain genetic predispositions also were exaggerated disproportionately—strength or dexterity or mental acuity in certain areas or reasoning. Ethics, morality, and social connections—the primary focus of their behavioral modification—proved to be the most volatile.

A volatility that was, in Thomas's medical opinion, quite likely to get him killed.

I can fix this. If I can just reason with Denholm . . . or at least force him

*back into the laboratory. Jarvis secured it, but it's still there. Then I could fix
this—fix Denholm and the others and make it right.*

The virus had not yet jumped from the hosts—he was sure of
that. There were only four members of the Apocalypse, and no
additional reports of other vigilantes or aberrant criminals, for
that matter. The disease seemed to be restricted to the blood-
stream thus far. All he had to do was contain them, hold them,
and find a cure. All he had to do—

"Thomas, what's wrong?" Denholm's voice echoed into the
cavern. It was closer now, near the entrance. "You wanted me to
be *good*. You wanted me to exact *justice* on the guilty, didn't you?"

Thomas felt his way further into the cavern. He knew instinctively that there was a small alcove just to the right of the
entrance. His father had forced him enough times to find it in
the pitched blackness of the cave. He swallowed hard and then
plunged down the tunnel, his right fingertips running along
the cold, slick, and irregular surface of the wall until it dropped
away into an abyss to his right. Thomas stepped into the void
and stopped.

He could hear the bats waking.

"That's what I've done, Thomas," Denholm's voice rebounded
throughout the cavern. "I've discovered the guilty of Gotham,
and it was a revelation . . . a pure, brilliant revelation. Thugs,
mobsters, thieves, robbers . . . they're just the branches,
Thomas. They're leaves that vanish in the fall and are born again
in spring."

Thomas felt awkwardly behind himself, hoping the cavern
wall was still where he remembered it . . . where his father had
forced him to find it.

"You know," Disciple said in a smooth, low voice just above
the sound of the river water rushing around him, "I grieve for
the innocent, too. Those orphans that died in the fire—it was

a terrible tragedy, a crime of unprecedented horror and callous cruelty. I wept for them. I wept for them all."

Patrick Wayne had a single refuge from his life. It had been coming down to this cave, where he could hide his drunken rages in the darkness and take them out on the bats overhead. He had returned often right up until the day he died, always leaving the tools of his private fury well oiled and ready.

"And I died with them, Thomas; you made sure of that," Denholm chuckled. "You burned away the impurities in my dark soul, killed everything that I once had been. Now I'll do the same for others, Thomas, just as you wanted me to do."

Thomas felt the cold, smooth steel behind him just where his father had left it.

"I've arisen like a phoenix from the ashes you made of me, dear Thomas," Denholm's voice resounded through the cavern.

Thomas ran his fingers down the barrel. He felt the mounts old Patrick had installed just above the action bar. The corrugated tube fixed parallel to the barrel, flaring wide at the end. The glass lens felt intact. He could only hope the batteries were still good.

"And who will pay for the screams of those children? Celia, who embezzled the money in the first place?"

Thomas gritted his teeth, his hands shaking as they closed around the mounted flashlight, feeling for the switch.

"Or perhaps Martha," Denholm murmured. "Dear Martha Kane, whose blind desire to assuage her own guilty conscience provided the money that fueled the fires of greed and desperation? Yes . . . she played a part in those children's deaths. She must pay, too."

In a motion, Thomas picked up the shotgun, using its upward momentum to cycle the pump-action. He held the heavy weapon against his hip with his right hand as he used his left to shove the switch forward along the length of the flashlight mounted to the gun barrel. The light brightened at once, its beam cutting a narrow circle of illumination through the void.

Denholm turned toward the light.

He was smiling at his prey from the other side of the cavern, the underground river flowing between them.

"Stand up. Damn it, boy!"

His father's voice emerged through the ringing in Thomas's ears.

"That's no way to hold a gun!"

"It's going to be all right, Denholm," Thomas said, his voice lacking the strength of his words even as he said them from behind the barrel of the shotgun. The light from the flashlight continued to dance shifting shadows across Denholm's still-masked face. "I'm going to take you somewhere . . . somewhere safe . . . and we'll figure this out. I'll make it right—"

"Make it RIGHT?" Denholm said through a vicious smile. "You made ME to make it RIGHT!"

"Hell or high water, boy, I'm going to make a man out of you!"

"Denholm, please," Thomas said, the light flickering atop the shotgun. His hands were sweating. "Just come with me. We'll go up to the house. I can help you."

"No, Thomas," Denholm's smile was malevolent. "It's me who's going to help you. It's in my blood—you put it in my blood."

"What?"

"The virus," Denholm said. "The gift. It lives in my veins. I'm going to give you that gift, Thomas. I'm going to give it to the world."

"There are only two kinds of people in this world: the hunters and the hunted—and you had better make up your mind right now that you're going to hunt!"

Denholm took a step into the river, the water splashing up

around the costume tights. The ridiculous, scalloped cape flared behind him as he moved. The scarf mask had bunched up at the side of his head, forming small, pointed folds. In Thomas's nervous state, he looked like a Sunday comics version of a bat.

"It's kill or be killed out there—not like that comic book world you live in!"

"Denholm, you're not well," Thomas said, his voice quavering. The gun felt slippery in his hands. The old batteries in the flashlight mounted next to the barrel were failing, causing the pool of light around Denholm to yellow and dim. "Please, just come with me and I can cure this."

"Come with you? But I've come *for* you, Thomas—my dear, doubting Thomas. Never truly committed to the faith of the convictions you espoused . . . always questioning yourself. But I've come to end your doubt, Thomas," Denholm the Disciple spoke from the dimming pool of light around him. "I've come to purge you of all that, Thomas, just as I've purged the souls of so many others. I'll purify you, too, dear Thomas. You can be free of guilt, free of fear. I've ushered many tortured souls into that peace . . . a peace that you brought to me, dear Thomas . . . and which I now return to you."

"And you're gonna learn how to kill today, son. You're gonna kill something!"

Thomas remembered to stand across the weapon, bracing against the back foot, pressing his shoulder hard into the stock. "Please, Denholm . . . I just want to help."

"You're sick, Thomas," Denholm snarled. "I'm going to *cure* you!"

"Be a man! Show me you're a man!"

Thomas had released the safety without thinking.

The cartoon bat leaped at him from the water's edge.

"DO IT!"

Thomas did not hear the gun discharge. He felt the sudden blow to his shoulder, his body bending and absorbing the recoil of the blast. His eyes opened to see the gaping hole in the costume's chest, the crimson stain blossoming outward like a tide across the cloth. Denholm reeled with the impact, staggering back to the river's edge.

"Kill or be killed . . ."

Tears were streaming down Thomas's face. Part of his mind was examining the wound in Denholm's chest, spinning through the steps necessary to have any chance of saving the patient. Broken ribs . . . punctured lungs . . . internal hemorrhaging . . .

"Atta boy! Show me!"

Thomas pumped a second shell into the breach, barely in time. Denholm, enraged, charged at him again, blood flowing down his chest, streaming from between his bared teeth.

The shotgun's roar echoed throughout the cavern. Thomas was not nearly as ready for it this time as before, the kick of the weapon nearly wrenching it out of his hands. The impact caught Denholm in the shoulder, spinning him around. He caught himself before falling, turned again, and screamed.

Thomas had regained his footing, the shell casings flying out of the ejector from the pump shotgun. Thomas yelled with every shot, his voice drowned out by the stream of explosions from the barrel of the gun. After the sixth shell ejected, Thomas pulled the trigger on an empty barrel.

Denholm was gratefully face down in the river, no longer recognizable from the carnage dealt by Thomas's hand. His body floated with the river a short way before hanging on the rocks at the cave's entrance.

Thomas walked out where the river flowed around the body of Denholm Sinclair, the shotgun now held loosely in his right hand. Thomas had promised to take care of him for Martha. It had all gone so wrong. He looked down at the body; the water was dark in the moonlight.

Denholm's virus-infected blood was washing down the stream, toward the Gotham River and the lit towers of the city beyond.

Batcave / Wayne Manor / Bristol / 8:59 p.m. / Present Day

" . . . ended any hope of containing the Richter virus to those who had been infected. As I watched his blood flow down the stream I realized the effects of the virus could be spread by contact with the infected blood or through other similar agents. I also knew that there were three more carriers still loose in the city . . ."

The mansion phone was ringing.

Bruce sat at his terminal in the Batcave listening to the continuation of the tape. It had taken him a while to locate an old reel-to-reel deck, but now it was playing the tape back into the cave. He had shed the heavily damaged Batsuit; its power was completely drained and the exomuscular system completely compromised. He was hearing the voice of a father he now realized he had never really known.

The mansion phone continued to ring.

" . . . Jarvis once again insisted on taking care of the problem, and I have wondered since if there was some ulterior motive behind his efforts. He certainly is the one man who had more leverage on me than I care to acknowledge. I suppose part of my reasons for making this record is so that my sons may not be threatened after my passing—so that the blame and the responsibility for all that has happened should rest on my shoulders rather than theirs . . ."

Bruce was slowly aware of the sound, wondering vaguely why Alfred did not pick up the phone. Then he remembered. He toggled the tape machine to stop and picked up the receiver.

"Wayne Estate," he said flatly.

"Yes, I . . . uh . . . I apologize for calling, but I was wondering if you might help me. I'm trying to get in touch with someone."

"Nurse Doppel?" Bruce said the words more as a statement than a question.

"Yes! I'm—is this Mr. Grayson?"

"Yes, everyone else is . . . out," Bruce answered. Alfred was gone and he was feeling his loss keenly. Turning in his chair, he gazed down at the video image of the unconscious Amanda lying on the divan in the reproduction of the study nearby. "Apparently I'm also the chief cook and bottle washer here now . . . not to mention babysitter."

"Oh, Mr. Grayson, I'm so relieved to find you," Doppel said over the phone. "I did exactly as you asked, but I haven't heard anything back from Amanda since I dropped off that book. She hasn't called back since and—"

"You can relax, Nurse Doppel," Bruce said, rubbing his hand across his eyes. "She's here with me. She's unconscious at the moment."

"You shouldn't worry about that too much," she replied. "That may just be an effect of her not receiving her medication on time."

"You would know better than I would." Bruce's voice sounded tired in his own ears. "Other than that, I don't think she's been harmed."

"Oh, thank God!" Doppel responded. "Can you bring her home? I've no car and without her medication . . ."

Bruce froze in his chair, staring with angry bewilderment down the metal catwalk that led to the elevator entrance to the cave. His eyes were fixed on something he knew for a fact had not been there when he had left for the Kane Mansion earlier that same evening.

There, propped against the railing, gleaming clean and well oiled, was his grandfather's shotgun.

"I'll bring her," Bruce said. "I'll be there in about twenty minutes."

His eyes fixed on the weapon.

It was the last thing he remembered seeing before he awoke.

CHAPTER TWENTY-FOUR

ATONEMENT

Academy Theater / Park Row / Gotham / 10:35 p.m. / Present Day

Bruce Wayne came slowly back to consciousness. He saw a bright blur in front of him surrounded by darkness. Thin, tinny music echoed around him, muffled as though by distance.

I was going to take Amanda Richter home. There was a phone call . . . Nurse Doppel . . . then my grandfather's shotgun . . .

A spray of sparkling laughter sounded in his left ear.

"Oh, Thomas, it's too funny!"

Bruce turned his head slowly, tentatively. He tried to focus his eyes. He seemed to be having trouble controlling his movements.

The hazy silhouette of a head atop a long, tapered neck filled his vision. Platinum blond hair shifted in and out of focus. The vague head tilted back, laughing again.

Bruce closed his eyes hard and then blinked them open.

The shape next to him came into focus. She was sitting just to his left in a row of theater seats while she laughed at something playing on the screen.

He shook his head, trying to clear it, and then looked again.

She was another version of Amanda Richter. Her long hair

was now piled up onto her head into a bouffant style vaguely reminiscent of the late 1960s. Amanda's makeup was carefully done to match the emerald green dress.

Bruce's eyes widened with the shock of recognition, his vision suddenly clearing.

The dark stains were still visible in the satin, radiating in an irregular pattern from the entry hole punched through the high scooped collar just above the left breast. The stain radiated undisturbed down past the cinched waist, where it broke up just above the knee into smaller patches and splatters.

It was her dress . . . IS her dress. Mother?

She turned to face him, her pupils dilated and unfocused. "Oh, Thomas, this really takes me back!"

Bruce turned to the screen. It had originally been a silent film, though he could hear a tinny piano orchestration playing from the theater speakers. Douglas Fairbanks leaped up onto the balcony after having defeated Noah Beery and started making eyes at Marguerite de la Motte.

It's that same damn movie. We came to the art theater retrospective that night. It was a charity event for the Gotham Arts Council.

Bruce looked quickly down. The tuxedo coat was unbuttoned, exposing the pleated, formal shirt beneath. There was a terrible dark stain on this garment, too, with two finger-sized holes within two inches of each other in the chest.

My father's tuxedo.

Bruce's hands began to shake. A short figure was seated on his right. He turned slowly toward it, dreading what might be there.

The Scarface ventriloquist dummy stared back up at him. It was no longer in its customary gangster pinstripe suit, but now wore a small tuxedo which was slightly too large for him. Bruce recognized it at once as his own, when he was a boy. He knew it from the pattern of the stains that were burned into his childhood.

Bruce tried to stand up at once, but his legs were unsteady beneath him.

"Sit down, Thomas!" Amanda urged. "You're ruining the show."

Bruce collapsed back down into the seat. He was finding it difficult to breathe.

Douglas Fairbanks stood next to Marguerite de la Motte and rakishly spoke to the cheering crowd below. A title card then appeared on the screen.

Have you seen this one?

Suddenly the film jumped on the screen. There was a loud pop and a grating sound. Then the scene changed to another crowd—also silent, and this time without the thin background music. It was the Kane Mansion ballroom . . . and Bruce realized he was seeing the footage of the ballroom shot that night by the newsman. There were scratch marks running through the film, but the image was still clear. There was the hodgepodge costume that looked more like a bat than any hero of popular imagination struggling against the Moxon mob at the end of the ballroom. There was Lewis Moxon being knocked unconscious.

"Oh, Thomas," Amanda cooed, wrapping herself around Bruce's left arm. "I never really saw you before that night."

"Amanda," Bruce said, "we've got to get out of here."

"Thomas! The movie's almost over—besides, that's *you*," Amanda purred back at him. "I think I started falling for you right then, when you punched poor Lewis. I don't think he ever forgave you."

The end of the footage grew bright and spotty, and then the sound rumbled once again, dramatic marching music playing through the hall. A new title, this one animated although still in black-and-white. It proclaimed, *"News on the March,"* and the title was shouted by an announcer's voice. The music continued as a second title card popped onto the screen.

NEWS ON THE MARCH

END OF AN APOCALYPSE
Vigilante Murderess Meets Gruesome End

FEBRUARY 1962

Bruce drew in a measured breath, his eyes fixed to the screen.
It's a message . . . for me . . .

"Blackgate Penitentiary!" the announcer continued in dramatic and deeply resonant tones as old stock footage of the prison walls splayed onto the screen. "Judgment isle for the first of the mass murderers known as the Apocalypse. Here, within these walls, came the grim end of Adele 'The Chanteuse' Lafontaine."

The newsreel footage showed the Chanteuse being led up the stairs onto the elevated gallows frame and the rope being affixed around her neck. She was wearing the same distinctive green coat she was always pictured in.

"Tried and convicted of sensational and often deadly crimes, Lafontaine was sentenced to be hung at midnight for her crimes, but met an even more shocking fate. Due to an error by the executioner, the length of her fall was miscalculated . . ."

Amanda averted her eyes.

" . . . and the result was a nearly complete decapitation of the criminal. It was too long a drop and too quick a stop for the woman who was once hailed as a vigilante hero and had since become one of the most flamboyant murderers in Gotham City. One Apocalypse down . . . three more to go!"

Bruce looked down suddenly at the Scarface dummy staring

back up at him from the seat on his right. He knew something of the history of Scarface. Those in the underworld swore the dummy was cursed, and the legend was that it had been carved from the wood of the Blackgate gallows by an inmate named Donnegan. Donnegan was a cellmate of Arnold Wesker, who escaped Blackgate with the carved figure. Wesker circulated among the underworld in the early '60s, right about the time the more extreme villains of Gotham began cropping up. Bruce stared back at Scarface.

Are you the source? Every super-criminal in the city infected with the virus you carried from the blood of the Chanteuse? That would mean every costumed freak who . . .

"We're leaving," Bruce said, standing up. "Now!"

"But the show isn't over, Tommy!" Amanda complained, gesturing toward the screen.

"I know how it ends," Bruce snarled, pulling Amanda to her feet.

He pulled her along behind him down the row, his feet still feeling a little unstable beneath him.

"What about Bruce?" Amanda wailed, reaching back toward the ventriloquist dummy.

Bruce ignored her. Many of the seats were in disrepair, hampering their passage. The theater had been closed for some time. He knew because he had bought it and closed it.

The projector continued to run from the booth high up on the back wall as he dragged Amanda behind him. He reached the rear doors of the theater and pushed against them. They moved slightly and then stopped. Bruce let go of Amanda's hand, gripping the inside edge of one of the double doors with his fingertips and pulling the double-hinged door toward him. It swung open easily . . . revealing a solid steel plate welded to the frame that filled the entire exit.

"Damn it!" Bruce turned, searching the room for an exit—any exit—except the one he knew would be open to him. The newsreels continued to play on the screen, their sounds filling the dilapidated theater and the next slate catching his eye.

NEWS ON THE MARCH

WAYNE FOUNDATION
CRUSADE AGAINST GERMAN MEASLES
All Citizens Tested for Virus in Face of Outbreak

AUGUST 1965

"The national outbreak of rubella—commonly known as the German Measles—has been ravaging communities from coast to coast . . . but today, thanks to the generosity of local philanthropist Dr. Thomas Wayne, Gotham has a new weapon against this scourge: a quick test for the virus for every citizen of the city and its environs."

Thomas Wayne smiled from the torn theater screen, waving at the camera. This was followed by a cascade of shots showing medical professionals drawing blood from people of many different ages and professions.

"An invaluable aide to possible quarantine efforts, Wayne Enterprises is funding this program without the use of tax dollars. Hospitals, clinics, and even your local doctor are all doing their part to make sure every man, woman and—that's right, Suzie—child in Gotham can benefit from these tests . . ."

Bruce snatched Amanda's hand once more into his own, bringing her with him toward the next exit as he turned over the newsreel in his mind.

The virus testing in '65 had to have been a cover—a façade. There was a rubella outbreak at the time and there were concerns about it, but the disease itself did not warrant a citywide testing for the virus. EVERYONE had the virus. The only reason to test the entire city was if someone was looking for something else. It was entirely funded by Wayne Enterprises—so his father must have been on the hunt, trying to find and isolate anyone who might have had contact with the Richter virus. Anyone with amped-up emotions, obsessive focus, or extremes in dress and behavior . . .

The second set of back exit doors also proved to be sealed. Each of the side exits proved blocked as well, until he came to the one he knew would open—the one that had opened so many years before.

Bruce turned to the woman wearing the last dress his mother wore in life. "Amanda! Listen to me!"

"What?" The woman seemed confused and dazed. "Tommy, who are you talking to?"

"Listen to me!" Bruce said, shaking her slightly. "I want you to stay in here, you understand?"

"Take me home, Tommy," Amanda murmured. "I always loved you the best. You know that, Tommy."

"Yes . . . yes, I know that," Bruce said. "I've got to . . . go out and take care of something. I want you to go back and sit with Bruce . . . you understand?"

Amanda lifted her face up toward Bruce, her eyes glazed but her smile beaming. "I . . . think so."

What if we had stayed a little longer? What if we had left by another door? What if . . . What if . . .

"You go back, you understand?" Bruce said, his voice heavy with emotion. "I'll come back for you."

"Sure, Tommy," Amanda said, patting him on the cheek. "You always take care of me."

Bruce watched her make her way back into the theater. She passed down the row once more and sat down next to the Scarface dummy, cradling her arm around it affectionately.

Bruce passed through the side curtain and came to the double-exit fire doors.

Crime Alley, he knew, lay just beyond.

He crouched down low, drew in a breath, grabbed the handles, and threw them open.

Crime Alley / Park Row / Gotham / 10:46 p.m. / Present Day

The territory was horribly familiar.

Bruce slammed the doors open, rolling quickly to the right. The alley was narrow, but he remembered there was a parking alcove to the right of the exit. There had been a car parked there that night of August 15, 1971 . . .

Bruce rolled against the curved bumper of the car. It was a 1966 Pontiac Grand Prix—white with a black roof—identical to the one that had parked in the same spot that night. He spun around in his crouch between the car and the wall of the alley, his senses heightened.

Nothing moved.

From the distance down the alley, he could hear a song playing. He remembered it as having being sung by an artist with the unlikely name of Gilbert O'Sullivan.

Footsteps approached from down the alleyway.

Bruce slipped around the car, moving down the opposite wall back toward the alley. There was a large dumpster there that gave him cover from whoever was approaching and, as importantly, was placed such that there was a dark pocket of shadow that could hide his presence. He slipped into the darkness—he owned the night—and tensed. He was prepared to take down this nemesis who had chosen this place—this *sacred* place—to torture him.

The figure stepped into the harsh circle of light cast downward from the exit-door lamp.

"Hello? H-h-hello?"

Bruce, astonished, reached out of the shadows and dragged the woman into his protected corner of the alley. "Nurse Doppel?"

"Mr. Grayson!"

"What the hell are you doing here?"

"I . . . I got a message," she said. She wore jeans and a jacket against the cold, and the same sensible shoes he had always seen her in. "It said that if I wanted Miss Amanda back, I should meet you here. I thought I heard someone behind me in the alley—"

"It isn't safe . . . you've got to get out of here," Bruce said, scanning the alley but seeing no movement. "It may be too late as it is."

"No, Mr. Wayne," said Nurse Doppel. "I think you're exactly on time."

It was 10:47 p.m.

The muzzle of the 9 mm semiautomatic pistol caught on Bruce's ribcage as the woman stepped back, causing the bullet to pass under his left lung. It was a hollow-point round expanding on impact and tearing tissue, sinew, organs, and veins in its short, growing path. The impact from the shell threw Bruce backward against the dumpster. He pitched forward, his hands closing over the gaping wound in his father's shirt, fresh blood spilling out over the old stain.

CHAPTER TWENTY-FIVE

DEAD BURY THE DEAD

Crime Alley / Park Row / Gotham / 10:47 p.m. / Present Day

Bruce struggled, pushing himself across the pavement, but he could not seem to get his legs under him. His hands tore at this shirt, the old, brittle fabric separating easily. He felt for the wound. The entry was not large, but the pain was excruciating. He knew the real damage was deeper than it appeared and far more extensive. He put pressure on the wound, but the blood kept coming.

Bruce reached up behind his right ear, triggering the subcutaneous transponder.

Alfred will come. He'll be monitoring . . . Oh, God!

No one would be listening. No reassuring voice sounded through the bones of his ear. He was alone.

"Help!" Bruce's shouts echoed down the alley. "Help me! Please! Somebody . . ."

"In this part of town, at this time of night?" the woman laughed. "Who are you expecting . . . Batman?"

Bruce Wayne knew that his clock was ticking now and that he was rapidly running out of time. "Ellen—"

"Marion . . . I'm Marion," the woman replied.

"Impossible!" Bruce spat blood as he pulled his knees up under himself. "Marion Richter died in Arkham in 1979. You would have to be—"

"Almost seventy years old?" Marion smiled, circling Bruce with the 9 mm in both her hands still trained on him. "Didn't I tell you the Richter women all carried their age well? It's an inherited genetic trait . . . one that my father's research greatly enhanced."

There was far more blood on the ground around him than he would have expected. Though his knees were under him, he seemed to be having far more difficulty straightening up than he should. "You? You have the Richter virus?"

Marion arched her eyebrow. "Of course . . . don't you?"

Bruce raised his head, glaring at Marion.

"Oh, poor Bruce," she chuckled. "Why do you think I've gone to all this trouble? I've done you a great service, Mr. Wayne: I've shown you the truth about yourself. Your family robbed me of everything—even the memory of my great father. He was erased, his existence forgotten along with his research by everyone . . . everyone except me, Mr. Wayne. Everyone except me!"

Bruce reached back with his left hand. The back of his father's coat was torn and slick with gore and blood.

Exit wound. I wonder how bad off I really am? Joe Chill stood under this same lamppost. Now I'm bleeding out into my father's coat.

Bruce tried to lunge up to his feet, but his muscles were not responding normally. He reached toward Marion with both his bloodied hands, surging toward her, but his father's dress shoes slipped in the blood on the ground. Bruce fell forward, the right side of his face slamming into the asphalt.

"Your father created monsters," Bruce croaked with a strange gurgling sound in his voice.

The gun barked again. Bruce screamed with the searing pain in his right leg.

"My father was a man five decades ahead of his time!" Marion shouted as she continued to hold the gun steady in her hands. "False memory implantation, chemical thought transference, base motivational modifiers all achieved through genetic programming and carried by a virus . . . ALL were his genius. I've spent my lifetime trying to understand his work. Thanks to modern equipment, I've even managed to perfect it! We'll have the utopia of my father's dreams. I'll bring it about, and when the day comes that crime is finally cured and peace reigns in Gotham, my father's name . . . *my* father's name . . . will be honored and shine like a beacon of hope to the world."

"Tommy?"

Amanda! I told her to stay in the theater!

"Better hurry, sister," Marion said. "The curtain's about to fall."

"Tommy! No!" Amanda said, rushing over to Bruce from the open theater exit. She fell kneeling next to Bruce, his blood soaking into his mother's death dress.

"May I present the *former* Miss Ellen Doppel," Marion said.

Bruce shook as the woman he knew as Amanda sobbed over him. "Tommy, tell me what to do!"

I feel so cold . . . and I don't feel anything at all . . .

"She's my masterwork," Marion sighed. "When my sister lay in Arkham I managed to harvest some of her memories before she died. This version of Amanda is a bit confused, I'll grant you, as I had to implant a number of false memories as well in order to reel you in. I'll straighten her out once you're out of the way."

"And so you plan to start this utopia of yours by torturing and killing me?" Bruce grimaced.

"Not just killing you, Mr. Wayne," Marion responded. "No,

you see, as a mental health professional, I felt an obligation to kill your soul as well as your body. I thought it important that you understand the depth of your father's betrayal—of Gotham, of my father, of your mother, and of you."

"What the hell are you talking about?" Bruce cried.

"Your father's cover-up," Marion answered. "The Wayne dynasty used its power, money, and influence to bury all its dirty laundry . . . and buried my father in the process, buried my family . . . and eventually buried my mother and sister . . . but it wasn't enough to destroy us. The initial virus spread to six prime carriers. Your father had to hunt them down as well. Without them, the virus would eventually mutate with every iteration, the genetic memory encoding would become corrupted, and the virus would die off. But as long as the original six lived, the virus could survive through them and that your father could not allow. He even patched things up with his old friend Lew Moxon, so that when the last of the six were found, they could all be taken care of quietly. Of course, *your* father only knew of the four Apocalypse and that *my* father had been infected."

"Who was the sixth?" Bruce was having trouble breathing.

"Unfortunately, while the equipment in the laboratory may have been state-of-the-art for the 1950s, it was inadequate to contain my father's work," Marion replied. "I suppose your father hoped Moxon would have his henchmen capture the prime carriers, but Moxon contracted a killer to take care of the problem for him. I think you probably know him . . . Joe Chill."

Punctured lung. Missed the heart, but the bleeding is bad. May have nicked an artery. Need to stop the bleeding . . . Getting cold.

"I wonder if your father knew as he lay where you're lying now," Marion mused, "that he had contracted his own killing?"

Bruce closed his eyes.

"Please, Tommy!" Amanda wailed. "It's me . . . Martha! Don't leave me! Don't—"

"So we pay for the sins of our fathers?" Bruce whispered hoarsely.

"One of us does," Marion said, lowering the 9 mm to Bruce's temple.

"NO!" Amanda screamed. The woman leaped up in the stained green formal, shoving Marion's hand aside just as the gun fired. The hollow-point projectile slammed into the asphalt, burying itself even as it flattened from the impact. Amanda— now Martha—launched herself at Marion, her fingers scratching Marion's hands as she clawed for the weapon. Marion stumbled backward toward the trash bin, shocked by the unexpected fury of Amanda's onslaught. Amanda threw herself into Marion without hesitation, slamming the older woman against the trash bin. The force pushed the air out of Marion's lungs.

The 9 mm Browning pistol fell, skittering across the asphalt of the alley and coming to rest in front of Bruce's face. He stared, blinking at the weapon.

Am I the monster? Have I become what I hate?

The weapon lay within his reach.

"Tommy! Help!" Amanda screamed.

Marion broke free of Amanda's clutches, lunging for the gun.

This is who I am . . . This is who I chose to be . . .

Bruce grabbed the gun . . . and slid it away from him with all the strength he had remaining, drawing in a painful breath.

"Martha!" Bruce yelled. "Help me!"

Marion fell to the ground where the gun had been moments before. She quickly got to her feet, turned to retrieve the weapon . . . and faced Amanda, who was holding the gun.

"Get away from him!" Amanda screeched.

Somewhere in Amanda's confused layers of false and implanted memories, she must have fired a handgun. She held the weapon rock solid in both hands and was braced to shoot.

Marion stood slowly upright, her hands held open in front of her as she worked hard to keep her voice calm. "Be still, sister! I'm Marion. It's almost finished . . . and then we'll be free."

"Free?" Amanda giggled the words madly. "You've killed my husband! You've killed my *son!*"

"No, *I've* killed our ghosts, dear sister," Marion said through a gentle smile. "I've killed the last man who stands in our way. The world will remember what they have done to us—we'll *make* them remember—and the Waynes will haunt us no more. I'll have you back with me, Amanda . . . and we'll be free."

Amanda cocked her head suddenly, the curls of the bouffant hairstyle bouncing on the shoulders of the stained emerald dress.

"Amanda," she said with a curious smile. "Who's Amanda?"

Marion opened her mouth to speak, rushing forward.

Amanda pulled the trigger.

The 9 mm Browning bucked in Amanda's hands. Marion was stopped by the impact of the shell at once, staggering backward. Her sensible shoes slipped slightly in the pooling blood around Bruce, but she regained her footing. Dark crimson was blossoming on her jacket. She screamed, "No, Amanda! Not now!"

"You killed him! You killed him!" Amanda screamed again and again as the Browning muzzle flared repeatedly.

Marion jerked with the next three shots before the impacts drove her back off her feet and she fell to the ground.

Still, Amanda continued to fire, moving toward the fallen form of Marion Richter. The cartridges continued to fly out of the handgun until the bolt stopped in the open position after the eleventh shot.

The last of the shell casings rang against the pavement.

Smoke drifted from the muzzle of the gun.

Marion Richter lay shattered and unmoving on the ground.

Amanda stood over the woman, her eyes wide. She blinked and then looked at the gun as though she had never seen it before.

"Amanda," Bruce groaned. "Get help! Hurry . . ."

Amanda's hand went limp, the weapon clattering to the ground. She cocked her head to one side, staring down at the gory mess at her feet.

"Ellen?" she murmured.

"Martha!" Bruce could barely speak. "Get . . . get help."

"Marion?" Amanda whispered. Suddenly, she threw back her head and screeched. "Marion! Where am I? Who am I? You have to tell me, Marion! You have to *tell* me!"

Amanda collapsed onto the ground, kneeling over the blood-streaked face of Marion Richter and screaming at the dead woman. "Who am I, Marion? You promised to tell me who I was . . . I . . . Oh, Tommy! What has she done to you? Where is my child? . . . Father? When is father coming home? Marion, you promised father was coming home . . ."

Bruce shuddered. He had seen men die and wondered what they experienced. Amanda, Martha, Ellen—all of them had vanished into a madwoman who no longer was anchored to any of them. Alfred was gone, and the ELT they had gone to such lengths to implant behind his ear would continue to broadcast his distress call on a frequency that now had no one listening to it. He lay in the alley where a young Master Wayne had died all those years ago only to die again.

"Alfred!" Bruce cried out. His vision was failing. "I need you!"

Father . . . Mother . . . we've a lot to talk about . . . a lot to forgive . . .

Bruce closed his eyes again. He knew it would be for the last time.

EPILOGUE

OBITUARY

Alfred Pennyworth stood within the center of Wayne Mausoleum and contemplated the column of moonlight that slanted in from the dome overhead. The structure resembled a small version of the Pantheon in Rome, complete with its own miniature oculus—a circular opening in the apex of the dome that allowed sunlight or moonlight into the chamber below. In the center of the floor, directly beneath the oculus, was a fountain arranged so that any rainwater that came in through the opening would gather into it. It required regular cleaning and maintenance, but Alfred did not mind the occasional intrusion among the dead. In many ways, he preferred it.

But his purpose tonight was not housekeeping. He was dressed in his finest suit and made sure his shoes had been polished to a mirror shine. He wore his camel-hair overcoat— the April weather was unseasonably cold, the aftereffect of a prolonged and difficult winter—and leather gloves. The rim of his bowler hat was now clutched in his right hand, while his left gripped a spray of flowers.

He stood before one of the crypts, gazing at the engraving in the stone.

BRUCE PATRICK WAYNE

FEBRUARY 19, 1963–

SON OF THOMAS AND MARTHA WAYNE

"I see they still haven't gotten around to putting in the deceased date," said the gruff voice behind him.

"One of those details I just haven't gotten around to, Commissioner," Alfred said, barely turning his head.

"Not that anyone is going to forget the date right away," James Gordon stepped up next to Alfred, his hands deep in his overcoat pockets. "August fifteenth—just over six months ago. It was quite a memorial service."

"You mean spectacle, don't you, Commissioner?" Alfred said, his eyes still fixed on the tomb. "I've never known so many people so anxious to get on the guest list for a funeral. You would have thought they all wanted him dead."

"I wasn't among them," Gordon replied, running his hand over his thick mustache.

Alfred gave the Commissioner a puzzled look. "My apologies, Commissioner. I thought I had included you on the guest list."

"Yes, you did," Gordon nodded, looking down at the ground. "And thank you, Alfred, for thinking of me, but . . . Well, I didn't want to say goodbye that way. He was a lot of things to a lot of people—good and bad—but to me he was just Bruce, a guy I knew with a quick smile who was generous to a fault and trying to cope with wealth and power he didn't ask for or particularly want. I didn't want to say goodbye that way—not with a big show and streamed mourning on the Internet. That's actually why I'm glad you asked me out here. It gives me a chance to say goodbye properly without having to worry about standing between some politician and a camera."

"I know what you mean," Alfred agreed. "It was a circus."

"I suppose you can hardly blame the moth for being attracted to the flame." Gordon shrugged with a sigh as he contemplated the tomb. "Bruce's death was international news for nearly two weeks before they ran out of things to say about him. The story had everything: fame, infamy, wealth, and power all brought down on the poor son of Gotham who died of a gunshot wound in the exact same place and same way his parents died over forty years before. Anyone who was anyone wanted to be seen as part of that kind of story."

"Half of them were here to be seen," Alfred corrected the Commissioner. "The other half most likely wanted to stick a pin in him to make sure he was dead."

"Then they were disappointed, I suppose," Gordon replied with a sad chuckle. "The casket being closed and all."

"You read the autopsy report," Alfred sniffed. "Several gunshots to the face. Horrible, really. The morticians simply gave up on reconstructing any reasonable likeness."

"Yes, well, that's why I asked to see you," Gordon continued. "Don't get me wrong . . . I appreciate the chance to come here, but why did you choose this place?"

"Because I like to think he's here somehow," Alfred replied wistfully. "I'd like to think what you have to say will bring his soul some peace."

Gordon glanced at the tomb, nodded, and went on. "We have a few things left to do to wrap up the investigation, but for the most part we think we have a clear picture of what happened. The Jane Doe you found at the scene remains just that. We haven't been able to identify her through our investigations and questioning her isn't going to help much. She changes personalities at the drop of a hat and claims to be everyone from Bruce Wayne's mother to a clinical psychologist who's been taken prisoner by a demon in her head. The shrinks at Arkham think that last one is a fixation on her therapist. Anyway, it appears she was living with the Doppel woman over on Pearl. Her prints are all over the weapon, along with some partials of the Richter woman. The ballistics were a solid match. We think they may have struggled over the gun. There was a lot of material in the Richter townhouse about Mr. Wayne, and we think the Jane Doe may have been stalking Bruce."

"What about the other woman—the other victim?" Alfred corrected himself.

"Ellen Doppel?" Gordon pulled out his notebook and pushed his glasses up his nose, but soon gave up trying to read in the soft blue moonlight illuminating the tomb. "Well, the gist of it is that she was living in the Richter townhouse because it had been left to her by the Richter family. CSU went over the house but didn't find anything except a weird stalker shrine in the library. The DA thinks Doppel had been trying to treat the Jane Doe, followed her into the alley, and was just in the wrong place at the wrong time. I understand Mr. Wayne had a habit of visiting that alley from time to time."

"Yes, Commissioner, a tradition which I hope to honor on his behalf," Alfred said. "So I suppose that's the end of it."

"Yes, as far as I am concerned," Gordon replied, pushing his hands back into his coat pockets. "It was decent of the man to leave you so much of the estate in his will."

"My employer was a most loving and generous man," Alfred nodded graciously. "Between Mr. Fox and I, we now hold a majority share in Wayne Enterprises."

"You gonna keep the name?" Gordon asked.

"That name has served Gotham well for some time," Alfred said. "I think it can still do so for a bit longer. The SEC is no longer interested in pursuing an investigation of the company; they could hardly press RICO charges against Master Wayne now that he is gone."

"Small good to come for so high a price," Gordon said. He stepped over to the tomb, placing his hand on the surface of the stone and resting it against the carved name.

"I'm sorry, Bruce," Gordon said. His voice became low and gruff, barely audible even in the stillness of the night. "I wish I had been there to help you. Goodbye, old friend."

Gordon turned, his head bowed down.

"Thank you for coming, Commissioner," Alfred nodded. "Take care on your way home."

"Sure," Gordon nodded to Alfred as he walked slowly from the tomb. "Call if you need anything, Alfred."

The new owner of Wayne Manor stood listening to the retreating footsteps of the police commissioner. When silence had once again descended on the tomb, he drew in a deep breath and turned to look up through the oculus to the starlit sky above.

"Did you hear that?" he said to the stars. "It's over."

"I did," answered a winged shape silhouetted against the stars. It descended in a whisper into the chamber, standing next to the old retainer.

"You have done an amazing job, Alfred," the shadow said. "Thank you."

"There's no need to thank me, Master—"

The shadow held up a warning hand.

"I meant to say there is no need to thank me," Alfred amended. "My father did not just teach me how to sweep the halls and dust the furniture. My training in England was not restricted to Eton. My father remained well connected with his OSS friends, and they served to, shall we say, broaden my education and vocational skills."

"You've demonstrated them well," the shape said in the darkness. "Why were you monitoring my frequency that night, Alfred?"

"Let's just say I don't give up easily," Alfred replied. "What about your own investigations?"

"Marion Richter was right," he answered. "The virus is a major contributing cause to the extreme type of criminal we face too often here in Gotham, but not *the* cause. It amplifies reactions and certain genetic abilities—but it doesn't *cause* criminals."

"You mean like Joker, sir?" Alfred asked.

"Interesting, isn't it?" the shadow mused. "Marion tried to coerce the Joker into helping her by manipulating his motivations. The one thing Joker cannot abide is control and order—the very things Marion was trying to instill in him. So he rebelled against Marion's programming and tried to save *me* from being drawn further into her web."

"And, I've been meaning to ask you . . ."

"No, Alfred," the shape replied. "I don't have the viral mutation. It wasn't passed to me."

"But, sir, I thought—"

"I am who I am because I've *chosen* this path, Alfred," the man said. "And now I've truly chosen it."

The shape stepped from the shadows into the moonlight. His cape flowed behind him as though it had a will of its own. The familiar cowl covered his head, rising to feral ears on either side. The symbol of a bat was fixed to the front of his exomuscular Batsuit.

Batman took a rose from Alfred's hand and laid it before one crypt.

MARTHA KANE WAYNE

DECEMBER 7, 1937–AUGUST 15, 1971

WIFE AND MOTHER

He then took a second rose and moved to the next vault. Here Batman paused and considered the inscription for a moment.

THOMAS ALAN WAYNE

NOVEMBER 26, 1935–AUGUST 15, 1971

HEALER, PHILANTHROPIST,
HUSBAND, AND FATHER

"Do you suppose we ever really know our parents, Alfred?" Batman asked.

"No, sir," Alfred responded. "And perhaps they are better left to live as we remember them rather than as who they really were."

Finally, Batman stopped at the third vault.

BRUCE PATRICK WAYNE

FEBRUARY 19, 1963–

SON OF THOMAS AND MARTHA WAYNE

Here he laid a third rose.

"A bit premature, isn't it, sir?" Alfred sniffed.

"Perhaps it's a bit overdue," Batman answered. "I wonder if Bruce Wayne died years ago and just didn't know it. Do we choose our fate, or does our fate choose us? Either way, the choice has now been made."

Gotham Herald OBITUARIES

BRUCE PATRICK WAYNE

Bruce Patrick Wayne, billionaire industrialist, philanthropist, and public figure of Gotham died tragically last Friday evening in Crime Alley off Park Row in the theater district of Uptown Gotham. The cause was multiple gunshot wounds. (See related story, "Suspicion Surrounds Wayne Murder," page 1, and special insert Section J, "The Wayne Dynasty.")

Wayne was a Gotham celebrity, known as much for making headlines as for presiding over one of the largest multinational corporations in the world. His life was marked by tragedy at an early age when his parents, Thomas and Martha Wayne, were both murdered in Crime Alley while then-eight-year-old Bruce watched. (See related story on page 6, Section J.)

At age 14, Bruce Wayne began a global journey, ultimately studying at Cambridge, the Sorbonne, and other European universities. However, he never stayed long and would often drop out after one semester. Beyond academia, Wayne successfully acquired various practical skills. His knowledge of so many varied disciplines made Wayne an unconventional and unpredictable individual. At age 20, he attempted to join the FBI, but after learning about its regulations and conduct, Wayne withdrew his application and returned to Gotham, taking up the mantle of the Wayne fortune on his 21st birthday. (See "Bruce Wayne Timeline," Section J, page 2.)

His early years led to considerable notoriety, and he was twice named most eligible bachelor in the world by Gotham Living magazine. He had reportedly dated Princess Portia Storme, Vicki Vale, and his bodyguard Sasha Bordeaux, with whom he was implicated in the death of another of his acquaintances, television personality Vesper Fairchild. (See "Wayne Manor Mystery," Section J, page 3.) Despite often being seen in the company of women of note, Wayne never married.

Wayne Enterprises, under his controversial leadership, grew into a formidable multinational corporation that included Wayne Aerospace, Wayne Biotech, Wayne Chemical, Wayne Electronics, Wayne Entertainment, Wayne Foods, Wayne Industries, the Wayne Institute for Advanced Studies, Wayne Medical, Wayne Research, Wayne Shipping, Wayne Steel, and Wayne Technologies. The philanthropic arm, the Wayne Foundation, supports causes all over the world. The Wayne operations are now under the direction of Alfred Pennyworth, who serves as president and chairman of the board of directors, and Lucius Fox, who serves as CEO.

In his later years, Wayne became more reclusive and shied away from the celebrity that had been his trademark in his younger years.

Bruce was the son of Thomas and Martha Wayne (both deceased) of Bristol. There are no surviving relations.